BETWEEN LIVES

EARL H. MCDANIEL

Copyright © 2012 Earl H. McDaniel

All rights reserved.

ISBN-10: 1475124422

ISBN-13: 978-1475124422

DEDICATION

To Cassandra

and

To Michael

I

They sat down to the most bountiful banquet in history.

They feasted on education, and they glowed in constant attention and analysis. They consumed hours of advertising fed to them via television, radio, newspapers and magazines. They wolfed down toys and games basted in the transformation from the machine age to the nuclear age. They quaffed rock, soul, metal and bubble gum music. They chewed up and spit out a president who sent them to war and a president who tried to steal the Constitution.

They drank in every pleasure they could, every game, every drink, every drug, every act of love, and they tossed into the garbage every rule that had been made for them.

They gorged themselves on bachelor's degrees and master's degrees and Ph.D.s. They gobbled up the ranks of corporate America and, after dinner, created their own companies.

Some of them who sat at the table had never been able to sit there before, but the many made room for the few, and everyone ate.

They ate and they ate, and they belched out a sense of entitlement and farted self-importance, and what they excreted, they thought was all their successors needed. Then they went back to the table for more. They sat down again and viewed the bounty, but now they saw others at the table, and they had to fight for what had previously been handed to them. Fewer and fewer of them won those fights until finally, there was no room at the table.

Not for them.

II

Mick Mackintosh surveyed the left knee of his big blue suit. He saw a speck of lint on it. Mick brushed it away, but noticed it did not go away. He brushed it again. No change. He ran his left index finger over the knee, which crossed over his right knee as he sat in the anteroom of the newsroom of the Twin Rivers *Independent*. "Damn," he said. It was a tiny hole. "Great. Just fucking great. It would have to be today," he muttered, barely audibly. Mick was waiting for the managing editor of the *Independent* to interview him for a job, and now he had a hole just above the knee in the pants of his big blue suit. One of his friends had first called it his "big blue suit" because it was so broad to fit his shoulders, but the coat just hung on his otherwise long, slender frame. Mick uncrossed his legs and put his right leg over the left knee and looked around the room. His knees throbbed from the arthritis that had plagued him for a few years. He saw coffee in the coffee maker and some cups, but the receptionist who had left him here, sitting just a few feet away, had not invited him to take any. Some coffee would be great. Getting this job would be better.

The door opened to his right, and he put his hands on the seat on either side of his thighs to push himself off the chair as his prospective supervisor entered the room.

"Are you Mick Mackintosh, Sir?" he said, extending his hand, looking up, way up, at Mick.

"Yes." Mick said, examining the brown hair and the blonde highlights on the top of this boy's head.

"I'm Christopher Post. So, like, how tall are you?"

"Probably about six-five or so. Or, not as tall as I used to be." He was conscious that he was trying to smile.

Christopher Post looked at him with puzzlement.

"People shrink a little as they age," Mick said.

Christopher Post held the door open so they could go through, and as Mick passed him, he said, "So, like, did you play basketball or whatever?"

"Yes, in high school. At Eastern Valley."

"Were you, like, the tallest guy in the league?"

He closed the door behind them.

"Yes."

"And were you, like, really good? I mean, if I told my dad your name, would he know it?"

Inside, Mick cringed a little. "Did he go to Eastern Valley?"

"No, he went to, like, Twin Rivers Area or whatever? But I'll bet he'd know your name if he heard it?"

Every utterance intoned like a question. Oh, wouldn't that be just delightful day after day, Mick thought.

"Maybe. Tell him 'MickeyMack.' That's what the newspapers and radio guys called me. Yacker Morris invented the name."

Again, Christopher Post looked puzzled.

"He did play-by-play of all the important games in the Valley about a hundred years ago, when your dad and I were kids. He was on WLV."

"Was that, like, a radio station?"

"It was very much like a radio station, with a tower — ." Mick caught himself. "I guess it went out of business or someone bought it and changed the call letters," Mick said. "So, you're the managing editor?"

"Oh, yeah." Christopher Post rolled his eyes as he walked slowly down a hall, half turned toward Mick as he talked. "That sounds so weird. I've only been managing editor for two weeks." He glanced at his watch. "Not even two weeks. I can't believe it. A guy my age running a newspaper? I mean, it's a pretty small newspaper, but it's a daily newspaper?" He looked down at the papers he held. Mick guessed it was his resume. "Well, not anything like the newspapers you've worked at, huh? I mean, a couple of these have, like, won Pulitzers, haven't they?"

"Yes, a few, uh, um, Mr. Post," man, did those words come hard, "but not when I was there."

"Topher."

"Pardon me?"

"You can call me Topher."

"Topher?" Mick asked. "Is that some kind of play on Tofu, or what exactly is that?"

"No," Christopher Post smiled shyly. "It's the last part of my name Chris-Topher? You know, like Topher Grace, the actor?"

Mick shook his head. "I don't know who that is."

"'That 70's Show?' It's a great show. Maybe you've never seen it."

"Or heard of it," Mick said.

Mick put his hands into the pants pockets of his big blue suit.

"Oh, wow," Christopher Post said. He wore a salmon colored short-sleeve shirt, not inappropriate for the first week in June — except, he was the managing editor and not a junior high science teacher — with a collar a size too big. Mick thought he might have been wearing a clip-on tie. He couldn't be sure.

"Hey, um, you ever, um, been in this newsroom, or — " Christopher Post said as he opened the door.

"Yes," Mick said walking through the door and into the newsroom. "A few years ago I came here for a couple of days as a consultant teaching narrative writing. Were you on staff then?"

"No," Christopher said as he closed the door to the newsroom and followed Mick into the room. "Heck, I was still in college."

"Of course," Mick said, following Christopher Post to a heavy oaken door, which led to a conference room. "I also interviewed here when I was in college, when Irv Peabody was the M.E."

"Oh, okay," Christopher Post said, unlocking and opening the door. "He's now, like, our history guy or whatever? His son's at the Boston Globe or something?"

"I know. I believe it was his son who got the job I interviewed for."

"Oh," Christopher Post said.

Christopher Post reached inside the room and turned on a light, then shoved the keys into his pants pocket. Mick stared at the long oaken table that dominated the room, then glanced back at Christopher Post. In all the newspaper conference rooms he had ever been in, he had never seen such an impressive conference table. Young Mr. Post gestured Mick inside. Mick stepped in and looked up at the front pages framed on the walls. He remembered some of them arriving at his parents' house, like the one with the thick, enormous headline "JFK DEAD"; and one just slightly smaller, "NIXON RESIGNS"; and a couple that had come to the house he and Constance had owned; the one from the fire that had claimed half of the Twin Rivers business district, even now still ruins; and the one that announced the closing of the last steel mill in the city. He looked at the highly polished wood shelf that ran below the window that looked out onto whatever was left of the city after the fire, the comatose economy and the teen gangs.

"Please sit down, Mr. Mackintosh," Christopher Post said.

Mick headed for the right side of the table as he faced it, and Christopher Post turned to the left. Mick sat down, bracing himself on the table with his hands because of the weakness in his knees. As he often did as a physical comma, he ran his hand back over his thick, hair, blonde turning ashen, all the way down to the split ends that hung over his collar, then stroked his goatee, now almost entirely gray. Christopher Post sat down opposite him and watched the procedure.

"Were you, like, a hippie?" Christopher Post asked.

Suddenly, Mick was conscious of what his hand had done.

"Oh, no," he said. A beat later, he realized that he would have to explain to the Christopher Posts of the world why a man his age wore long hair, as though it had to be part of some uniform. "It's just who I became at a very young age, and I just stayed this way."

"Oh," said Christopher Post.

Mick thought maybe Christopher Post was slightly disappointed with the answer, as though the boy had envisioned Mick as some sort of historic icon.

"And I was in a band once," Mick said, trying to recover some of the boy's admiration.

"Oh, that's so cool. What did you play?"

"Trombone."

"So, like, what kind of band was it?"

"Did you ever hear of Blood, Sweat and Tears?"

"Huh-uh," he said looking down at the table. Then his face brightened. "Wait. I think maybe my dad has a record or something with that on it? He made us listen to that when we were kids? Were you in that band?"

"No." Mick looked at his long fingers and started to pick at a nail. "The band I was in was kind of like that," he said to his fingers. He lifted his head, crossed his left leg over his right knee and noticed the tiny hole again. He leaned back in his chair and his finger ran over the hole. This would limit him to only one suit, the charcoal gray one. He suddenly felt weary. "It was a rock band with a sort of jazzy, big band sound. I like jazzy big bands."

"Oh," Christopher Post said and looked down at the papers he had set in front of him. Christopher Post dropped one page of Mick's resume onto the floor. "Oh, uh, sorry," he said, dipping to the floor to pick it up. He spread the papers out in front of him. His fingers waggled as he arranged the three pages of the resume, fidgeting with the corners to make them all line up. He scanned the pages, then looked up at Mick with a nervous smile across his fair face.

"I've never seen a three-page resume," he said. "I mean, I can't believe someone with your experience, your accomplishments is even applying for a job at the *Independent?* Your resume is, like, so awesome. You've even written a book."

"Well, it's a very short book, and it was self-published. I'm lucky the Eastern Valley schools use it in the fifth-grade program."

"Oh, so it's, like, a textbook?"

"Well, I didn't envision it that way. It's a history of Twin Rivers that I wrote for a grad program I was in many years ago. The program rejected it because it was too elementary, which I think means people who didn't go to MIT could understand it." Mick realized that he sounded a little bitter and maybe even pathetic. He sat up and re-crossed his legs and brushed his hand through his hair and over his goatee. "So, I quit the program, but I got that book out of it, so, I sort of shopped it around, and they use it for their local history class. But, you know, it's a one-time purchase. If they wanted more, I'd have to republish it."

"And you used to teach high school?"

"A long time ago, for a few years."

Christopher Post shifted his pen from his left hand to his right hand and brushed his left hand back and forth through his short hair. He looked down at the papers, the way a confounded student would look at his homework when asked a question. "Um, so, I mean, how come you left *The Sun*? That's, like, such a good paper."

"I didn't leave so much as I was downsized. I went there in early 2001. On my fourth day, they announced layoffs, but only for the union. It's a Rust Belt city, as you know, bigger than this one, but its transforming itself from manufacturing to education as its biggest employer, what with the colleges up there. Not much ad revenue to be had since manufacturing dried up. People living there just out of habit. Anyway, the paper's profit margin was down, and, as you've probably read, the CEO of the chain could not abide a profit margin of less than twenty-three percent. Hence, the layoffs. Of course, *The Sun* was not the only paper hit. I'm sure you've read about cuts across the chain, except in Philadelphia and Miami. A few months later, things were no better. They bought out about twenty people, which meant my staff was decimated. I didn't have enough people to cover all the topics I had to cover."

Christopher Post looked puzzled.

"We had topical beats instead of geographical beats. You know, like education and local government and courts and transportation and the like."

"Oh, we only have geographical beats."

"Yes, I know."

"Oh, right. You said on the phone, you've been reading this paper since you were a kid, huh?"

"My parents got married the day my dad was mustered out. Uh, after World War II. They moved here, where my dad had grown up. They subscribed the day after they moved in. I look at it online to keep up. Should I go on with why I left *The Sun*?"

"Oh, um, I mean, yeah." Again, Mick thought Christopher Post looked overwhelmed.

"When the World Trade Center went down and the stock market quickly followed, no one — I mean, no one — was buying ads. By the first of the year, they decided they had to get rid of one more position, and because of how hard the previous layoffs and buyouts had hit the union, it had to be an editor. I was the last one in, so I was the first one out."

Mick felt his nail snag on the edge of the hole in his pants, and he instinctively pulled it away, pulling a thread with it.

"Oh, wow, that's really tough. And that's been, like, a year, right? What have you been doing in that time?"

"More than a year. Oh, I've been looking for a job, going to grad school," Mick said. "Mostly, economizing."

"Oh, I see," Christopher Post said. "So, um, you're in grad school?"

"Yeah."

"Same program?"

"No."

"Are the classes at night? Cause we're a p.m. newspaper, so I'd need to have you here during the day."

"I know. The classes are all at night."

Mick tried to tuck the thread back into the tiny hole, but poked his finger into the hole, making it a little bigger.

"So, um, this job is something like an assistant metro editor job? 'Cause, I'm, like, the metro editor? Even though I'm, you know, managing editor? So, like, do you have, like, an editing philosophy?"

An editing philosophy, Mick said to himself. He'd bet his next mortgage payment he was this kid's first interview.

"I consider myself more of a coach than an editor," Mick said. "Like Ron Patrick Clift says, you can fix copy or you can coach writers. If all you do is fix the copy, you never get done fixing copy. If you coach the writers, you can help them give you better copy every day. In order to succeed in the long term, everyone has to grow and adapt."

"Who's Ron Patrick, um — ?"

"Clift," Mick said. He put his hand over the hole. "He and his partner, Dan Free, are the foremost writing coaches in the country for newspapers. Ron," Mick said, conscious of how pretentious he would sound to an adult, "is at the Painter Institute for Modern Media, and Dan now works as an independent coach."

"Yeah, okay. I've heard of Painter. So, like, you're a writing coach?"

"I was full-time at one newspaper. I've done that unofficially at my past two papers. Each of them had me working with the interns every summer. I did workshops for them in-house, and I always had at least one of them on my staff. And I did a few brown-baggers at both of those last two papers."

Christopher Post looked confused.

"What's, um, a brown-bagger?"

"Lunch-time coaching session for a large group. Whole newsroom is invited. Very good for a young staff."

"Yeah, cool. We're a pretty young staff, so that would be helpful."

"Yes, I think so," Mick said. He re-crossed his legs so he wouldn't see the hole in the pants.

"So, um, how do you think we have to do stories?"

"As everyone in newspapers must realize, we never do first-day stories anymore, unless they're about meetings nobody else covers or breaking — I don't know — scandals or leaking announcements. Things like that. But even, if, say, the school board is approving a teacher contract that ends a two-month strike, TV will be there, so the paper is still very late, and because this is an afternoon newspaper, our readers won't see the story until at least eighteen hours after the fact, unless the reporter files online first. Do you file night stories online? I mean, on your Web site?"

"Um, no. Only stories that break during the day, and, uh, we, like, update stories after the paper gets, like, on the street, until, um, six o'clock?"

"Okay, so mostly you break stories on newsprint instead of online. Then, I think we have to coach the writers to write second-day stories, more of a feature approach or an analytical approach. Or we have to start breaking stories online. We did that at the past two newspapers I worked at."

"Yeah, wow, you're right. Yeah. That's cool. Um, so, how do you think you would make our staff better?"

"Other than with what I know and my experience coaching writers? What time is your copy deadline?"

"Nine-thirty."

"Then at around ten, we might have, at least once a week, a brown-bag session in which we go over some writing and reporting issues or maybe critique the paper. And the other days, I could use for one-on-one conferences with my staffers, a different one every day. Does that sound feasible?"

"Um, yeah." Christopher Post fidgeted with the knot of his tie, so maybe it wasn't fake. He nodded his head two or three times, then made some notes.

"Um," Christopher Post looked quickly at Mick, then back down at the resume, "we don't pay anything like what you made at *The Sun*? So why are you applying here and not at the *Chronicle*? Or even the *Standard*? I mean, we don't pay anything like that."

"You have a job open and they don't, and I wouldn't work for the *Standard* on a dare because I worked for them once before, and I don't like how they do business. Plus, any job either of them would have open would probably be a night desk job, and then I wouldn't be able to go to grad school."

"Oh," Christopher Post fidgeted with his pen, "so did you apply there?"

"I've applied to a lot of places." Mick thought Christopher Post had just asked him something he had no right to ask. "Newspapers, magazines, school districts. I can write, and I can edit, and I can teach, and I've applied for any number of jobs that would allow me to do any of those things."

"Yeah, okay. Um, so how much money would you need to work here?"

"How much does the job pay?"

"Um, I mean, like, we never pay our copy editors — that's what the position is called, even though it's more like an assistant metro editor — we never pay them more than about twenty-seven thousand dollars, but," Christopher Post looked quickly at Mick, then, seeing his eyes, shifted his glance away from Mick and toward the door, "maybe we could go as high as, I don't know, like, um. thirty?"

Mick smoothed his pony tail and rubbed his goatee. He re-crossed his legs again and folded his hands across the front of his knee, hoping to hide the hole. "That's thirty thousand more than I'm making now."

Christopher Post broke into a grin.

"Yeah, I mean, you're right," he said. He leaned back in his chair for first time, Mick noticed. "I mean, the cost of living isn't all that bad here, and you're living out of state right now, so you could move back and your tuition would go down if you were here, right? Yeah, and you know, if you lived really close, I mean, you could even take the bus to work, right? It stops right in front of the office."

Mick nodded and watched Christopher Post as the dam burst with stories about the people on the staff. Apparently, he had been nervous that Mick would expect the kind of money he had made before at those metros. This meant Christopher Post would have to explain to the other copy editors why Mick was making more than they, although maybe they would never know. Mick certainly knew enough not to talk about salary in the shop. But there was also the issue of breaking the budget on one position.

Christopher Post talked about the reporters and his perception of their weaknesses and quirks, then talked about the other two copy editors, who clearly, from what Christopher Post said, didn't know anything close to what Mick knew. Then he launched into a dissertation on the paper's business side, none of it flattering. Next he divulged that the owner, the great-granddaughter of the state senator who had founded the paper in the late nineteenth century, was going through a messy divorce, and that her soon-to-be-ex-husband had been cheating with the membership secretary at their country club, founded, in fact, by the senator. "She was, like, re-e-e-ally pissed," Christopher Post said with a grin.

Christopher Post stood up. Mick stood up and an edge of his watch band caught on the hole and tore it a little wider. Christopher Post reached across the table and shook Mick's hand and headed for the door. Christopher Post explained that his wife knew someone who knew someone who worked for the lawyer who represented the husband, and she said her boss was trying to get a share of the newspaper as part of the settlement, so Christopher Post really wasn't sure what the future held for the paper, not that it mattered all that much anyway since the owner — Christopher Post called her "Evelyn" — was almost never in the office anyway. Her only real influence over the paper, other than signing checks, Christopher Post said with a nervous laugh, was to tell them to endorse Al Gore in the last presidential election.

"So, um, how soon could you start?"

"All I have to do is find a place to live back here and put my house back there up for sale," Mick said. "How soon do you think you'll be making a decision?"

"We have a few more people to interview? But they don't have anything near the experience you have? It would be, like, re-e-e-ally great to have someone like you around I could learn from."

"That would be my pleasure," Mick said.

Christopher Post opened the door onto the anteroom, and extended his hand again.

"It was a pleasure to meet you, Mr. Mackintosh, and I'm sure we'll be talking soon."

For the first time in the interview, Mick smiled without effort as he took the younger man's hand. "I think you should get into the habit of calling me 'Mick.'"

Christopher Post smiled again and vigorously shook Mick's hand. He opened the door that led out of the newsroom to the anteroom.

"Okay, Mick. Nice to meet you."

"My pleasure," Mick said, truly grinning now.

Mick walked out of the newsroom. A young man, thin, like a distance runner, wearing a suit coat, white shirt and tie, shirttail hanging out of a pair of dark blue jeans, and white running shoes, looked up at the door. He scratched his head through the highlights in his brown hair. Mick could feel Christopher Post coming through the door behind him, standing in the doorway.

The young man stood up. "Duuude," he said, pushing his fist toward Christopher Post. Mick stepped aside to give the young man room, and he saw Christopher Post extend his fist to bump the young man's.

"Duuude," Christopher Post said, and the young man entered the newsroom.

Mick waited for a few seconds as the door closed. He turned and looked at the newsroom receptionist, who lowered her head back to her work. Mick put a hand on the wall, then took a couple of steps toward the stairs. He descended them gingerly because of his arthritic knees. He walked out through the art deco lobby, where classified liner salespeople spoke into headsets and typed ads into computers, behind the long desk that wrapped around the lobby and under the series of clocks telling the time in London, Berlin, Moscow, Tokyo, Los Angeles and New York — installed decades ago, when they were thought to be indispensable to every newspaper. He burst into the mid-August sunshine of the decrepit city and walked the couple of blocks to the parking garage where he had parked and climbed stairs, not without pain, to get to the level where he had parked. He opened the car door and stepped in, sat down and looked down at his big blue suit and at the expanding hole. This was a suit he could never wear again, but it wouldn't matter, he told himself. Soon, he would have a few bucks in his pocket with which to buy a new big blue suit.

That kid, wearing the running shoes with his suit, was probably a reporter candidate. No editor would be that young, he told himself. But Christopher Post was, he allowed himself to think. And he knew that some kids came right out of school and into editing jobs without ever having been reporters. Mick didn't like that. An editor who had never reported couldn't truly understand how news was gathered, might not understand the nuances of local governments: councils, school boards, authorities of various types. Not wise, Mick thought. This kid had to be a reporting candidate.

Had to.

III

Mick drove out of the parking garage and headed out of the city. The radio played news, and the announcer talked about casualties in the war in Iraq. "Wasted lives," Mick said. "Wasted fucking lives." Then the announcer told the latest news about the president's economic plan. Mick shook his head. "Asshole," he said, reaching for his tuner. "His only economic plan is to drive the middle class into poverty and to enrich the upper class even further. Fucking asshole." He popped in an Artie Shaw cassette.

He pointed the car toward home, a two-hour drive on two different state turnpikes, boredom bathed in asphalt, followed by a couple of burgers under his broiler. Then he had the revelation: He was about to come into some money. He was a new man, reborn in a salary and job respect to come. He not only would buy himself a new suit, but today, this very day, he would stop at one of the restaurants in one of the suburbs on the way to the turnpike and have himself something good for dinner. So, he settled back and headed for Route 30 until he saw the sign indicating that his home township was coming up in just one mile.

Hell, if he could buy a new suit and he could eschew his home-broiled burgers for a restaurant meal, he could damn well buy himself a house. He followed the signs to Westinghouse Township, though God knew he didn't need any signs. He had grown up here. He and his ex-wife, Constance, had bought a tiny house there right after they got married. They were both teaching at Eastern Valley Area High School, and they had accumulated enough for a down payment for that bungalow on Victory Road in a post-World War II plan whose developer had won a Silver Star in the European Theater. Mick drove past it and slowed down, then pulled to the curb, putting the car into park. He studied the mustard-yellow clapboard and burgundy trim and wished he and Constance had thought of painting it that way. In the fifteen years since they had moved out, someone had replaced the multi-paned front window with a bay window — one large dominant pane in the middle and two vertical panes on either side. He noticed an old-fashioned weather vane on the roof, and he realized someone had cut down the pine trees on either corner of the front of the lot. Mick had teased Constance that if things went bad, even two years running, they'd still have a Christmas tree. Maybe things had got bad for whoever lived there. Or maybe one of the trees got in the way of the wires extending from the telephone pole to the house. Or maybe somebody didn't like picking up pine cones. Mick frowned.

Mick pulled the car out of park and into drive and pulled back onto the road. It wasn't the same house at all, Mick told himself. Somebody had fucked the whole thing up. Not really, Mick admitted to himself as he left Victory and turned onto Eisenhower. Someone had made it better than Mick and Constance had ever envisioned the house. After all, they had never planned to stay there. They had never planned to build it into the family homestead. It was too small for the family they had planned to grow, so the only upkeep they did was what needed to be done at the moment. Constance was in grad school, and Mick was still playing with the band on weekends, and picking up every bus chaperoning or other extra-curricular assignment the school would pay him to do. Constance volunteered with the literacy council, sang in the church choir (as did Mick) and served on the Altar Guild. They'd had neither the time nor the interest to make the house into anything more than it needed to be for them for the time being.

Mick saw nothing on Eisenhower for sale, then turned onto Churchill Road, where one of his high school friends had lived. His buddy's house wasn't for sale. He guessed that someone had painted over the autographs he and Vincent had left on the basement walls when they were in junior high school. The sprawling side yard where he and Vincent and the Mecklin brothers had played Wiffle Ball now suffered a great gash from home plate through the pitcher's mound to where the clothes pole that was second base used to stand. In the gash, Mick could see from the road, was turned-over-dirt sprouting skinny posts to which tomato plants were tied. Mick knew other vegetables grew there, too, but he couldn't tell what they were. He didn't know if Vincent's parents were alive or dead, but he knew they didn't live there. No way, Mick knew, would Vincent's dad have spent time in the garden, cultivating dirt, nurturing sprouts. Vincent's dad had spent little time doing anything other than cultivating Vincent's mother and nurturing an Iron City.

Mick turned the corner at Vincent's old house and moved onto Farmhouse Lane, where he saw a yellow brick ranch house he had always admired. It was L-shaped, with a walk that extended along both sides of the L, broadly enough to accommodate a round metal table and a couple of chairs. An overhang came off the roof and sheltered the walk. Someone had alternated petunias and geraniums in pots along the length and breadth of the walk. He guessed that, as he had when he owned his houses, the residents brought the geraniums in every year to keep them going. Mick thought that would be a great house for him if it were for sale.

A few houses down was a house for sale, two stories, and the oldest house on the block. He remembered Vincent's father saying that house had been the center of a small farm, part of the former Heath estate, when he was a boy before World War II. Mick pulled over and put the car into park. The house needed to be painted, and the yard could use some flowers or trees or something instead of just the grass that crept from the wrap-around porch — which Mick loved — to the curb. Mick leaned his elbow on the open window of the driver's side of the car and leaned his chin on his fist. The windows might not have been replaced since the 19-teens, when Vincent's dad had thought the house had been built. They would have to go for better energy efficiency and for better appearance. His gaze rose and he wondered how old the roof was. No garage, he noted. He thought he remembered a stand-alone garage in the back of the house from his youth. Must have fallen down. He could live without a garage. Maybe he could get a book or two to edit to build a little nest egg for building a garage. There was plenty of room in the yard, after all. Mick grabbed a small yellow lined pad from his glove box and wrote down the address, the realtor's name and the phone number. After he was sure he got the job at the *Independent*, he would make a call about this house.

He passed a few nondescript houses on sale on the couple of streets between the old farmhouse and his childhood home. At those places, he stopped only long enough to write down addresses and not to indulge in a detailed inspection.

He felt tugs of memory and relief and anxiety as he turned onto Heath Road. He stopped the car on the side of the road. He got out of the car, carrying his pad and pen and walked along the road. The old house on the corner had fallen when he was in college to accommodate a gas station that had closed in the '80s. The property now sprouted weeds in cracks in the asphalt, and weather or time or both had eroded the corner of the corner block at the top of the building. The large picture window in the front was now covered with plywood, if indeed there was even glass behind it anymore. He shook his head. "Asshole oil companies," he muttered. The old couple who had lived there when he was a boy had kind of adopted his parents. Many times he had been inside the house that was no longer there. He could still see the ornate — to his childish eye — banister along the stairs to the second floor. He remembered the flowers Mrs. Cioffi had tended along the curving walk from the road to the porch. On that porch, which lived on in Mick's mind, he had played Junior Scrabble with the Cioffis' grandson, who had disappeared at Woodstock and never resurfaced. Mr. Cioffi made wine back in the day, and he remembered the summer night his dad and Mr. Knoop woke him up singing Dean Martin songs on the way from the wine cellar under the Cioffis' garage, past the four houses in between, and all the way into the kitchen, where his dad had poured coffee into Mr. Knoop to try to sober him up for Mrs. Knoop. Mick's mother had got out of bed to make something for them to eat, and she had allowed Mick to come out of his bedroom and join the party.

"Fucking oil companies."

He walked down the street, which was the same as he remembered it, despite new asphalt laid over the decades, layers milled, then new layers laid, over and over, yet the manhole remained in the same place and the storm sewer still opened right in front of O'Connells', and there still was no sidewalk, just a lip of asphalt reaching upward to the property fronts, all the way to the end of the cul-de-sac ("plural: culs-de-sac," his editor's brain told him automatically), where Mick stopped and stared — .

At a For Sale sign.

On the house in which he had grown up.

Mick walked a little more quickly toward his parents' old house. He'd lost track of how many people had lived there since he had sold it after his mother died, which wasn't long after his dad had died. After a few seconds, he found himself jogging, as much as his knees would allow. Then he stopped at the asphalt lip right in front of the house. He surveyed the property only for a minute.

Mick's mouth dropped open, and he stared at the slightly worn house, the center of an estate in the mid-nineteenth century. By the late 1890s, the Heath family that owned it had squandered its wealth. That might not be fair. Mick didn't know exactly how the wealth had dissipated, but the Heaths had started selling off lots to small farmers, who, in turn, after World War II, sold their farms to developers building the suburbs. In the 1930s, the surviving Heaths sold the house and left the area. A series of people owned it — or at least lived in it — until Mick's dad and uncle had bought it after the war. By that time, there was very little property to go with the house, but the house was big enough for Mick's parents and one uncle and the woman he planned to marry. His uncle never did marry that woman, so he went back into the Army and sold his share of the house to Mick's dad. That made finances more than a little tight when Mick was a boy, especially when the mills slowed, as they did from time to time. But at those times, Mick's dad tended bar at a dive a friend of his owned. They cut corners wherever they could, and they made it.

They had never been able to restore the house to the showplace it must have been in its glory days, but they had kept it looking better than it looked now. A few of the bricks on the second and third floors poked red through the ghastly white paint some idiot had put there. The roses on the east side of the house, Mick discovered as he walked somewhat involuntarily onto the property, fought for survival against a couple of different species of vines and spindles of spiky weeds. Mick walked faster the closer he got to the roses. He remembered his mother kneeling in her house dress, gloved hands pulling weeds, then holding the shoots of the bushes to trim and to cut roses she would take into the house and up and down Heath Road to neighbors suffering everything from sunburn to broken limbs. Even after her stroke, Mick's mother worked in that garden. The roses and his mother's nurturing of them always defined summer in the neighborhood, the same way the Pirates' games on the radio did.

Mick dropped to the knees of his big blue suit, not caring if grass stained them, leaning on his hands, crinkling his eyes at the pain in his knees. No matter. He would be buying a new big blue suit. He reached into the poorly defined borders of the rose garden and grabbed vine shoot after vine shoot and pulled one after another violently, tearing the shoots, not at their roots, but from deeper in the shoot. He tossed the refuse into a pile to his left, as his mother always had. He wrapped his fist around one spiky weed, cutting into his palm, and pulled it out, breaking it at the root. "Fuck." He tossed the weed, then looked around and felt around until he found a plastic pop bottle under one of the rose bushes. He tore the back of his hand on an angry thorn pulling the bottle. He clutched the bottle with both hands and dug into the dirt around the reluctant weed root. He dug away dirt and pebbles and ancient pieces of mulch until he could get one of his mitts around a few inches of root, and he pulled. His hand slid off the moist root. He reached back into his right hip pocket and pulled out his white handkerchief, and he wrapped the handkerchief around the root and pulled. The root broke loose of the dirt, completely, full of soil clinging to the strings, and Mick yelled, "Aaaahhhh!! Bastard!!!" And he tossed the root onto his refuse pile. He reached deeper into the garden for another, seizing it with his handkerchief first and pulling. He felt his pants slide on the grass. He yanked vine after vine, encroaching on the dirt with the knees of the pants of his big blue suit. With every victory over every invader, he said, "Yeah," or "Ya bastard" or some other triumphant utterance.

Mick heard a screen door slam in the undercurrent of his mind, then he heard noise like a person yelling. Depositing a weed in his pile, he turned and beheld a matronly woman bulging out of a teal sweat suit, short dark hair framing her wrinkling face.

"Hey," she yelled, "what the hell are you doing?"

"Huh?"

"What the hell are you doing? Get out of there!"

"I'm saving my mother's roses. Do you think they weed themselves?"

"Get the hell out of my roses." She pointed a cell phone at him. "Get the hell out of my yard before I call the police."

Mick watched her for an instant, then pushed himself off the ground and onto his feet, wincing as his knees straightened. Instinctively, he rubbed his knees, brushing dirt off them.

"You live here?" He breathed heavy.

"Where the hell do you think I live?" She shook the phone at him, punctuation her words.

"I want to buy your house."

She put the phone back to her side. "Who are you?"

His breathing slowed a bit as he put his hands on his hips.

"Mick Mackintosh. I grew up in this house. My mother planted the roses. My father and my uncle laid the cement block from the porch to the mailbox."

"You grew up in this house?"

"Yeah. I just said that."

"My husband grew up on this street. Second house on the right."

"Dickie? You're married to Dickie?"

"No. On the right as you go out. Kenny Barker."

"Yeah?" Mick thought Kenny was an ass, not fit to live in this house. Made sense that the damned thing was falling apart. "Kenny was one of the guys on the street who played Wiffle ball in the back yard, and — " he pointed to the woods beyond the back yard. "Those were our Ardennes."

"Your what?"

"The Ardennes. Battle of the Bulge." Mick waved the thought away. "Look, you selling?"

"You're a genius. You can read."

"I'm moving back to the area. What are you asking?"

"Can you read the name on the sign? Call the agent."

"Geez, all I asked is what you're asking."

"I don't negotiate. I don't talk to anyone about the house. You want to buy the house, you talk to the agent. Virginia Crandall."

"You're charming, you know that? I can see what Kenny sees in you."

"Okay, whatever-the-hell-your-name is, off the lawn or I call the police."

Mick headed for the street, then turned and said. "Mickey Mackintosh. Tell Kenny Mickey Mackintosh wants to buy the house. I'll call him."

He turned away again, then stopped.

"Pull the freaking weeds. My mother poured her life into those roses. Ask Kenny. They were the pride of the neighborhood, and she knew it. Pull the freaking weeds."

"When you buy the house, you can pull the weeds." She took a breath. Mick saw her eyes go to the knees of his suit pants. "If you can afford it." She took another breath, then called after him. "Asshole."

Virginia Crandall, Mick repeated to himself. Hmm. Name sounded familiar. He'd have to look her up on the Web. Then give her a call. She didn't know it yet, but she was going to sell Mick his old house.

"Hey," she yelled, "what the hell are you doing?"

"Huh?"

"What the hell are you doing? Get out of there!"

"I'm saving my mother's roses. Do you think they weed themselves?"

"Get the hell out of my roses." She pointed a cell phone at him. "Get the hell out of my yard before I call the police."

Mick watched her for an instant, then pushed himself off the ground and onto his feet, wincing as his knees straightened. Instinctively, he rubbed his knees, brushing dirt off them.

"You live here?" He breathed heavy.

"Where the hell do you think I live?" She shook the phone at him, punctuation her words.

"I want to buy your house."

She put the phone back to her side. "Who are you?"

His breathing slowed a bit as he put his hands on his hips.

"Mick Mackintosh. I grew up in this house. My mother planted the roses. My father and my uncle laid the cement block from the porch to the mailbox."

"You grew up in this house?"

"Yeah. I just said that."

"My husband grew up on this street. Second house on the right."

"Dickie? You're married to Dickie?"

"No. On the right as you go out. Kenny Barker."

"Yeah?" Mick thought Kenny was an ass, not fit to live in this house. Made sense that the damned thing was falling apart. "Kenny was one of the guys on the street who played Wiffle ball in the back yard, and — " he pointed to the woods beyond the back yard. "Those were our Ardennes."

"Your what?"

"The Ardennes. Battle of the Bulge." Mick waved the thought away. "Look, you selling?"

"You're a genius. You can read."

"I'm moving back to the area. What are you asking?"

"Can you read the name on the sign? Call the agent."

"Geez, all I asked is what you're asking."

"I don't negotiate. I don't talk to anyone about the house. You want to buy the house, you talk to the agent. Virginia Crandall."

"You're charming, you know that? I can see what Kenny sees in you."

"Okay, whatever-the-hell-your-name is, off the lawn or I call the police."

Mick headed for the street, then turned and said. "Mickey Mackintosh. Tell Kenny Mickey Mackintosh wants to buy the house. I'll call him."

He turned away again, then stopped.

"Pull the freaking weeds. My mother poured her life into those roses. Ask Kenny. They were the pride of the neighborhood, and she knew it. Pull the freaking weeds."

"When you buy the house, you can pull the weeds." She took a breath. Mick saw her eyes go to the knees of his suit pants. "If you can afford it." She took another breath, then called after him. "Asshole."

Virginia Crandall, Mick repeated to himself. Hmm. Name sounded familiar. He'd have to look her up on the Web. Then give her a call. She didn't know it yet, but she was going to sell Mick his old house.

IV

I hope you will join me in standing firmly on the side of the people. You see, the growing surplus exists because taxes are too high and government is charging more than it needs. The people of America have been overcharged and, on their behalf, I am here asking for a refund. (Applause.)

Some say my tax plan is too big. (Applause.) Others say it's too small. (Applause.) I respectfully disagree. (Laughter.) This plan is just right. (Applause.) I didn't throw darts at the board to come up with a number for tax relief. I didn't take a poll or develop an arbitrary formula that might sound good. I looked at problems in the Tax Code and calculated the cost to fix them.

A tax rate of 15 percent is too high for those who earn low wages, so we must lower the rate to 10 percent. (Applause.) No one should pay more than a third of the money they earn in federal income taxes, so we lowered the top rate to 33 percent (Applause.)

This reform will be welcome relief for America's small businesses, which often pay taxes at the highest rate. And help for small business means jobs for Americans. (Applause.) We simplified the Tax Code by reducing the number of tax rates from the current five rates to four lower ones, 10 percent, 15, 25 and 33 percent. In my plan, no one is targeted in or targeted out. Everyone who pays income taxes will get relief. (Applause.)

President George W. Bush
February 27, 2001

V

Mick stopped for gas at one of those multiplex stations with eight or ten islands, two pumps to an island. He went in to pay and grabbed a couple of burgers from a warming tray and drew a fountain drink big enough to keep him wet across Death Valley. He would eat at a nice restaurant some other time.

A couple of miles later, the burgers consumed, Mick got onto the turnpike heading west and settled into the left-hand lane, passing old people hunched over the wheels of compact cars and tractor-trailers that threatened to mash him into the jersey barrier median on left-leaning curves. He passed exits he had never taken and exits he had wandered up in his youth. He passed the time fixated on the morning's interview, imagining better answers he could have given, then pushing the regrets from his mind. He had the job. Finally. He had the job. He had been looking for so long, much longer than he had ever anticipated he would look. He was known in the newspaper industry because of his coaching work, but no one was expanding staff and no staffers were leaving with the economy so uncertain. And now he had the job. Probably. The picture of the other young guy with highlights in his hair flicked at the back of his brain.

"Duuude."

Leaving the Pennsylvania Turnpike for the Ohio, he envisioned himself owning the house. He knew he would never have been able to afford it if it had been in good condition, but Kenny had let it deteriorate and it could not bring top price anymore. Besides, the neighborhood in general was deteriorating. An abandoned gas station always attracted vermin of various sorts, including, often, drug dealers who argued about their deals late at night. Most of the houses on Heath Road were less appealing than Mick remembered them. Mick guessed Kenny wanted more money than the house was worth. He'd have to find out how long it had been on the market. He'd have to find out why and how soon Kenny wanted to sell. If it had been listed for several months and if Kenny and his lovely bride were eager to move, maybe Mick could get the house for less than Kenny's supposed bottom line.

Mick would buy the house and make improvements bit by bit, depending upon the time and money he had. Grad school would take a major bite out of each, but he would sell the house he lived in fairly quickly, so he would have money to navigate both grad school and home improvements. He wondered, as he stayed on Interstate 76 and left the Ohio Turnpike, how much it would cost to get that hideous white paint off the house and get those bricks re-pointed. He wondered what the inside looked like. He remembered the house as bright and cheery when he was a boy and his mother was well enough to keep the house up. He remembered the grand piano in one huge room on the first floor, left perhaps from the days of the Heaths and which no one in his family could play, and which he left there when he sold the house. He wondered if it was still there. He remembered the built-in book shelves in the library, which the family could never fill with books. He remembered fondly the colonial motif throughout the house, including the fife-and-drum wallpaper in the long first-floor hall. Knowing Kenny, Mick thought as he pulled on the straw of his fountain drink, he had painted the whole thing over in lime green or some damned thing.

But Mick would make it right. He would restore the house, and he envisioned his inspiring the rest of the neighborhood families to fix up their own homes. The value of everyone's property would only increase as people painted and landscaped and replaced roofs and old mailboxes and weather-beaten fence posts and such. Mick would return Heath Road to its former glory, sort of like a Romantic hero returning to his hometown to rid it of evil.

As Mick passed the big antique store just off I-76, his thoughts turned to the newspaper and how he would fix it. He wished he had brought some copies of the paper so he could look over the stories, recognize tendencies and make notes about his goals for each reporter. No matter, he could those stories online. Wouldn't it be great, he thought, to have each reporter go into some depth about the biggest issue facing each council or board on his or her beat? Wouldn't it be great, he thought, to teach them all to write about those problems in a good narrative style? Wouldn't it be great, he thought, to meet with the reporters, the photographers and the graphic artists — if the *Independent* had any — and page designers to plan packages, to ignite the front page with enough excitement to leap off the page and grab the readers by the throat? Wouldn't it be great, he thought, to wake up the entire Valley and get everyone talking about the *Independent*, and help to spur circulation and advertising and win some awards? Wouldn't it all be great, he thought.

He felt something shoot through him, a cold charge surging through his veins, the same thing he used to feel before his high school basketball games. He felt brighter in his soul, though he would never have said such a thing out loud. The gloom that had enveloped him through months of unemployment flew off him. He welcomed the flood of purpose and self-confidence that replaced it. He had always worked, and he had always worked long hours. He had always worked stressful jobs. In fact, he had quit one job because he didn't feel like he was doing enough work, that he was stealing the employer's money. He wanted to be drained at the end of every day. He wanted to go home knowing his writers were better than they had been the day before. He wanted to be a force in the newsroom — Hurricane Mick, blowing out the rotted prose, forcing a rebuilding, a rebirth, a freshness of reporting perspective, a freshness of prose, a freshness of purpose.

It wasn't just about the money, although the ever-widening tear in the pants of his big blue suit reminded him mile after mile of the need for more cash. He needed to restore his self-respect. It was not the Mackintosh way to not work, to live off one's retirement, as Mick was now doing. It was not the Mackintosh way to lie in bed until mid-morning, shorn of a purpose to get out of bed and produce something. It was not the Mackintosh way to watch daytime television, even if it was CNN. He could tell himself that he was keeping up with the news, keeping his mind sharp, staying ready for the right opportunity to jump back into a newsroom. But he knew he was wasting away, at least intellectually, and he was getting into bad habits, like a nap in the middle of the day, like staying up late watching movies he'd seen a hundred times, like playing computer solitaire until — in one instance — he had drifted off to sleep right at the keyboard. Work, Mick knew very well from his family, enriched not only the wallet, but also the soul. It was part of the Protestant ethic his family had instilled in him. His father had worked long hours until the day he died, keeling over from a heart attack in front of the blast furnace at the mill. His mother had never turned on the TV during the day except for a half hour of the news at noon with Bill Burns on KDKA. Each day she had set housekeeping tasks, and if a church committee meeting was scheduled for a day she had planned deep cleaning for a certain room, then she would clean that room starting at 5 a.m. if necessary in order to finish in time to clean up and be on time for that meeting, which she would walk to. As sick as she was just before she died, she baked coffee cakes for a church bake sale. Pending death would not cause her to shirk her duty.

And Mick knew, as he pulled off of the interstate and onto the county road that would take him home, that work made him feel whole, and soon he would feel whole again, working for the Twin Rivers *Independent*.

VI

From: Mick Mackintosh [mailto:mickeymack@fastconnect.com]
Sent: Monday, June 24, 2003 11:56 AM
To: B.D. Butterfield
Subject: Something good (maybe)

B.D., what's shakin' in the Great Northwest? I read your piece about the eco-terrorists. Scary stuff. But I had to look all over the site for the sidebar about the woman sitting in the tree for six months. Your webmaster must not have set up the link properly.

Hey, I think I'm getting back into it. I had an interview with the Twin Rivers Independent. Twin Rivers is the town outside Westinghouse Township. It's where everyone in our area of the Mon used to shop every Saturday afternoon when I was a kid, and where you went if you wanted to see a movie in a theater. Had a coupla "still mills" when I was a kid. My dad and everyone else's dad worked in one.

Paper's kind of shitty. The editor has asked for a bike without training wheels for his next birthday, but it's a newspaper, and it's a place I can help get better and I can stay in the master's program. As soon as I get the official word, I'm putting this house on the market and moving back home. I'm gonna buy the house I grew up in. It's for sale. Can't wait for you and Denise to come out.

Truly, man, the best part of this is that I can get a little dignity back in my life. I can stop shopping at Sprawl Mart. Good lord. That can't happen too soon. Once I was consigned to shopping there, I realized that one of the reasons Sprawl Mart can sell stuff so cheaply is that they keep their costs down. One of the ways they keep costs down is to employ fewer people than they really need to keep customers happy. So, when we shop there, we make a deal: You give me cheap peaches and apples and oranges, and I'll let you treat me like crap in any number of ways. You can make me stand in line for about as long as it takes for the trees to grow the next batch. You can give me "associates" in the store that have less knowledge about the products they're selling than they have about computer engineering. And you can put the milk all the way at the back of the store and give me painfully narrow aisles to walk through, crowded with old people and people with built-in oversized loads driving those little battery-powered shopping carts.

I'd like to shop somewhere where the management has some respect for my time. Sprawl-Mart keeps just enough lines open that everyone has to wait for at least three people ahead of him in line. And their express line is for 20 items, which is a problem for shoppers — and there are many of them there — who get lost somewhere in the double digits, so they bring 25 or 30 items to the checkout, and no one tells them they can't. So, the wait is interminable. I was in there this a.m. for just bread and milk and cherries — the one week they're available for less than my mortgage payment a pound — and I waited so long that when I got to the cashier, and she said how good the cherries looked to her, I said, "You know they were green when I got in line." She just looked at me. I know, they don't run the place. They're not the enemy. And I know they're getting paid like pre-union seamstresses, but I just want to say to the managers: This standing in line business might fly in some parts of the country, but here we have better things to do with our time. For example, we know how to read.

Oh, well. As soon as Skippy the boy editor calls me, I'll be done with that.

Later
MM

VII

Mick's ex-wife called him late the next afternoon. Got him out of bed from his pre-dinner nap. Mick saw that it was closing in on 3:30.

"I heard you were back home this week."

"You're kidding," Mick said. "You live about six counties away from Westinghouse Township, and you heard I was back home?"

"I still have friends there, Mick. Do you? You didn't have many when we lived there."

"No, Sweetheart. I'm not a social butterfly. I am the iconic loner. You told me that's what drew you to me."

"So, what took you back home? In a suit."

"I had a job interview."

"Good. I hope you get the job."

"Thank you for your good wishes," Mick said.

"You're going to need the money."

"Why, are you divorcing me again?"

"Your son needs your help."

"Which son?"

"Sean."

That was one in college.

"Why?"

"He has to go to Ireland."

"Sweetheart, none of us has to go to Ireland. We left Ireland a hundred and sixty years ago. We were starving to death in Ireland."

"You do realize, don't you that Sean's major is Gaelic studies? Or are you no longer in touch with your children?"

"I don't need the attitude, Constance."

"It would be nice if he got to Ireland," she said.

"You'll just have to tell him no."

"That's not what good parents do. Good parents find a way to say yes to their children. You kept telling me when the boys were little: 'Every parent wants his child to have it better than he had it.'"

"Yeah, well, the world's changed since the boys were little. My father died on the job. I got downsized."

"Your dad never told you you couldn't do something."

"Of course he did. He told me I could never get Jeannie Carpenter to go to the prom with me. He was right. She wouldn't go with me."

"Probably because you were the iconic loner."

"I've always thought it was my anti-war stance."

"Mick, Sean is going to Ireland. You knew that when he entered this program. He told you that. You were supposed to be saving for it."

"Right. And al-Qaeda was supposed to stay the hell in Afghanistan, and the economy was supposed to stay strong, and I wasn't supposed to lose my job. What the hell do you think my life has been like for the past two years? I can't believe that fu — " Mick remembered Constance hated that word. "I can't believe that judge didn't lower my child support payments."

"It's because you have assets."

"I have a house. And a mortgage. And. No. Job."

"You have your retirement to live on."

"Until it's all dried up." Mick was yelling now. "I've been living on that for two years. It's how I pay the fu — . It's how I pay the damned mortgage. It's how I eat. Nobody's hiring. Constance, I had to lower myself to an interview at the Twin Rivers *Independent*. They won't pay me half what I'm worth."

"Then maybe you'd better try for a different kind of job. And you'd probably better stop thinking about buying your parents' old house."

Mick didn't say a word for a moment.

"How did you know about that?"

"I know you called that Virginia Somebody person at Westinghouse Township Realty."

"Virginia Crandall. Ginny. She's an old classmate of mine. And how do you know I talked to her?"

"And I know she told you there were teaching jobs open at the high school."

"How do you know all this shit? I just made that phone call yesterday."

"I still have friends there. And I read my e-mail."

Mick held his head in his free hand. "How did you — . You don't even know Ginny Crandall. Do you?"

"It's a small town, Mick. You grew up there. You taught there. Everyone there knows you, even if they don't like you. People see you, word gets around."

"Un-fucking-believable."

"Watch your mouth, Mick."

"Yes, you're pure as the Holy Mother, working on your second husband, with whom you slept while we were married. I love a good

Christian, you know, like you, Jimmy Swaggart, and all the rest of the adulterers and fornicators."

She let a moment pass without filling it with the sound of her voice.

"Mick, I even know Ginny Kramer had a crush on you in high school."

"Crandall. Good lord."

"And her husband plays softball with a guy on the school board. And, if my sources are accurate, the president of the school board used to be one of your teachers."

"Ex-husband," Mick said. "He's a good Christian, too. It's a wonder you two didn't meet while we lived there."

"Am I right?" she asked.

"Yes."

"Then you need to get back to Ginny Kramer — ."

"Crandall."

"Crandall, and you'd better get a resume in the mail and make a phone call to the board president — ."

"Who is it?"

"How do I know? Ask Ginny Kramer."

"No, I'm not asking Ginny Crandall anything. I'm going to get the *Independent* job. That's in the bag. The kid who interviewed me all but offered me the job the day I was there."

"So, then what's the problem? You'll have money for Sean."

"Constance, you aren't listening. They aren't going to pay me half of what I made before."

"I'm done listening, Mick. I'm calling my lawyer."

And she hung up. Of course.

Mick looked at his watch and scratched his head. He turned on CNN to find out what was going on in the world. He got out of bed and moved toward the kitchen. The phone rang again. He took it in the living room, so he would not be tempted to lie down.

"Mr. Mackintosh, this is Vera from Western Area Junior College."

"Good morning."

"Mr. Mackintosh, you sent us a resume in response to an ad we placed for someone to join our public relations staff."

"Yes."

"I'd like to invite you to come for an interview. Are you free later this week?"

"Tell me something about the job," Mick said, leaning back on his chair and stretching out his legs onto the desk.

"It's part time," she said, "twenty hours a week. You'll be an assistant to the head of the communications department."

"And what will I be doing?"

"Whatever he needs you to do." Mick imagined the PR guy Eastern Valley Area had hired early in his public school teaching career. He was the nephew of the woman the superintendent was screwing. A tall guy with too much hair that wouldn't lie right no matter what he did with it. At school board meetings, everyone could tell he had no idea what he was doing, asking a hundred questions about what had just happened. And when the monthly newsletter came out, it screamed unprofessional. And now that Mick had spent time in newsrooms and had tangled with a number of PR types, he was sure this guy would be even worse than that poor bastard from a hundred years ago. "You might be writing press releases. You might be proofing things other people have written."

Mick knew he wouldn't take the job because he knew he'd be taking the job at the *Independent*, but he wanted to make a point.

"So, how many people are in the department?"

"Um, let me check my org chart." Mick could hear her clicking on her computer keyboard. "Uh, looks like six people besides the director."

"How many are part time?"

"All six. Three work the eight to noon shift, then three others work from noon to four. Once in a great while, if something big happens and the staff needs to stay on and manage a story through the night, people get extra hours."

"I see," Mick said. "Why not just hire three full-time people and stagger them through the day?"

"Mr. Mackintosh, do you want to interview for the job or not?"

"I don't think so. I couldn't afford to move just for part-time work."

"Thank you," she said in a clipped tone. Mick had found out since being unemployed that human relations people get pretty testy when you ask about the part-time set-up. They know their companies keep part-time positions so they don't have to pay benefits, and they know everyone else knows that. Mick just wanted to make them say it. He wanted to hear them admit how cheap and exploitative their employers were.

Mick emptied a can of condensed tomato soup into a bowl, mixed it with water and put it into the microwave. While the microwave hummed, Mick turned on the computer in the office so it would warm up. He went back into the kitchen and got out a sleeveful of crackers, and when the microwave beeped, he pulled the soup up and broke about half the sleeve of crackers into it. He took a bottle of hot sauce out of the refrigerator and shook a liberal portion into the bowl, then stuck a tablespoon into the bowl. Cradling it with a potholder, he carried the bowl into the office and sat down. Holding the soup with his left hand, he clicked on this and that to make his computer pull up his e-mail. At the top was a message from Christopher Post. Mick opened it up to see when he'd be starting.

"Dear Mr. Mackintosh:

"Thank you for your interest in the Twin Rivers *Independent*."

At those words, Mick's heart thudded faster inside his chest. He knew what they meant.

"We have filled the position for which you applied. Feel free to apply for any other position in the future for which you feel qualified. We have no other positions available at this time. The *Independent* wishes you good luck in your future journalistic endeavors.

"Sincerely,

"C. Post"

Mick felt the ire rising. His face felt hot. His hands trembled. "Mr. Mackintosh." "C. Post." "Good luck in your future journalistic endeavors." What the fuck was that? He wondered who had composed this message. This was not the voice of the wide-eyed kid who had told Mick in-house gossip about the people who ran the *Independent*. Mick hit the reply button. The screen hesitated to come up, perhaps sensing his burgeoning wrath. He clicked on the reply button again. And again. And again. Each time with increasing intensity. Finally the screen popped up. He set the soup down on the desk to the right of the screen. He typed furiously, his fingers pounding keys imprecisely, producing only gibberish. He could feel his eyes vibrating and he could barely see the screen. Mick finished his note, then cleaned up all the typos that had raged through his fingertips:

"What happened? You all but signed me up for benefits when I interviewed. Did someone more qualified come along? I don't understand. What did I do wrong?"

Then he aimed the mouse at the send button. Then he aimed his index finger at the "right-click" button on the mouse and jabbed it as hard as he could.

His fury launched Mick out of his chair, and it recoiled backwards and thudded onto the carpet.

He paced the room, first staring at the tan rug, nap flattened by years of trampling. He put his hands on his hips and stared straight upward at the knick-knacks adorning the cherry-stained wood-grain shelf hung a couple of feet from the white ceiling. He reached the end of the room and spun around, staring at and marching toward the family pictures hung on the pale blue wall above his desk. He spun around again and stared straight ahead at the framed front pages below the shelf, pages that carried his stories or his staffers' stories, flanking the state press association awards he'd won for news-, editorial- and column-writing, plus the publisher's award from a paper where he had led a yearlong, newsroom-wide project.

"What the fuck happened?" he roared. "I had that job. I HAD THAT FUCKING JOB. How could I not get a job at a puke-ass fucking newspaper like the fucking *Independent*? Fucking bastard doesn't know a third of what I know." He caught his breath. Mick's head pounded. "How could he not fucking hire me?"

One word stuck in his mind:

"Duuude"

He steamed out of the office and around the corner into the living room. He collapsed onto the overstuffed couch and threw his right arm up and across his forehead. He stared at the ceiling.

"The fucking *Independent*. The fucking *Independent* didn't hire me. I can't fucking believe it. I GOT BEAT OUT BY SOME FUCKING KID WHO WENT ON PANTY RAIDS WITH THE BOSS A COUPLE OF WEEKS AGO. I CAN'T FUCKING BELIEVE THIS."

Again Mick caught his breath. His head continued to pound. He had to compose himself. He thought he could have a stroke. He stood up and looked out the window of the front screen door. He could see the hedge lining the bottom of the front yard. He could see the petunias he had planted along the driveway and the rose bushes that lined the walk up to the porch. He could see a neighbor across the street coming home from work. He wanted desperately to come home from work.

He closed his eyes and remembered what it had been like to win that publisher's award. The entire newsroom had been gathered in the community room for the presentation of several annual awards. Everyone had assumed the winner would be the two reporters who had investigated the sexual harassment allegations against the district attorney. Mick himself had nominated them, had written a note to the publisher that those reporters had to be the first consideration, and no one was even in second place. Sitting in the last row, right in front of the refreshment table laden with coffee urns and cookie trays, Mick had just stuffed a peanut butter cookie into his mouth and slurped a little coffee when the publisher ripped the plain brown wrapper off the publisher's award and started to read the citation. Hearing the first three words, Mick knew it was him. Adrenaline flooded cold through his system. He couldn't chew. He couldn't swallow. A staff member two seats away from his leaned over and clutched his hand, crushing a part of the cookie. Mick had just stared at her, trying to force down that cookie. Then the publisher said his name, and he wobbled up from his chair and set his paper coffee cup on the seat and lurched forward, still chewing, making the long walk past applauding co-workers. He saw the two reporters he assumed would win smiling broadly and clapping hard. A couple of his staffers in the middle of the room stood while they applauded. The rest of the room followed their lead. Mick just shook his head, still chewing the remnants of that cookie. He reached the podium behind which the publisher stood. She handed Mick the large, framed citation, done in Old English script. She shook his hand and leaned in and kissed his cheek. He shook hands with the editor, who leaned in and kissed Mick's cheek, then turned to face the staff, some dopey grin hanging on his face. The staff roared. At that moment, Mick knew what every awardee had ever meant when he had said, "I'm humbled by this award." To have the people who mean the most in your professional life make such a display of love and respect changes the world. The music writer yelled out, "Speech."

 Mick forced the last of the cookie down his gullet and cleared his throat. He opened his mouth and his eyes filled and his words could not get past his emotions.

 "I — ."

He just shook his head. He tried again.

 "I, um — ."

He thought he would try a different tack.

 "I really just came for the cookies."

The staff roared and applauded. The editor squeezed the top of his shoulder. The publisher patted his back.

"I, uh — . Thank you." The publisher hugged Mick and the editor shook his hand again, and the room applauded again, then Mick, carrying the award, wobbled back to his seat.

Mick's staff took him to dinner that night — Constance declined an invitation to join them — and they had a grand celebration. Mick went home that night flushed with joy that someone had appreciated the work he had done, that his co-workers had embraced his triumph, even if he still thought someone else was the better choice. When Mick got inside the house, Constance tossed a quick, "Congratulations" at him, then went back to the television program that mesmerized her. Mick reached a beer out of the refrigerator and sat down in his recliner and replayed the day over and over, never noting what moved and spoke in front of him on the TV. He also thought about the hours of labor he had put into the project, working late into the night, filling in for an editor with more pressing duties than the project, directing reporters who weren't sure what thrust to take on their stories, negotiating with senior staff for more bodies for the project. He had even given up a vacation when it looked like the whole project would fall through, and he stayed home and nursed it over its wounds. Work was Mick's essence. Not friendships, not travel, certainly not family. Work. The publisher's award validated his work, validated him.

That thought gave Mick some comfort as he lay back down on the couch, his temples squeezing his brain. He could do work, and he could do work well.

Christopher Post could never have known a moment like that in his nascent career. Mick told himself the kid had had no right to not hire him. He had no right to sit in judgment of Mick in any respect. Mick lay sprawled on the couch, right leg bent, foot resting on the far arm, left leg bent at the knee, foot flat on the floor. He shook his head and said softly. "I can't fucking believe it."

After a few minutes, Mick lifted himself from the couch and trudged back into the office and to his desk. Christopher Post had responded. Mick opened the e-mail.

"Mr. Mackintosh:

"We simply decided to go in another direction.

"C. Post"

Mick leaned back in his chair, now incapable of rage. He ran his right hand over his face.

They would never give a reason. Fear of lawsuits now sent every manager in America cowering. Mick would never know what kind of person was better than himself in the eyes of Christopher Post or whoever had made that decision.

So, he wouldn't be going home. He wouldn't be leaving his imprint on the newspaper he had grown up reading. He wouldn't be buying the house he grew up in. He wouldn't be buying a new big blue suit. He wouldn't be earning any money to send his son to Ireland, which, Mick knew, meant that Constance's lawyer would be going to court trying to attach his mutual funds. Most of all, Mick knew he wouldn't be working.

Mick told himself that Christopher Post was some kid who couldn't know what he had sitting in the board room the other day. He could tell himself that, from the time he had read the first book about journalism he had ever read, preparing to teach a high school "J" course, he knew that the *Independent* was a piece of junk, and he could conclude: No wonder it's a piece of junk; they never hire anybody any good. He could even tell himself that all his life, his father had told him that you have to know someone to get a job, so that's was this was about. He could tell himself all of those things, but he couldn't understand. Not really.

In his head, the monologue played: What could I possibly have done differently to win this job? Did Christopher Post notice the hole in my suit pants and think I had come dressed inappropriately? Did he ultimately fear that I would want to usurp his position and challenge his every decision? Did I talk too much, going on about things he didn't care about, and did he fear I would become the newsroom orator? Did the owners think my salary demands were out of line with the salaries of the rest of the newsroom? Was I too old?

Good lord.

He thought of the PR job. If only that woman had called after he'd read Christopher Post's e-mail. He wouldn't have been so smug. He shook his head. Didn't matter. He couldn't live on twenty hours a week. He'd never find a place to live.

What would he do? Who would hire him? Should he just sell the house? How would he pay for school? How would he send Sean to Ireland? How would he buy his parents' old house? His head hurt.

He conceded to himself that maybe he would never have another job in journalism. Maybe he would never have another job. He thought of those pathetic men he would see on the streets of Twin Rivers when he was a boy. Bums, his dad called them. No matter the time of year, they walked the streets wearing an overcoat, maybe a scruffy hat, scuffed, filthy shoes, sometimes torn where the leather should have met the sole. Sometimes, a grimy bare foot protruded from the tear; other times, a sock of an indeterminate color covered the foot. Some of the bums carried a bundle slung over their shoulders. Some pushed a battered shopping cart. Is that the figure he would someday cut, Mick asked himself.

Or maybe he would simply find a dreary job somewhere, doing something utterly uninteresting to him. He knew people — and pitied them — who dragged themselves out of bed each morning and trudged wearily to the car or bus stop on the way to jobs they hated, jobs they did only because their dreams had not worked out.

Mick would never know what silly reason Christopher Post or someone else had for keeping him away from the *Independent*. All he knew was that in the two years since the *Sun* editors had recruited him to help them revive their newspaper, he had gone from someone prized to someone inconsequential. For years he had looked with pity upon every basketball player who eventually discovered he lacked the speed and power to drive to the hoop or every baseball player who discovered that he couldn't hit a breaking ball or couldn't throw hard enough to impress scouts. Or every aspiring writer who found out in college that she lacked the power of language or insight to engage readers. For years, as he climbed toward his ultimate potential, he had looked with pity upon people who had lacked the talent or the skill to work in a job with some prestige. Now he was one of them.

Mick closed his eyes.

***

The phone rang. Mick leapt up from the couch, startled. The clock on the VCR said 1:22. He picked up the phone.

"Mick, it's Ginny Crandall."

"Ginny," Mick straightened himself into a sitting position. "How's it going?"

"Fine. How are you?"

"Okay, okay. So, what's up?"

"I talked to the owners of the house. Did you have a run-in with them?"

"I had a, uh, discussion with the lady of the house."

"Kenny's wife."

"Apparently. Until she told me that, I was thinking she was the sadistic housekeeper."

Ginny giggled. "Yeah, she's not very well thought of in the neighborhood. They called the police once to escort her out of a school board meeting."

"I'm not surprised," Mick said. "Why the hell did Kenny marry her?"

"Knocked her up. He did the honorable thing."

"Should be a statute of limitations on that. So, what did she say?"

"She said if Mick Mackintosh was the really tall guy with long hair, the price just went up ten thousand dollars."

"Shit."

"What did you do to her?"

"I weeded her garden."

Mick heard only silence for a moment.

"Does that mean what I think it means?"

"I doubt it. I literally pulled the weeds out of the rose garden my mother had. They were choking the roses. She came out and saw me and got pissed. I may have said harsh words to her."

Ginny giggled again.

"Well," she said, "she's not selling to you at the list price. I tried to tell her what a good guy you were."

"And Kenny was no help?"

"Oh, Mick, you haven't talked to Kenny in a while. Kenny doesn't make any decisions in that house."

"Aaah. Just like his dad."

"But if you want to come out here, I'd be happy to show you as many houses as you want to see."

"Well," Mick said, letting out a sigh, "let's put that off for a while. I didn't get the job at the *Independent*. I just found out."

"What? Why not?"

"They won't say. Probably hired some half-literate kid."

"Oh, Mick, I'm so sorry."

"Ginny, my ex called this morning. She knew all about my talking to you about the house."

"I'm sorry," Ginny said. "I was just so excited about one of the old gang coming back, I must have told too many people."

"Don't worry about that right now. But, look, you told me yesterday there were teaching jobs open. Do you know if any of them are in English?"

"No. I could make a few calls."

"Thanks. Ginny, who's the board president?"

"Remember Miss Gaynor?"

"Junior high English."

"Yes. Well, she married a doctor."

"Okay, I knew that. Dr. Petrovich. He gave the athletic physicals."

"Well, I didn't know that, but that's who she married. She quit teaching to have kids, and she's been on the board for years."

"And now she's president."

"And now she's president," Ginny repeated.

"Cool. Who's the superintendent? Well, never mind. I can get that on the Web. They probably post openings on the Web, too, but if you can find out and give me a call, that would be great."

"I'll be happy to. Anything that brings me closer to those ten thousand extra dollars you need to buy your parents' house.

"And, Mick," she said.

"Yeah?"

"If you come out for an interview, let's have lunch or something."

"Um, sure. We should do that."

Mick and Ginny said their goodbyes and hung up. This would be perfect. His school district had always hired alumni. Well, alumni were in the second tier when Mick was a kid, he remembered. First tier were political hires, people whose relatives worked for the Democratic Party or family and friends of people in the school administration, though Mick wasn't sure there was any difference in that distinction. Then came alumni. That's how he got the job the first time. Apparently no politicians' or administrators' kids were English teachers. When all else failed, Eastern Valley hired people who were qualified. Mick smiled to think that he was all three. Ms. Gaynor had loved him when he was in junior high, because he was a great grammar student and was editor of the ninth-grade newspaper, which was little more than three or four mimeographed pages stapled together. And he was an alumnus, and he was qualified. He was the trifecta. No way could they find any teaching candidate who could work better with writing students than he could. And Mick knew that was important because he had read that the SATs had added a writing component. That was his selling point.

Hell, Mick realized, he was even a vendor, since they had bought his book for their elementary history program.

Mick picked himself up off the couch and scurried into the office, awkwardly until his knees loosened up a little. He did a search for the Eastern Valley district. There it was. An ad for a high school English teacher. He would be teaching American Lit and English 9. Okay. That could work. They listed all of the high school teachers by department. He knew some of them from when he was there before. Of course, they would be late in their careers, nearing retirement, and he would be coming with a fresh perspective. He also recognized names exactly like the names of students he had had. Maybe they were the same people. It might not be a bad thing to teach. He'd have summers off for grad school or to write some freelance pieces. Maybe they'd even reimburse for tuition. Man, that would be sweet.

But the application process was pretty involved. He needed to get some letters of reference. He wrote letters to the guy who had been principal when he taught, which he found on an on-line telephone directory; the editor from a couple of newspapers ago who had made him a writing coach; and one of his profs from the grad program, who had expressed admiration for his presentations. Fine. He wrote letters to the state to get criminal check and child abuse clearances. He wrote for transcripts to the college where he had earned his bachelor's degree, then to his master's program. Finally, he found the standard state teacher application on line and downloaded a copy to fill out.

The final page of the state application asked him to write an essay about his philosophy of teaching his discipline. Mick thought back to his teaching career, remembering what had succeeded for him and what had failed for him. He remembered the bright student who simply couldn't grasp grammar and blamed him for her D. He remembered the closed-circuit television news broadcasts he did with his journalism class each year. He remembered his slowest lit section reading "To An Athlete Dying Young" and the hard case who, without raising his head involuntarily muttered in wonder, "He's dead." Mick remembered how much he enjoyed teaching writing, how much he enjoyed reading and correcting what the students had written. He always wrote extensive notes. He remembered his best writing student, Janet Winslow, who could paint awe-inspiring pictures with her words, who could give characters realistic dialogue, who could create a voice you'd want to spend your life with. And who died in her freshman year in college. Once, she complained that Mick's notes back to her were longer than the papers she wrote. Of course, they were. She had the potential to make a living as a writer, and Mick wanted her to know as much as she could know. It occurred to him that he had kept a couple of her papers as models for students who would come after her. He wondered if he still had them. His philosophy of teaching English would be to make sure the Janet Winslows of the world had every shred of his knowledge to apply. Or reject.

Of course, he knew that was the last answer that any bureaucrat in any school district, much less Eastern Valley, wanted to read. So, he threw together some claptrap about teaching to the breadth of the English discipline and developing the potential of students, whether they were college bound or headed for vocational training or whatever. He filled the page and saved it.

Next he found the superintendent's name. Dr. Franklin F. Fosburg. Never heard of him. Who else was in the administration? Aha! Dr. Edward J. Webb was the high school principal. Eddie Webb. Not a bad guy. Taught science when Mick was teaching. A little older than Mick. That's good.

Mick composed a quick letter to the superintendent:

Dear Dr. Fosburg:

Please consider me a candidate for the high school English teaching job you advertised on the school district Web site.

I grew up in the Eastern Valley Area School District and taught there in my first years out of college. I also spent more than twenty years at various newspapers, doing an array of writing, editing and management jobs. I also wrote the history of Westinghouse Township that your elementary school teachers once used. My extensive experience makes me an outstanding candidate to help your students learn.

Please find my resume and my state application enclosed. I will send transcripts, letters of reference and state clearances under another cover.

I look forward to the opportunity to interview with you.

Thank you.

Sincerely,

Michael P. Mackintosh

    Then he created another resume file and copied his resume into it, then revised it so it would be appropriate for an education job.
    Mick couldn't believe how excited he was about this. He was moving forward. Fuck the *Independent*. Fuck journalism. Mostly, fuck the dude. Mick was a teacher before he was a journalist. Even when he was an editor, he'd been a teacher. So, teaching was his past and his destiny. He would get back to it and inspire the children of Eastern Valley, the way he'd been inspired.

Mick printed everything out and put all of the sheets into an envelope, and typed a label he affixed to the envelope.

Then he went back to the Eastern Area web site and clicked on the e-mail link for Eddie Webb.

From: Mick Mackintosh [mailto:mickeymack@fastconnect.com]
Sent: Wednesday, June 5, 2003 2:37 AM
To: Dr. Edward J. Webb
Re: Touching base

Eddie,

I hope you remember me as an English teacher in the 1970s. I taught mostly American lit, but I also taught some writing.

I wanted you to know I just sent a resume to Dr. Fosburg. I'm applying for the English teaching job you have on your web site.

In case you haven't heard, I've been in newspapers for years and years, but I lost my job after 9/11. I need to move back to the Pittsburgh area because I'm in a grad program at Pitt. Teaching at Eastern Valley would be great. Perfect, actually. I don't know how the decision-making process works there now, whether you get your choice or if you and Dr. Fosburg talk things over or exactly how things work, but I thought you would want to hear from me personally that I had applied. I look forward to interviewing with you.

Thank you.

Michael P. Mackintosh

Mick then took his packet to the post office. The woman at the counter looked it over.

"You want to be a teacher?" she asked. "All of your other applications were for newspaper jobs."

"Well, that and PR jobs," he said. "But, you know, I have teaching experience. That could be fun again." She didn't say anything, but she looked up at Mick from under her eyebrows while she suspended her scanning of the envelopes. "I know what you're thinking," he said, "but the longer I'm out of work, the more different jobs I think I could do."

"And what do I always say? 'You'll find something,'" she said, resuming her task. "You have to have faith. I'm praying for you. And from now on, I'm praying for you to go back to teaching."

Mick thanked her and hurried home.

On the drive home, it occurred to him that he didn't have to settle for Eastern Valley Area. He certainly had the qualifications to teach at one of the wealthy school districts in southwestern Pennsylvania. He raced into the house and got back on line. He called up the web site for the state Department of Education and looked at the map. What the hell, he told himself, I'll just flood the region with resumes.

VIII

From: Mick Mackintosh [mailto:mickeymack@fastconnect.com]
Sent: Thursday, June 26, 2003 6:41 AM
To: B.D. Butterfield
Subject: Nothing good (for sure)

I didn't get the fucking job. I don't know why. They won't say. No job. No house.
B.D., I swear, if I weren't so deep into this master's program, I'd take you up on your invitation to apply for a job out there. It would be great to work together again, but I've already invested a ton of money in this program, and I can't let it go without getting the degree.

For two days, I felt free of the constraints of joblessness, or at least that I would be soon. Now I'm back to being the guy on the block with no job.

Between Lives

I'm back to pinching pennies on everything I buy. They just opened a grocery store cheaper than Sprawl Mart called Bargain Foods. I guess I'll have to check into that, along with all the people dragging food stamps to the cashier and the old people talking about how much they saved on a can of green beans compared to what they would have spent at the big grocery store on the highway that also sells cut flowers. This is so depressing.

Do you know how long it's been since I bought I book that I didn't need for a class? I know, I can go to the library and borrow books, but I'm used to OWNING them. Especially the non-fiction books, history and sports, that I go back to time and again for details I've forgotten.

I know. There are people in real poverty in America, and I shouldn't complain. But many of those are people born into poverty. Some of them — and I belie my streak of liberalism here — play the system to stay in poverty and take government handouts. And still others had opportunities for education or athletics to take them away from their poverty, and they dismissed it like a hot blonde waving off the fat guy in a leisure suit.

I did all the right things. I went to college, and I got good jobs and worked hard to advance into better jobs. Then the roof falls in exactly when I'm supposed to be in my peak earning years. I'm so fucking angry, I couldn't sleep last night. I just lay in bed cursing the terrorists and cursing the newspaper industry and the profit margin whores who own the papers and the president and Wall Street. And snotty boy editors who don't hire people who know how to do things.

There was this kid who went into the office when I was coming out. A friend of the editor's. Didn't know how to dress for an interview. Probably can't spell "cat." Probably can't write a fucking sentence. Probably has no clue how to structure a story. But because he and the editor learned to tie their shoelaces at the same daycare — LIKE, LAST WEEK — he gets the job and I get to try to figure out how to pay a mortgage, put two kids through college, pay my own tuition and, oh by the way, eat three meals a day.

THIS IS SO FUCKING UNFAIR.

This is just beyond belief.
Shit.

MM

IX

A few weeks later, while Mick was digging through his boxes looking for old lesson plans, the phone rang.
Constance.
"Now what have the tom-toms told you?" Mick said.
"Shut up," she said. "This is serious."
Mick knew the tone.
"What's wrong?"
"It's Sam."
"What's wrong?" Mick repeated.
"Well, he dropped a bombshell last night."
"What?" Mick hated the way she had to drag everything out.
"He's made a career choice."
"Tell me."

"He wants to tell you himself."

"Then—Put—Him—On. Somebody better freaking tell me."

"I'll get him."

Mick waited. What career choice would have Constance upset? Sean wanted to — well, Mick was never clear what the hell Sean wanted to do with a major in Gaelic studies. He sure wouldn't be an English teacher.

"Hi, Dad."

"Sam, your mother said you had news. What's up?"

"Dad, I've made a big decision."

"Yeah, I know." Mick was losing patience. "What is it?"

"Don't get mad."

"Unless you've decided to be a drag queen at the Cuban Heel, I won't get mad," but his voice was rising. "Now, what is your decision?"

"What's the Cuban Heel?"

"Samuel-Polk-Mackintosh."

"I'm joining the army."

Mick didn't say anything for an instant. Two instants.

"The army," Mick said quietly.

"Look, Dad, I know you're having trouble getting Sean through school, and if I go to the army, they'll pay for college."

"If they don't get you killed." Mick realized he was shouting.

"Well, I can go to some school that won't put me on the front lines."

"You can go to some school that won't put you in Iraq. I suggest Penn State. They accepted you, if I remember correctly. You're supposed to start in a couple of months."

"Just to a branch campus. You know that, and I know you can't even afford that."

"'Even'" Mick muttered under his breath. Sam was too young to understand how that word felt.

"Dad. Really, I'll be okay. And they'll pay me an arm and a leg to go to Iraq."

"No. No. No. You'll lose an arm. Or a leg. Or maybe both. You're not going to Iraq. You're just not."

Mick could hear Sam talking to his mother, even though Sam muffled the sound with his hand over the speaker.

"Mick." It was Constance.

"No. He's not going to Iraq."

"Well, I told him you'd be mad. I told him. He thought you'd take it like an adult."

"Constance, he's not — . Where the hell did this come from?"

"A recruiter sent him a letter. Sam just tossed it aside until he heard about Sean."

"No. No. This was no recruiter. This was your fucking husband. What about Sean?"

He could feel Constance fuming on the other end.

"I think I'm going to hang up now, Mick. I don't like the language, and I don't like your insinuations."

"You married a freaking Neo-Con, a right-wing nut job, and — ."

"He heard me talking to you about Sean, and he realized you wouldn't be able to put him through school."

"Who?"

"Who what?"

"Who heard you talking about Sean?"

"Sam, you imbecile."

"Yeah, well, I'm not Sam's only parent. Your right-wing nut job is a county commissioner, right? He's got to be pulling down serious money from that job, and his salary on top of that."

"You're an ass. Carl is not taking graft or anything. You think everybody's taking graft."

"That's because I've actually read the newspapers and read political history. You should try reading. Carl should try reading."

"This is not about Carl. This is about your inability to provide an education for your sons."

"I had a pretty damned good career going until Nine-Eleven. I made pretty good money."

"And since then, you haven't worked a day, and your sons are suffering for it."

"What do you know? You don't know anything about the industry. There just aren't any jobs out there."

"So, get into another industry."

"I'm fifty-two years old. You want me to maybe start a career as an engineer?"

"Maybe your girlfriend Ginny Kramer can get you a job at the high school."

"Girlfriend?" Mick responded to exactly the wrong thing. On purpose. He didn't want to give Constance the satisfaction of knowing that he'd already applied for the job. "Yeah, well, listen, Constance, I'm coming out there. It's a little after four. I'm gonna get a shower and be there in three hours or so. You tell Sam to meet me at the food court at that mall near you. Tell him at Davey's. Let's say seven. Make it half past seven."

"What are you going to say?"

"Well, I'm gonna just tell him — ." Mick was struck by the thought that telling him wouldn't do. He remembered what happened when his dad had told him he had to accept the basketball scholarship he was offered. "I'm not sure. I just — .

"Constance, are you in favor of this?"

"Mick, I'm a political wife of a conservative Republican. What do you want from me?"

"Your baby might die."

Mick heard a sniffle on the other end.

"We raised our sons to make their own decisions," she said. "We raised them to — " nothing for an instant — "to observe, read, ask questions, seek counsel, and make their own best decisions."

"I know, but — ."

"And we taught them that no matter what decision they made, they had to live with the consequences, and that we would never bail them out."

"The army?"

"Everything, Mick. Now, don't try to get around me. I know how you work, Michael." Her voice rose. "I'm not having it. You have to do what you have to do. But I'm his mother, and I have to live here. You don't know what it's like. You don't live here." If Constance knew Mick's tactics, Mick knew hers. Her anger and what Mick thought of as a non-sequitur, were attempts to forestall the tears, but Mick heard them. "I'm his mother, for God's sake."

Then she hung up.

Mick hung up, looked at the twin frames containing pictures of his boys, then peeled off his shirt and headed for the shower.

The water hit his face, and he turned to let it run all over him.

His mind drifted over his conversations with Constance and Sam, with his anger, with his past, and thudded on one word: Christians.

X

From: Mick Mackintosh [mailto:mickeymack@fastconnect.com]
Sent: Thursday, July 10, 2003 4:22 AM
To: Audrey Kleffer
Subject: Anti-war movement

Dear Ms. Kleffer:

I am a dedicated pacifist since the Vietnam War, but I have sat on the sidelines through this disaster the dumbest president in history has dragged us into. Now, however, it's time for me to get involved because my son is going to enlist in the service with the express purpose of going to Iraq.

Between Lives

I have cast about for what I can do, and I have remembered that I saw a news story about a demonstration Christians Against the War held in Cleveland.

I am interested in joining your group and participating however I can. I have a long career in newspapers, and I might be able to help you get your message — our message — into the media, print, anyway.

I am about to drive to a meeting with my son to see if I can dissuade him from taking this step, but I am interested in talking to you about what I can contribute to the anti-war movement and how I can undermine this idiot's plans to light a fire that will consume all of the Middle East and devastate our young people.

You can write to me at this e-mail address, or you can call me tomorrow at the number in my sig below. I'm eager to discuss this with you.

Michael "Mick" Mackintosh

XI

On the drive to meet Sam, Mick thought about what he might say, how he might approach the topic. He knew what he couldn't do. He couldn't tell him what to do. That's not how he and Constance had raised the boys. And he knew he couldn't lecture Sam. When he was a boy, people lectured to kids, and Mick and his contemporaries were expected to just listen. At some point, the Boomers stopped just listening. The popular mythology was that the Boomers started asking uncomfortable questions, such as "Why?" Mick wasn't sure he remembered that part. What he remembered were a lot of arguments, himself with his dad; his buddies with theirs.

He and his dad didn't argue about Vietnam the way a lot of

sons and fathers had. Even though his dad was a decorated veteran of World War II, the old man did not want his son to go to war. He didn't want anyone's son to go to war. He used to say that Lyndon Johnson had no idea what he was doing in running the Vietnam war, that he couldn't decide whether to win it or not. He was just like that damned Harry Truman, who had not let MacArthur have his way in Korea. Johnson had never served. Oh, he was in the naval reserves or some damned thing, his dad knew, but he hadn't been overseas, hadn't seen men die, hadn't been forced to kill anyone. Mick's dad had coached little league baseball and midget football and PAL basketball and had been a Scout leader until Mick had shown no interest whatsoever in Scouting. Because the old man had had so much contact with so many boys in Westinghouse Township, he didn't want any of his boys going. He wanted all of them to go to college and get deferments. He used to say, if Johnson had "a goddamned brain in his goddamned head" he would bring back all the men from World War II and turn them loose on the Viet Cong, and they'd wrap things up in a couple of weeks. Mick envisioned a bunch of paunchy old men in bowling shirts, carrying bowling bags and shotguns jumping out of helicopters and looking for the enemy. Of course, Mick came to understand as he got older that his father didn't want to go into war again, but that he would have been happy to go if that would spare Mick and all the other boys he had helped coach and mentor.

Mick remembered when the newspaper reported that Wally Deere had been killed in Vietnam. His father was in the living room reading the paper, and his mother was setting the table for dinner. "Honey," his dad had said, "Wally — ." And the word stuck in the old man's throat. And Mick, reading on the sofa, had looked over at his dad, and asked, "What, Dad." The old man did not put down the paper, did not look at Mick. "Wally De — ." And that's all he got out before the gurgle hit. The old man got up and went into the kitchen, careful not to let Mick see his face, and he showed the paper to Mick's mother. And Mick's mother tried to take the paper, but his father held fast and pointed. Mick's mother had said, "Oh, my God. They've gone and killed Wally. That goddamned Johnson." And it was the only time Mick had heard his mother take the Lord's name in vain.

Mick had got up from his reading to see what all of this was about, but when he got close to his dad, his dad set the paper down, turned his back on Mick and stormed out the back door. He went right to the car and started it up and drove away. Mick never knew where his dad had gone, knew he shouldn't ask, shouldn't risk seeing his dad expose his emotions like that.

No, no one in the family was a fan of the war. But his parents were also not ones for demonstrations. His dad would serve picket duty when the mill went out on strike, but he wouldn't carry a sign. He always chose "third trick" for his picket duty so no one would see him. When Mick joined an ad hoc anti-war student group at the high school, Mick's dad lectured him, lectured him about staying in his place, lectured him about working within the system. Mick did not ask why. Mick shouted at him. And when it came time for the basketball scholarship to Pitt, Mick wouldn't have it. Pitt had been the old man's dream for Mick, and he was the proudest guy in western Pennsylvania when the basketball coach offered his boy a scholarship. He was The Man at the VFW and at the mill. But, as a committed antiauthoritarian, Mick would not play for, in his perspective, the aggrandizement of an institution. Mick's dad had no money to send him to Pitt on his own dime, and he couldn't understand why Mick wouldn't just take the education to spite the bastards. The old man lectured him about money, about dreams, about responsibility to the family, about the future, about opportunity. Mick tuned him out or shouted at him. Mick had prevailed, but he knew he had paid the price for winning. Everything costs, Mick told himself as he pulled into the mall parking lot.

No, he would not lecture Sam. He would not shout at Sam. Mick had been a pretty good staff manager at the various newspapers. He had often been able to convince his reporters to do what he wanted to by a series of questions. "Ask why five times," he believed, a business model American industry had rejected and for which rejection it had paid a price. Mick would ask Sam why five times. He'd get Sam to the root of his own thinking. He'd get Sam to see the folly of his choice.

On a Friday night in June, Mick found the Lakeview Mall a sea of teens. Mick stood on the aisle looking over the well into the food court. Floating and mingling in homogeneous and heterogeneous groups were boys of every race, some with the sides of their heads shaved and the middle slicked and sticking up, with hues varying from boy to boy; some sporting completely shaved heads; some wearing Pirates', Indians', White Sox' and Yankees' baseball caps of traditional and untraditional styles askew on their heads; some with cornrows, with and without do-rags. Almost all of the boys wore oversized T-shirts over pants whose crotch seemed to reach to their knees. Most of the boys flirted with or gawked at girls wearing oversized T-shirts, jeans and tennis shoes, or wearing belly shirts and shorts and sandals, or halters or tube tops or ridiculously short skirts. Mick was pretty sure Sam would have a shaved head, but he may or may not be wearing a cap cockeyed.

He moved toward Davey's Dogs, a business that operated out of a small, square, brick building on the lake when Mick's parents brought them to the resort in the late 1950s and early '60s. Mick sliced through groups of boys, who glanced up at him and stared at the hair over the collar and the goatee. Mick had got to know Davey over the years because his mother was a fiend for hot dogs. Davey, like Mick, loved the Pirates and told Mick stories about Ralph Kiner and Arky Vaughn and other old-timers. Every time Mick visited the boys since Constance had married Carl, they ended up at Davey's.

A girl with most of both boobs pouring out of her top giggled at the old man weaving his way through the crowd. And Mick always wondered if Davey was still alive. Or if any of the employees at this franchise even knew there was a real Davey instead of just a corporate nickname.

"Dad."

Mick looked toward the sound and saw Sam get up from a small, rectangular table against a brick dividing wall topped with a planter filled with ferns. Sam reached out his right hand and took his dad's while putting his left arm around his dad's shoulder, pulling him close for a brief hug. Mick reciprocated.

"Pirates' hat," Mick said, as they moved toward the table. "Cool. I missed their pastel blue phase." He had to raise his voice above the near din, which reminded Mick of nights in his favorite college-town bar. He settled into the swiveled seat, which barely swung out far enough for Mick to slide his long legs under the table.

Sam looked around and pointed to a tall, broad black kid moving away from the Subway restaurant. "Do you remember the Yankees cherry red period?"

Mick turned to look, then shook his head. "I'll bet you didn't know," he told Sam, "that until the late '40s the Pirates' colors were red and blue. Dark blue."

"Yeah, Dad, you told me that a few years ago."

"Huh?" Mick leaned his head in turned his ear to Sam.

Sam raised his voice.

"I said you told me a few years ago."

Mick nodded his head.

"And I suppose I told you that Roberto Clemente was the greatest Pirate ever, no matter how many home runs Barry Bonds ever hits. Remember, he hit all those homers as a Giant."

Sam nodded his head. Mick wasn't sure Sam had heard what he had just said. Sam looked away. Mick looked in that direction and thought maybe Sam was admiring the brunette with the soulful eyes who seemed only tangentially a part of the crew of girls who fluttered around her. Yes, Mick thought to himself, that's the one I would have chosen, too.

Mick looked his son over, as he did every time he saw one of them after time had elapsed. He had never inherited Mick's height, as Sean had. Instead, he was short, like his mom, although he had

Mick's broad shoulders, this evening stretching a T-shirt proclaiming some band Mick had never heard of.

"What?" Sam asked, loudly.

"If your mother hadn't objected, you would have made a great wrestler. Somewhere in the 130-, 140-pound range."

"I know. Whatever." This was another discussion they had had before, part of the colloquy of the man separated from the boy. Sam's dark eyes darted from side to side. Mick assumed he was checking out one girl after the other.

"I guess you ate already," Mick said.

"Huh?" Now Sam leaned in to hear.

"You had dinner?" Mick shouted.

"Yeah, mom made flounder. Really good. Did you eat or — ? You wanna get a dog or — ?" Mick hated that his son had adopted the speech pattern that trailed off after an "or" at the end of the sentence. Christopher Post had done that. Mick hated that his son hadn't been the iconoclastic teen he himself had been back in the day. No, back in *his* day, Mick told himself.

"Nah, if you ate, that's OK."

"I guess you want to talk about this army thing."

Mick realized he had been reluctant to start down that road, though it was the reason he had come. "Knowing how way leads on to way," Mick recited in his mind, though he could hardly hear himself do even that.

"Yeah, but not here. It's a lot louder than I expected."

"Friday."

"Huh?"

Sam lifted his head and raised his voice. "I guess you don't go to many malls on Fridays."

"No, Son, at my age, Friday is past my bed time." Mick stood up. "C'mon."

Mick took two steps toward the stairs that led out of the well, then he turned to wait for Sam. Sam did a fast, loose handshake with a kid in sunglasses, then came to Mick's side. As soon as he did,

Mick started to break through the crowds, his size opening holes for his smaller, yet muscular son. In a minute or two, they emerged from the din onto the main floor of the mall, near an ice cream stand. Mick walked up to the counter and ordered a cup of chocolate. He turned toward Sam, who waved him off and grabbed a table in the corner. Mick got his ice cream and sat down across from Sam.

"How's your sugar, Dad?" Sam asked in a normal voice, over just the hum of the freezer.

"It's okay, Sam."

"What's it gonna be when you finish the ice cream?"

"Well, I haven't had dinner, so it's probably low anyway. The ice cream won't hurt. Plus, it's no sugar added."

"Ah," Sam said.

"Now, Sam," Mick said, a spoonful of ice cream an inch from entry, "tell me where this army idea came from. Why do you want to do this?"

One "why."

"Well, like I said on the phone, I know you haven't been working. I know just getting Sean through school is hard for you. The army is a good opportunity for me. I'm gonna go to cryptology school. My recruiter said my grades were good enough for me to do that."

"So, they're not sending you to Iraq?"

"Oh, yeah, I signed up for that."

Mick stuck the spoon into the scoop of ice cream like a flag in the ground, shook his head, then leaned his head into his hands. Through his fingers, he said, "Why in God's name would you sign up to go to that hell hole?"

Two "whys," though perhaps this one was more desperation than design.

"Oh, Dad, check it out. The pay for a tour in Iraq is more than you made at *The Sun*."

Mick dropped his hands and leaned his long frame over so far that he almost touched Sam's face with his own. "Son, you can't collect that money if you're dead."

"Yeah, but it's all over over there. It's just mop-up stuff now. I might not even get over there before it's all over."

"Don't believe that 'Mission Accomplished' stuff, Sam. We'll have a long occupation over there, and you do follow the news, don't you? You do know that they're killing Americans over there, don't you? The Sunni are killing them, and the Shiites are killing them, and probably the agnostics are killing them."

Mick knew that he had missed a "why." He'd come back to it.

"I don't know how many agnostic Iraqis there are, Dad."

"Sam. Look. I don't understand. The whole time you were growing up, we were a pacifist household. Neither you nor your brother owned a toy gun. When your Grandfather Polk wanted to take you hunting, we said no."

"But when Pap brought deer meat we ate it."

Mick felt sure he'd had an opportunity for a "why" in there, but Sam had probably pre-empted it with his point about Constance's dad's deer meat.

Mick glared at Sam. "Different argument, Son. Let's have one debate at a time. Where the hell did you get the notion that it was a good idea to grab a gun and start shooting Muslims?"

Mick thought that was a "why." He might not have used that exact word. For that matter, he probably hadn't phrased any of it the way he should have. Sam probably understood that was a "why."

"They killed thousands of people at the World Trade Center."

Mick pushed aside the ice cream in which he had lost interest, lay his forearms on the table, hands clasped, and leaned into Sam. "I can guarantee you — . I promise you, on a stack of Bibles, that not one person in Iraq killed anyone on September 11. Guarantee you."

"Well, no, they didn't fly the planes, but they hate us."

"They hate us, if they do, because they chose to stay in the seventh century and the United States moved on."

"They hate us because of our lifestyle."

"Son, if you say 'They hate us because of our freedoms,'" Mick said in his imitation of the president, "I'm going to take you home and lock you up in a room and make you listen to Al Gore tapes non-stop for a week."

Okay, not a "why," Mick knew, but a good line. Sam would give points for a good line.

Same chuckled. "Well, that is true, isn't it?"

"It may be true of some Muslims. You can damn-betcha that the Iraqis didn't hate American freedom when we helped them fight their war against Iran in the seventies. And you can damn-betcha that Osama bin-Laden didn't hate American freedom when the Americans were shipping the Mujahedeen arms to fight the Soviets in Afghanistan."

Sam leaned back in his chair and draped his left arm over the back. "Well the president couldn't say that stuff if it wasn't true."

"Of course, he would. He lies. They all lie. Did you believe Bill Clinton when he said he never had sex with that woman? The president isn't Jesus. No president is. They all lie. They want us to support them in whatever idiot thing they want to do. The last thing they have in mind is to do what's good for the country, to do what's good for you. They want to do what's good for them. If the two happen to be the same thing, why that's just a happy coincidence." Mick pulled the ice cream back, brought a spoonful to his mouth, then pulled it away again. "And they probably wouldn't even realize it if it did benefit you. They don't know you're out here. They know you as white-male-not-of-voting-age. That's how you show up in the polls.

"And, Son, please do not confuse al-Qaeda with Iraq. Two different things. Even the president says that Iraq had nothing to do with the World Trade Center attack. He says it every Monday, right after Cheney goes on the Sunday TV talk shows to say they're the same thing. The difference is that Cheney tells millions of people watching Meet the Press, and the president tells Barney."

Mick knew he was talking way more than he should have. This was started to feel oddly familiar, in a through-the-looking-glass sort of way.

"Who's Barney?"

"The president's dog — " Mick took a spoonful of ice cream — "who has higher approval ratings than the president, by the way.

"Son, please, please, PLEASE do not go over there and waste your life."

Sam shot Mick a hard look. "Are you saying that everyone who dies over there has wasted their lives?"

"His life. Or his or her life."

"Are you saying that to defend your country is to waste your life?"

Again Mick dropped the spoon and held his head in his hands. "God, no. Of course not." He dropped his hands. "But, Sam, they're not defending — . Iraq didn't attack anyone. Bush wanted to do this from the get-go. Wolfowitz had the plans already drawn up when he took office. Nine-eleven was an excuse, not a reason."

Sam shook his head. Was he afraid to open his mouth or did he think Mick unworthy of oral response?

"But, Sam, the fact remains: This is not how you were raised. I don't know what kind of influences you've had to — ."

Sam leaned back in his chair and watched himself pick dead skin off his fingers. "Mom said you would do this."

"Do what?" Mick spread his arms wide.

"Blame Carl."

"Well," Mick said, lowering his head, looking at the table, then right back up at Sam, "now that you mention it, he is the only influence you've had that wasn't your mother and me."

"Mom's okay with this."

"Is that what she told you?"

Mick felt guilty, and instead of looking at Sam, he had another spoonful of ice cream.

"Yeah, she said if I was sure that was the best move for me, that's what I should do."

Mick nodded his head up and down as he tilted the cup toward him, "Oh, I see."

"What?" Sam leaned forward.

"Oh, nothing." Different tactic.

"What are you saying, Dad? Are you saying she doesn't want me to go?"

"You'll have to take that up with her, Son." Mick spooned out the last melted drops of ice cream.

Sam leaned back again. "Oh, I get it. You're not telling me anything. You're not lying to me; you're just letting me think something that's not true."

"Yes," Mick said, leaning his face across the table toward Sam. "I'm practicing to be president."

Sam shook his head and picked at some dry skin separating from his thumb.

"Sam, I'll get money for school."

"How could you do that? You don't have a job. Where are you going to get that kind of money?"

"Oh," Mick waved his hand dismissively, "I could sell the house, I could sell my mutual funds, I could even go into my IRA. Don't worry about that. I'll make you this deal: You go to your recruiter and have him tear up the papers, and you call Penn State or write them a letter or whatever you need to do, and I'll find the money."

Mick watched his son puzzle over that. Sam chewed the inside of his cheek, the way Mick did, the way Mick's father had, and his uncle and his grandfather. Sam shifted in his chair and put his hands on top of his head and pushed the cap back and forth over his head.

"What do you think Mom and Carl are going to say if I don't go?"

"What do I care what they say?"

Sam grinned and put his hands back on the table. "Yeah, but you don't have to live with them."

"Oh, Sam," Mick said, "in ways you'll only understand when you grow up and have an ex-wife of your own, I live with your mother every day of my life."

Sam chuckled. "Well, I'm not planning to have an ex-wife."

"Well, you know," Mick said, relaxing now, crossing one leg over the other, showing a bit of a wince to do so, "an ex-husband. Who am I to judge?"

Sam reached across the table and punched his dad's arm.

"Ow, damn it. You're strong. Should have been a wrestler. If you'd have been good enough, Penn State would have given you a scholarship."

"I don't know why you always push wrestling," Sam said. "Why didn't you want me to be a basketball player like you?"

Mick shook his head while he looked down at the table. "You could only be a basketball player like me if you were tall and slow. Instead, you're short and quick. You could have been a guard, but you're not that quick. Besides," Mick smiled the way he had when he had insinuated his son was gay, "only the best of the best get to play basketball. They invented all those other sports for guys who weren't good enough for the hard court, for the hoop, for the cage."

"Cage?"

"An archaic term, probably invented by headline writers who couldn't fit 'basketball' in thirty-six point type into an eight-pica column."

Sam looked up at his dad and smiled. "I didn't understand one word you said other than 'archaic.'"

"Actually, the game was once played in a cage. But, listen, Penn State has an excellent journalism program. You can learn all about all that stuff there."

"Dad, you didn't push me to play basketball, so you shouldn't push me to be a journalist. Besides, you're a journalist, and you don't even have a job. It's like you waste — . I mean," Sam shifted in his seat. "Not that you wasted your life. I didn't mean to say that."

Mick nodded.

"I mean, like, nobody reads newspapers anymore. There won't be any newspaper jobs. But you're a great journalist. Even Mom says that. She says you were a great writer in your day. I mean, not that your day's over." Sam sat and didn't say anything for a minute. He stared at the wall, then shifted in his seat again, still avoiding Mick's gaze. "I don't know what I mean, Dad. You're my dad, and you're a great guy."

"I'm teasing about the journalism. I don't care what you major in as long as you're happy. I just don't want you to go to Vietnam."

"Vietnam? Geez, dad.

"Iraq." Mick said, covering his eyes. "It's the same war, Son. Really and truly, it's the same war."

"But if you want me to be happy, you should want me to go to Iraq."

"Son, I don't want you to die. Even if you die happy."

"Not everybody dies in Iraq, Dad."

"Too many do. And don't think it can't happen to you. In D.C., there's a list carved into granite of 56,000 men and women who thought they wouldn't die."

Sam stared off into space for a while. Mick tried to envision him as a boy in a Little League uni, leaning on the knob of a bat upside down in the dirt of the ball field, but the picture of Sam in a soldier's uniform: desert camo with the U.S.-style Wehrmacht helmet shoved it away. For the eight millionth time, Mick regretted breaking up with Constance and losing touch with the boys, losing influence with the boys, ceding influence to some warped Neo-Con who thought Ann Coulter had invented logic. For the eight millionth time, Mick cursed the president and the vice president and Defense secretary and the assistant secretary and the national security adviser. He thought of the lyrics Eric Burdon sung at the height of the Vietnam War, that war was good for nothing. In Mick's view, that hadn't changed in more than thirty years. And now, a bunch of guys who had never been in a war had made war attractive to a new generation, a generation that had not watched "Combat" on TV every Tuesday night, or even "Baa Baa Black Sheep." Mick couldn't understand why this idiot wanted to kill so many people.

"Dad, I can't pass up the money."

Mick slammed his hand on the table. "No! No! This cannot be about money. I told you. I told you! I TOLD YOU!"

"Hey, pal," the manager said, "keep it down over there or take it someplace else."

Mick waved a wordless apology. He leaned in to Sam and said softly, "I told you: If you want to go to college, I'll find you the money. But, SamSamSamSamSam, please — PLEASE — do not hand over your life to that sonofabitch in the White House."

Sam stood up. "I know you're pissed, Dad, but I'm goin'. I'll be okay. I'll be a cryptologist. I won't even see any action."

"Sam, they're killing guys who are carrying nothing more lethal than laptops."

"You wouldn't fight for your country when it was your chance. Now it's my chance, and I'm not dodging my responsibility." Sam walked away.

"Is that — ?" Mick looked up to see he was talking to the wall. He turned in his chair. "Is that what Carl told you? Did Carl go to Vietnam? I'll tell you: he didn't." Mick stood up and followed Sam out of the store. "He was the same place during the war that I was. College. He wasn't at the same college, but he was in college. When you get home, ask him why he didn't sign up if that was such a goddamned good idea. I'll tell you why: he had a choice." Sam kept walking. "Sam. Wait. Sam, the guys who went to Vietnam, by and large, except for the guys who came out of West Point, they were drafted, and they were drafted because they didn't go to college." Sam started running, nimbly avoiding oncoming people and strollers, as well as window shoppers going in his own direction. Mick picked up his own pace, dodging the same people Sam had already passed by, but soon his knee ached, and he lost his breath and had to stop. Mick dragged his bad knee to the nearest bench and sat down and tried to see Sam. He even looked on the other side of the chain of islands of kiosks, indoor plants and benches. Sam never returned.

Mick ran his hand over his face and down the back of his head.
"Why the hell did I do that?"
The final why.

XII

From: Mick Mackintosh [mailto:mickeymack@fastconnect.com]
Sent: Saturday, July 13, 2003 9:56 AM
To: B.D. Butterfield
Subject: Talk with Sam

Well, I had a chat with Sam last night about joining the army. I couldn't talk him out of it. I fucked up the whole thing, to tell you the absolute truth. What kind of blind spot does more than half — excuse me, but did I just suggest that a MAJORITY of Americans voted for this bastard in 2000? Silly me. But what the hell do people see in this guy? One good thing: he has proven himself to be such a goober that the Democrats could run Snuffy Smith and Barney Google and beat this outfit in '04.

No, I haven't heard from the school district about an interview. I'll call them Monday and see when they start the interviews. It will be nice to be back home in a good job. They won't pay moving expenses, but those will be deductible. At least I know some Gen-Xer isn't running the school district.

I'll tell you what I have done, tho. I've connected with a group called Christians Against the War. I'm going to write some op-eds for them and make some media contacts. Of course, I know everyone at The Sun, and they have a branch in Pittsburgh (Christians Against the War, I mean), and I've worked with a lot of the people at the newspapers around there. And I'll probably participate in a demonstration or 12.

Talk to you later.

MM

XIII

Mick frittered away much of Monday morning, reading the paper online and watching CNN. Just before 11, he called the school district.

"Yes, good morning," he told the woman who answered. "I've applied for the English teaching job, and I wondered when you would start interviews."

"All the interviews have been scheduled, sir. If you haven't heard from us, then you are not among the finalists. I'm sorry."

"I find that hard to believe. Would you double-check, please? I'm Michael P. Mackintosh."

"All right," she said. "I remember your resume. You used to teach here. Let me find your file. May I put you on hold?"

Mick had a bad feeling about this. It couldn't happen a second time. He was pretty sure Eddie Webb didn't have a "Duuude" on his interview list, and he couldn't imagine anyone named Dr. Franklin F. Fosburg having a "Duuude" on his interview list.

"Mr. Mackintosh," the woman said, "your file is in the second tier of candidates. You would be called for an interview only if none of the others were hired."

"Second tier? Ma'am, I'm a published author. I have teaching experience. I've been teaching professional writers how to write. Who could teach the kids writing better than I could?"

"Mr. Mackintosh, these are not my decisions. I can't tell you what specific thing about your resume would put you into the second tier. I can tell you the qualifications for getting an interview."

"I'd like to know what they are."

"Okay, the form says — ."

"What form is this?"

"Oh, there's a form created by the school board that dictates what characteristics the successful candidate will have. Each resume gets a form, and the criteria listed on the form are checked off or not, depending upon whether or not the resume contains those qualities. Did I explain that clearly, Sir?"

"Yes."

"Okay, the first group of criteria is academic: At least thirty-six credit hours in your major. State teaching certificate. Praxis score in the eightieth percentile or above — ."

"Did you say 'Praxis score?'"

"Yes."

"What's that?'

"That's a test teacher candidates take, usually before they finish college. It tests subject mastery."

"Never heard of it."

"The state has required those tests for a few years."

"Oh. I've been living out of state for some time."

"Actually, sir, all states use them, I think."

"I see."

"Shall I continue?"

"Yes, please."

"Grade Point Average of three-point-oh overall and three-point-five in your major.

"Those are the academic requirements," she said. "Should I continue with the character requirements?"

"No," Mick said. He knew that she could see his file, and he knew what lines in the form were checked off and which were not. "I wonder if I may talk to Dr. Fosburg."

"Sir, the groupings are final. If no one from the first grouping is hired, then we'll probably call you for an interview."

"I just want to discuss the criteria with Dr. Fosburg. I mean, he knows that these cold numbers aren't the only predictor of success in teaching."

"Sir — ."

"In fact, what you mentioned may not predict success at all."

"Sir — ."

"I just want to talk about, maybe some other strengths I have, like experience. I want to know if that was overlooked and maybe it shouldn't have been.

"Sir, there is no appeal process. The decision has been made. I'm sorry, sir. Maybe another school district. Maybe none of these in the first tier will work out for some reason. If I can do anything for you at all, I'll call you."

"I grew up in your district."

"Thank you for calling, sir. Maybe another time."

Mick hung up and went to the list of school districts to which he had applied. He called the first one on the list.

"Is there a minimum Grade Point Average required to teach in your district?"

"Let me check." Mick was put on hold. "Sir? Have you applied for a job here?"

"Yes."

"Well, you have to have a Grade Point Average of three-point-oh overall and three-point-five in your major."

He called another one. Same answer. He called a third. Same answer.

He ran his hand over his face and down over the back of his head. This couldn't be, he told himself. Who the hell ever decided that you had to have these great grades to be a good teacher? Some of the best major league managers couldn't hit or pitch. Some of the best basketball coaches couldn't play a lick. What the hell had happened? If he couldn't work for a newspaper as lousy as the *Independent*, and he couldn't teach in the district that had once employed him, what the hell would he do to make a living? What the hell was he going to do?

Eddie Webb. He would call Eddie Webb. The job was in his building. Eddie must have some influence over who would work in that building and who would not. He'd call Eddie Webb.

He dialed the number, and a woman answered.

Yes, sir, Mr. Webb was in the building today, but he has stepped out for a lunch meeting. … Who is calling, please? … And what is this about, Mr. Mackintosh? … Oh, I'm sure Mr. Webb is always happy to speak with an old friend. … I certainly will, Sir, just as soon as he gets back into his office. … Oh, I have no idea, Sir. He's meeting with a couple of the department chairs, and I know they have a lot to talk about. But as soon as he gets back in, I'll give him the message.

But Mick waited for an hour, and he had no return call. He cut the grass and came back in and checked his messages. No return call. He went back outside and worked on the trim along the driveway and the walks and the equipment shed in the back yard and came back in, knees throbbing. No return call. He would take a shower and get the sweat of the yard work off of him. He kept the bathroom door open so he could hear the phone, even through the pounding of the shower. Drying himself off, he walked to the phone to see if a message was blinking. No return call.

"Not good," he told himself.

He called the high school.

Yes, Mr. Mackintosh, I gave him the message, but I'm afraid he had another appointment out of the building this afternoon. ... Well, he hasn't finalized his schedule for tomorrow. ... Well, I don't think he'd want to make an appointment to talk to an old friend. ... Well, sir, I'm sure he'll call you, maybe this evening.

Mick knew better. Her tone this afternoon was very different from her tone this morning. This morning, as soon as he had mentioned that he was an old friend, her tone had lightened, but this afternoon her tone was more professional. Eddie knew why he was calling. He didn't want to talk to Mick, and he had told the secretary to hold Mick off. Of course, Eddie's schedule was firm for tomorrow this late in the day.

Mick poured himself a glass of iced tea and went outside to the deck to smell the newly cut lawn and consider his identity. A school superintendent had tossed aside his application to teach. Mickey Mackintosh, a published author, a recognized authority on newspaper story forms, an accomplished teacher back in the day, a man whose presence filled a room, whose stature and persona kept a high school classroom in control, a man whose knowledge of the fundamentals of writing, even before his years on newspapers, brought a few handsful of former students back to him every Thanksgiving as long as he taught to thank him for preparing them for their freshman comp courses — that Mick Mackintosh had been denied an interview to teach in a high school in which he had taught as a young man. A high school principal, who had been a teaching colleague in those days, a guy who guzzled beer and munched pretzels and chips with Mick at all those floating Monday Night Football parties in the '70s would not return a phone call. How did all of this happen? How could the world have changed so drastically in such a short period of time? He wouldn't allow that, of course.

Not as a teacher, not as a reporter, not as an editor would he allow himself to be ignored. He would not even allow it as an unemployed middle-aged — whatever he was.

He would start his summer class on the next Monday, which meant he had to go to Pittsburgh in the evening. But during the day, he would do what he had told his reporters to do when public officials did not answer the phones or return phone calls. He would go to the high school and wait for Eddie Webb. Just sit in the office until Webb would let him in.

But if he couldn't talk Webb into interviewing him? What the hell was he going to do?

Consult.

Of course. He had heard of people, executives losing their jobs, whether they had taken buyouts or their companies had closed or they had been released before they were vested in their pension funds — a favorite tactic of one of the nation's best known conglomerates, Mick knew — and taking on brand new careers as consultants. Mick had done some consulting when he worked for newspapers. He had led a number of sessions at various workshops, and a couple of newspapers had hired him to come for an afternoon and talk about story forms. He had even spent two days at a nearby university, where an old friend was the newspaper advisor. She had asked him to spend a couple of days with her journalism classes and with her newspaper staff. The university gig he had done for nothing, but the newspapers had paid him a little.

Mick leaned over to take hold of the railing of the deck so he could push himself off the chair. After cutting the grass, his knee always ached and felt a little weaker. Mick allowed his knee to settle into whatever place it needed to be so he could walk, and he dragged himself into his office. He went to the Internet and found newspaper trade associations of a few neighboring states and compiled himself a mailing list. He then composed a letter offering his services to work with staffs over the course of a day or the course of a week or any time period in between. He would even structure a program in which he would work with a staff for a few days, then return periodically to refresh their memories, to check on progress, to do whatever remedial or follow-up work he deemed necessary. He listed all of the workshops in which he had been a guest speaker, and he listed the newspapers that had hired him to consult. He would not be shut out of a way to earn a living. How many of his own students had he told, how many students at career days in three states had he advised: Learn to write, because if you learn to write, you can do any number of things. Well, Mickey Mackintosh knew how to write, and he would always find a way to earn a living.

Fuck you, Duuude.

XIV

Mick got up early the next Monday, read the paper online, then jumped into the shower. One thing Mick knew: He could always be charming in person. He was a killer interview, and once he got in the door, he always got the job. Well, he said, envisioning young Christopher Post, there was a time he always had. Or maybe he was just deluding himself. Shit.

But this was different. He knew Eddie. Eddie knew what he could do in a classroom. Mick knew that the kids always told their favorite teachers who the good teachers were and who the lousy teachers were. Kids had always told him how much fun Eddie had made chemistry and physics, and he assumed they had told Eddie how effective Mick was as an English teacher. And, hell, Mick remembered, the last year he had been in the school district, he had been nominated in his own building in the state's Teacher of the Year competition. He had not made the cut at the county level, but it was something to have been nominated.

Funny, Mick thought, how he had forgotten about that in all his years in a newsroom. Funny how little Mick thought about teaching all those years. He had even missed this Praxis business, though he knew about No Child Left Behind. Well, he knew it existed without knowing every jot and tittle. But now, nothing was more important to him than teaching. Nothing was more important to him than that job. The job he used to have. When he was young. It was as though his professional life was this parabola, in which he had started at one point, then swung way out to a place quite distant from the starting point, and now it was coming back to the starting point. Not exactly the starting point, because he was twenty-some years older and because he knew so much more, had experienced so many triumphs and, lately, so many defeats. So, no, he was not at the same point, but, like the parabola, he was at a point parallel to where he had begun.

Mick was on his way out of the house when the phone rang. It was Constance.

"He signed up."

Mick didn't say anything. He wiped his hand over his face and down the back of his head.

"Is it irrevocable?"

"What? What do you mean?"

"Is it final? Can he take it back? Can I go to the fucking recruiter's office and take a goddamned pick-ax to every drawer in the building until I find the papers and burn them in front of God and the joint chiefs and the idiot president and everybody? That would mean they are revocable. Can we get him out of it somehow?"

"Don't scream at me, and don't take the Lord's name in vain. This isn't my fault."

"Well, how about I drive up there, and take the guy whose fault this is, and drag him out into your front yard and beat him until he bleeds like a stuck pig out of every orifice of his adulterous body?"

"It isn't Carl's fault, you ass. You have no one to blame but yourself."

"Constance, — ." Mick stopped. Fighting about his losing his job served no purpose here. "Constance, I'm going to say this slowly and calmly: Can — We — Get — Him — Out — of — This?"

"He signed a contract. He's eighteen. The contract is enforceable." Neither of them said anything for a few seconds. "I don't like this any better than you do."

"Oh? I thought you and your neo-con husband were such big fans of the semi-literate the Supreme Court appointed president and this fu — and this war he started so he wouldn't, like his father before him, become one of the most non-descript presidents in the history of the United States."

"You're impossible. I just thought you'd want to know what you did to your son."

And she hung up. Of course. Mick slammed the receiver down into the cradle, once, twice, thrice, banging it down harder and louder each time. Then with every bit of power in his body, he pulled the phone off of the desk and yanked the wire out of the phone jack and hurled it against the farthest wall. It clanged and fell in pieces onto the rug, leaving a gash in the plaster.

Mick's head spun, and stars blinked in front of his eyes. He collapsed onto the couch, drained of energy, devoid of strength. He held his head in his hands and sobbed.

Had he done this to his son? Maybe he was selfish to have started the graduate program when he lost his job. But he couldn't know the economy would never bounce back. He couldn't know that he'd never find a job back in the Pittsburgh area. He slumped back on the couch. As soon as he lost the job, he contacted the biggest paper in the city, the *Chronicle*, the one he'd always wanted to work for. However, competition from a well-funded upstart conservative and, in Mick's view, unethical paper, the *Standard*, had bled the *Chronicle*'s ad revenues, and it was not hiring. In fact, a guy he knew on the *Chronicle* sports desk had told him that in the past two years, they had lost three editors, but had not replaced them. Now, Mick's friend was editing twice the number of stories and designing twice the number of pages he had when he had started there. He couldn't do as good a job, but all the *Chronicle* cared about was getting the pages out, and as long as they got out by deadline, they saw no need to add staff. In fact, since the top editors had seen that all of those pages could get out by deadline, they had realized they could cut back on the news and features desks, too, and those jobs would never come back.

He had even lowered himself to interview at the *Standard*. He had seen the ad online, but had ignored it until he got a call from the managing editor, who had seen Mick's resume posted on a trade magazine web site. Mick had tried to beg off, saying that he had worked for the *Standard*'s sister paper in the next county over and had not enjoyed it. The ME was insistent, and Mick made the trip for the interview. It did not go well. The top guy at the paper had asked Mick how he had liked working for that sister paper, and Mick had told him. The editor said that Mick didn't understand how the newspaper had worked, and he had not been able to see the big picture. Mick answered that the editor had not been there during those years and couldn't possibly judge the validity of Mick's judgments about the paper. Mick took the copy editing test, which the Pulitzer Prize-winning *Sun* had not required him to take because of Mick's references and reputation in the industry. Mick had found one aspect of the test ridiculous and had not finished it. He had walked out and that was that.

Even without walking out, Mick figured, he would not have won the job because of his candor with the editor. But had his candor and his pride cost him the job that would have given him the money to send Sam to college? Had his candor and pride cost him the job that would have kept Sam out of the Army? Out of Iraq? Mick sat on the couch and shook his head. Television programs aimed at the Baby Boomers in the 1950s and '60s always taught that integrity, fidelity to oneself, led to a satisfying life. Teachers and parents and Sunday school teachers reinforced those messages. And it was all bullshit. The requisite stance when faced with authority was obsequiousness. Sell out and kiss ass. That will get your kid to college. That will keep you out of Sprawl-Mart. So, what, if you lose your self-respect? How much self-respect do you win yourself when your kid comes home in a body bag? Your kid does something he thinks is noble and pays for it with his life, and you mourn the loss of your kid for the rest of your life. And unless you take your own life, you can damn well betcha that God will make it a long and painful one.

So, now what could he do? He had to get into his car and drive to a place he had left many years ago to make his fortune and his name in journalism and beg a guy who doesn't want to talk to him to interview him for a job for which he, Mick, was ridiculously overqualified. Mick thought about his alternatives. None. There was not another thing he could do. He had no other opportunities. Well, he'd had a feeler from an old friend of his in Texas, who was running a small paper, but Texas was not for him, and small newspapers were no longer for him. Small newspapers were for young people who didn't mind working twelve hours every day and didn't mind doing line editing and copy editing and taking an obituary and running out to cover a fire if no one else was around.

No, he'd done that. He'd done that in a few different places that weren't home. And he was done. He belonged at home. He belonged in Westinghouse Township. He belonged in the house he grew up in. He belonged somewhere near his sons.

But he had no money to buy the house, and one son was in college, and another was on his way to Iraq. Just where the hell did he belong?

He didn't know. He guessed belonging was for another time. He had to go where he could. So, he would drive back home and talk to Eddie Webb. Maybe something would come of it. Probably not. Unfortunately, "Maybe" was his most promising option.

Mick dragged himself off the couch, stretched slowly into a standing position until his knee settled into whatever it settled into, then he headed for the car.

XV

"Mr. Mackintosh? Why is that name fam — ? Oh, I spoke to you on the phone yesterday. Why, you live out in Ohio. Did you drive all the way here just to talk to Mr. Webb? I hope not."

"Nope. I have a class at Pitt tonight."

"Oh, my. Well, sir, at least you didn't waste the drive, but you'll have to find something else to do between now and your class. Mr. Webb is booked solid all afternoon."

"Ma'am, I can think of no better way to tell you and Eddie how important this job is to me than for me to drive out here without an appointment. Please tell Eddie that I've done that."

She sighed, and she wagged the fingers of her right hand holding the pen, making it bounce off the counter at each end. "I just don't know what to tell you."

"Tell me you'll go talk to Eddie."

"I feel bad, Mr. Mackintosh, because Helen — do you remember Helen? She's the guidance counselors' secretary, and she says she knows you and that you're a very nice man and a very good teacher and that you grew up here and all of that, but — ."

"Ma'am, please. Take one minute. Duck your head into Eddie's office and tell him I'm here. Please."

Again she sighed.

"All he can say is 'no.'" Mick said softly.

She rolled her eyes and spun on her tennis shoes and disappeared down a hallway.

She was gone for a couple of minutes, longer than she would have if Eddie had just nixed the idea, Mick figured. His knee ached, so he sat down in one of the chairs generally occupied by some recalcitrant student. The office was totally different from when he taught here. Mick couldn't remember what was where in the old days, but he knew this wasn't the set-up. One thing he did recognize was the painting of a steel mill at night done by a classmate of his when they were seniors. It still dominated the far wall, though he guessed the current students must wonder what the hell it is. Mick couldn't remember the classmate's name, but he could see his face in his head. Died of a drug overdose. The people his age who had survived Vietnam and the drug culture and the AIDS epidemic were supposed to be the smart ones. "Smart lad to slip betimes away/From fields where glory does not stay, … ."

Yep, that's how it worked.

"Mick," Eddie said, tearing Mick's attention away from the painting. Mick noticed the voice did not express the joy of an old friend rediscovered. Mick stood up and stepped toward the counter. It occurred to him that Eddie, wearing a pale green golf shirt and black slacks, stood right in the shadow of the hallway and was not moving closer to Mick. He had lost a lot of hair over the years, and his nose had bulbed into a dark pink. The secretary took a seat at her desk.

"Hey, Eddie. Congratulations on the principalship."

"Thanks, Mick. I've been at it for a few years. A lot different than it used to be around here.

"Look, Mick, I wish you hadn't driven all the way out here." Eddie shook his head. "There's just nothing I can do for you. I understand you're upset about not getting an interview. I get that. Really, I tried to talk Frank into bringing you in, but, you know, what with NCLB — ."

"What?" Mick asked.

"Oh, No Child Left Behind. With all the rules about that, the board would just go through the roof if he hired someone who wasn't qualified."

"Eddie, I have a permanent teaching certificate. I'm qualified."

Eddie threw up his hands to hold off the argument. He lowered his head a tad. "No. No. I'm sorry, Mick, but the rules have changed. Having a certificate no longer makes you qualified. It's a very involved explanation, and I'm up to my elbows in getting state reports out for the past year and setting things up for next year, and I just can't take time to explain it. But you'll just have to take my word for it that your undergraduate grades don't cut the mustard, and I can't help you."

Mick opened his mouth.

"Mick, I'm sorry, but I just can't discuss this with you anymore. I'll tell you what: I'll be happy to write a letter of recommendation for you for anybody else. Happy to do it. I'll dictate it to Julie before I go home today. Leave your address with her, and it will go out in the morning mail."

Eddie waved as he backed into the darkened hallway. "Good to see you, Mick." Another step. "You're lookin' great." Another step. "Looks like you could still dunk the ball." Mick could see only the far half of Eddie's trunk. "Take care of yourself, Mick." The voice became more faint. "Good luck." Mick could barely hear the last.

He looked at the secretary. "Would you like to give me your address?" she asked, pen poised.

Mick gave it to her, so softly at first that she had to ask him to speak up. Then he trudged out of the office and into the sunlight. He squinted into the parking lot for his car. As he walked toward it, all he could think of was "What now? What now? What now?" He crossed the driveway between the building and the lot. He felt cheated that he had not had the chance to make his case to Eddie. He was good at words, and he had a strong presence, but he had not had the chance to present himself. He knew he had important things to say. On the other hand, he had heard Eddie's message that the decision was irreversible. Still, the words kept echoing in his brain: "What now?" He had no answer for the "What now?"

He took the keys out of his front right pants pocket as he always did long before he got to his car. He passed the handicapped spaces. He passed the spaces reserved for the principal and the two guidance counselors and the athletic director. He walked on to the spaces marked for visitors. Then he stopped and turned around and looked once more at the spaces reserved for the school officials. Each car was parked head in against a curb, with a sign on a metal post planted into the asphalt. Mick turned back and finished the walk to his car. He smiled and thought of one of his favorite books, *Shoeless Joe*, which had been made into the movie *Field of Dreams*, which he'd seen only about a dozen times. He got into his car and waited and thought about Kevin Costner and James Earl Jones, or, as the book was written, Ray Kinsella and J.D. Salinger. He stretched out his leg as far as he could in the car that was too short for his frame. His knee hurt. He put the key into the ignition and turned the engine over. He backed out of his space and turned to his left, away from the building and away from the driveway leading to the highway. He drove to the end of the parking spaces in the shadow of the trees at the edge of the property. He turned left again and drove toward the road along the last row of spaces, the row that abutted the end zone seats of the football stadium. But he stopped and backed into a space. Just ahead of him was the space reserved for the principal.

He looked at his watch. A little before 11 a.m. It would be a long wait for Mick until Eddie left for home. And he had to be careful not to be late for his class. Geez, he couldn't be late the first night.

He hated to just sit. He read his favorite chapters from a textbook that he had left in the back seat at the end of one of his grad courses, but he tired of that after a while. He found the bottle of Armor-all on the floor of the backseat and found a rag he thought wasn't too filthy, and he wiped down the dashboard of his car, giving the top of it, which caught the sun, an extra coat. None of this took long enough. He thought about the futility of all of this. Why didn't he just drive out to the local Sprawl-Mart and apply for a job. But what if even THEY didn't hire him?! Jesus, Lord in Heaven, how could he handle that? He envisioned himself driving halfway across the Westinghouse Bridge and making a hard right into Turtle Creek. The creek, not the town. Nope. Not going to do that. He reached over to clean out the glove box. He stared at the houses beyond the high school. He twisted around to look at some kids playing on the basketball court. He had the urge to join them, but if his knee hurt just to stand up out of a chair, how the hell could he bounce around on the asphalt? Nobody on the asphalt court had any size or much game anyway. Still, he watched, checking back to see the front door of the building from time to time. He saw the athletic director leave the school and Julie and Helen (and he resisted the urge to get out of the car and say hello; Helen was just a couple of years older than Mick, and Mick had lusted after her when he was a younger man). Of course. They were going out for lunch. Maybe Eddie would go out for lunch. The guidance counselors left, and Mick kept his eye on the door.

Finally Mick saw Eddie Webb come out of the building, tan blazer thrown over his left arm, a briefcase hanging down from his right hand, rocking back and forth. Mick guessed Eddie had his own problems with his legs or his knees or his feet. Where would Eddie want to go for lunch? He thought again of the nose and guessed a sports bar he had passed on the way. And he guessed he would be pretty anxious about getting there. Mick watched Eddie cross the driveway and wobble around the trunk of his car to the front seat. In an instant, Mick started his own car and threw it into drive with his foot gunning the gas. The car leapt forward. Mick barreled across the rows of empty spaces. Eddie threw his blazer and briefcase into the car, onto the passenger seat and spun his head around to investigate the noise. Mick pulled right up to the back bumper of Eddie's car, and he rolled down the window.

"Eddie, how you doin'? Know what I was thinking? I was thinking you and I ought to have lunch."

Eddie shook his head and put his hands on his hips. "Sorry, Mick. Got things to do." He waved his hand at the passenger side of the car. "Got a briefcase full of papers to read and work on over lunch. I'm just going home and have Karen make me something so I can work on my computer."

"Eddie, get in. I haven't been to Dirk's. That's the bar that Dirk Moran opened on the highway, right? I'll bet there are a bunch of photos of him abusing quarterbacks hanging on those walls. Shame about that leg, wasn't it? He might have been another Steeler in the Hall of Fame."

"Mick, back up. Let me out."

"You know, out where I live, if I go to a sports bar, I have to look at photos of Jimmy Brown and Paul Warfield and Bernie Freakin' Kosar. What the hell is it with those people and Bernie Kosar? What the hell did he ever win? Brown, I can understand. Warfield. Oh, geez, I loved Warfield, even with Miami. If I remember correctly, you won some money on that Miami-Minnesota Super

Bowl. That was the night we had the Super Bowl party at Lou Crain's. Is he still alive?"

"Mick, pull away, or I'll call the police."

"No need. Instead, call Karen. Tell her I'm in town, and you wanted to have lunch with me. You know she loves me."

"Mick, there's not a damned thing I can do for you."

"You can listen, Eddie. Just listen. You have no idea how desperate I am for a job. Just give me a hearing, and if I can't convince you, what have you lost?"

"Fosburg won't budge."

"Come on, Eddie. I brought my credit card. It's on me. Is Lou Crain still alive?"

Eddie stared hard at Mick and opened his mouth to say something, then closed it and shook his head. "No, Mick," Eddie said slamming his car door shut and walking toward Mick's car. "He took a heart attack a few years ago. Those goddamned cigarettes he was so damned proud of smoking finally killed him." Eddie opened the passenger door of Mick's car. "Not Dirk's. My niece works there. If she sees me eating anything other than lettuce, she calls Karen. Diabetes."

"So, where?"

"Butch's."

"That place still open?"

"Yes. And all they know about me there now is that I come in after work."

Mick backed the car up. "How do you know?"

"I go there every night for a couple of screwdrivers. I spend a day here, I need a drink before I see Karen."

Mick started the car forward. "Not good for the diabetes."

"You, too?"

"Uh-huh."

"I can't eat bread at home," Eddie said. "Or much of anything else. It's not that Karen's a terrible wife or anything." He looked at Mick. "You and Constance split up, didn't you?"

"Uh-huh."

"Does that have anything to do with your desperation here?"

Mick turned the car right, toward Twin Rivers.

"Nah, not really. I don't know. Maybe."

Mick told the story of the gradual distancing between himself and Constance, how she stopped supporting him, how, maybe, he had stopped supporting her. Mick didn't want to talk about his employment situation until they sat down, until Mick could look Eddie in the eye and gauge his reaction. He needed to know whether Eddie could really do anything about his not getting an interview or not. He didn't know enough about No Child Left Behind to know what the rules were. He didn't know whether Eddie was telling the truth or just avoiding him. He asked Eddie how he made the trek from classroom teacher of the first degree to principal, but he didn't listen to much of it. He tried to remember if he had done something as a teacher that would have made Eddie uncomfortable about hiring him. He couldn't remember any sort of outburst, any lapse of professionalism, nothing about any improper relationship with any of the students.

He thought about any social situations he might have been in with Eddie. He never hit on Karen; he knew that. He never drank any more than Eddie had at Monday Night Football parties or end-of-the-year barbecues; at least, he didn't remember any instance like that. He knew that all of his evaluations were strong. He had taken all six years allowed — three plus the three-year extension — to get the credits the state required for permanent certification, credits required to convert the temporary teaching certificate license into a permanent one, the one good for ninety-nine years or an idiot president, whichever came first. As he pulled into Butch's parking lot, he felt himself verging on the same resentment and anger he had experienced when Christopher Post told him he would not be hired at the *Independent*.

Mick and Eddie found a table along the far wall of Butch's.

"Geez, Eddie," Mick said looking around. Pictures of sandlot baseball teams from decades past caught his eye, as did pictures of old-time Twin Rivers, the town Mick remembered from his youth. "I don't think I've been in here since, hmm. I think I came in here after a game in the Y league. The team we played was sponsored by Butch, and we drank free after we played them. Beer, that is. Of course, lots of guys were into harder stuff, and we all bought food and dumped money into the pinball machines. Some of the guys bought cigars or cigarettes. Butch made out. Is he still alive?"

A middle-aged woman smoking a cigarette came to the table and called Eddie, "Doll" and noted that Eddie was there early. She asked Eddie if he wanted a screwdriver, then looked Mick over before asking what he wanted. Mick ordered a draft. Eddie told her to bring him a menu.

Eddie pointed to the two young women wearing too much makeup, sitting at the bar, smoking and looking over every guy in the place. "You think they'd be here if Butch were alive?"

"Oh, are they hookers?"

"Low end. And too damned young to be in here, I'll bet. Butch never ran a sophisticated joint, but he was careful about kids being in here, and he wouldn't allow hookers or cross-dressers."

Mick laughed. "I wasn't aware of cross-dressers coming in here."

"Maybe you had already left town. One came in here one night, and when Butch found out he wasn't a woman, Butch took a baseball bat and chased him down Mulligan Road until his wind gave out. At least, that's the story I heard."

Mick nodded his head. "Yeah, I can see that."

The woman brought the drinks. Mick looked her over. As she left, he said, "When I was coming in here, the waitresses were younger and better looking."

Eddie watched her go to the end of the bar and snuff out her cigarette in an ashtray. "So, they were your age."

"Yeah. And not bad looking."

"News for you, pal. They're still your age."

"Oh, Jesus, Eddie." Mick took in her weathered look, the gray hair peeking through the platinum dye job. "Did you see her hands? They were all, I mean, gnarled and wrinkled." Mick looked at his own hands. "Mine don't look like that, Eddie."

"Well, she's had a hard life," Eddie said, taking something more than a sip. "Why else would she be working in a place like this? She sure isn't making anything in tips. I can tell you that."

Mick burst through the opening.

"Maybe she got downsized by a newspaper and can't get a job teaching at the high school where she used to teach."

Eddie cocked his head to one side and moved the screwdriver from directly in front of him to off to his right.

"And so it begins. You have exactly two screwdrivers' worth of time, plus — " Eddie opened the menu and pulled out his glasses and put them on — "a bacon-cheeseburger and fries to tell me whatever you want to tell me. But first, understand, I'm really sorry about this, but there's really nothing I can do."

Eddie waved and the waitress came over and took their orders.

"Okay. Drink slowly. All right, so here's the thing: You're the building principal. Don't you have any pull with the superintendent?"

"It's not about pull, Mick."

"Eddie, I'm not asking you to, to, to give me a job. I mean, all I'm asking you to do is give me an interview."

"I can't." Eddie watched his hand move the glass back to the far left. "You don't have the qualifications."

Eddie took a smaller sip. Mick watched and gauged what was left in the glass.

"Meaning?"

Eddie bored in at Mick. "What the hell did you do in college, for God's sake? I looked at your transcripts. You got a D in a course that looked an awful lot like algebra I."

"You want me to teach math or English?"

"I want somebody who could carry a B average in college. Jesus Christ, Mick. You're a smart guy. You didn't even maintain a B average in your major."

"So, what? You're not giving me an interview because thirty years ago I didn't bury myself in my dorm room and read short stories by Kafka? Look at what I've done since then. Eddie, I wrote a book, a book your school district used to use to teach history to elementary students. I was a professional writing coach at newspapers." Mick watched Eddie take another sip and quickened the pace of his delivery. "I've been a presenter at writing seminars all over the country. Eddie, after one of my presentations, a Pulitzer Prize winner came to me and asked me all kinds of questions about story structure."

Eddie moved the glass back to the right and tried to make a point, but Mick wouldn't let him.

"Do you have any idea what I could teach your students? Eddie, listen to me: When you and I worked together, I was pretty good. The kids always told me how much they'd learned. Eddie," Mick leaned toward Eddie and jabbed his finger into the table next to the screwdriver, "I know about seven hundred times more now than I did then. Do you realize what I'm saying? When I was hired to teach here, I could barely count my balls twice and come up with the same number both times. Now — NOW — when I know so much more and, arguably, the need for students to learn more about writing is greater — NOW — I can't get hired because of something I did or didn't do when I was a child. Does any of this make sense to you, Eddie? Jesus Christ."

"It doesn't have to make sense to me. It makes sense to the federal government, and it makes sense to the board. How the hell do you think I can explain to nine adults, one of whom can barely spell his own name, and none of whom has a background in education, that I should choose someone who came out of college weak in subject area mastery instead of someone who came out of college with a four-point-oh in his major and Praxis scores off the charts?

"Mick, do you know anything about No Child Left Behind?" Eddie took a drink. Mick noted that he was nearing the bottom of the glass. The waitress brought their food and Eddie ordered another drink.

Mick rubbed his hands over his face, still leaning forward. He shook his head no.

"The law," Eddie said, "says every teacher of a core subject has to be 'highly qualified.' That means he has to demonstrate competency in his subject area. Now, how the hell are we supposed to determine competency? Grades."

"That's not the only barometer, Eddie. You know that," Mick said as he watched Eddie take another sip. "You know, Eddie, you're really throwing that drink down. That's not good for your digestive system. Slow down. And don't eat so fast. You're not chewing your food slowly enough to enhance digestion."

"I appreciate your expertise in the gastro-intestinal system, Mick. Look, the grades, it's all that most candidates have. Most candidates have never taught high school, so all we have to measure is their college grades."

"Okay, okay, I get that." Mick leaned forward and chopped his hands lightly into the table to make his point. Eddie saw his glass jump slightly, and he picked it up for a drink. "But here's the thing," Mick said, eyeing the level of orangish liquid in the glass as Eddie set it down. "I have more for you to measure. I mean, I have a track record. I have seven years in a high school classroom, in which my — a bunch of my kids were able to skip their freshman comp courses."

"How many?"

"How the hell do I know? It was a long time ago. I know Rosie Patterson did. I remember her writing to me when her first semester started. And I think — what the hell was his name? The wrestler. Heavyweight. Went to states."

"Andy Polesewich?"

"Yeah, yeah, that's the guy. I think he did."

"So," Eddie said, waving what was left of the screwdriver as he talked, Mick hoping he didn't spill any as the drink sloshed back and forth against the sides of the glass, "the quantification you have that you think should make me disregard some kid right out of college who was in the honors program is that you know one student who was able to opt out of freshman comp and another guy who you think did. You really believe that's the ammunition you want me to stake my reputation on with my superintendent? Is that right, Mick?" Eddie had another sip of the drink and looked around for the waitress.

"Okay," Mick said, "but there's this: You know I can control a classroom. You know I have an engaging way of conveying information. You know that my kids can come talk to me. Huh? That's important stuff, right? You don't know if that brainiac — ."

"Brainiac? Christ, Mick, are you fifteen?"

"You know what I mean. You don't know if your honors student can do any of that stuff. It's all about relationships, Eddie. You know I can establish the right kinds of relationships with kids. You KNOW I can. You don't know if your recent grad can."

The waitress brought over a second screwdriver as Eddie finished the first. She took away an empty glass. Mick watched her take it away and figured it was halftime.

"That's why he's on probation and we do frequent observations." Eddie dug into his fries, stacking three, four, five on his fork, then dipping them into the catsup on the side of his plate.

"Eddie," Mick said, shaking his head and looking at the beer he still had not touched, "I won't have to be on probation. I have tenure. I have a permanent certification. All you have to do is make sure I'm not schtupping the sexy senior in the third row near the windows."

"You're not helping yourself," Eddie said, arms folded.

"Let me tell you something," Mick said. "A story. And slow down, here. Are you in that much a hurry to get back to work?"

"I'm in college, and, as you say, I'm not the most industrious student in the program. You're right. I spent a lot of time with anti-war politics and a lot of time playing intramural sports and a lot of time chasing women I had no business chasing. And I might have spent a night or two drinking when I should have been studying. OK, I get that. So, I get into my teaching methods course, and I figure I have one thing going for me, and that is that I am the most charming motherfucker in the room. I know that cause when I hold court in the dorm, I have everyone in the palm of my hand. I can own that room, Eddie, even at twenty years old. You've seen me do that, right?"

Eddie nodded and took a healthy sip. Mick watched the glass and not Eddie.

"Okay, so the list comes out, I mean, the schedule for teaching classes, and I have to teach right after Gretchen Van Doven. Now, Gretchen is without question the smartest student in the program. She's been dating the basketball star, an all-American boy type, since the day they arrived on campus. She's pretty as a starlet, and she has a laugh every guy would die to evoke. And, as if God hasn't blessed her sufficiently, she has this presence when she walks into a room. Conversation stops, and everyone just wants to listen to her. I think I'm pretty good, but she's, like, fucking Oprah or something."

Eddie squinted, cocked his head and said, "But I thought you were the most charming motherfucker in the room."

"Testosterone Division, Eddie. I can't compare with this, you know? She's gorgeous. Anyway, I have committed to teaching the gerund. You laugh, I know. Scintillating, right? But I know it. I know how to make gerunds dance. But Gretchen comes in and teaches, I don't know, the themes of inadequacy in *Hamlet* or some damned thing. And she has a projector and shows fucking Olivier playing Hamlet, and she has handout sheets and a great question-and-answer. I mean, she owns this room for an hour.

"Okay, so I'm up during the next class. I've repressed the details, but I didn't do quite as well as she did. Sidney Poitier didn't do as well in *To Sir With Love*, you know what I mean? So, Gretchen gets an A, and I get a C. Okay, you've seen my transcripts; I always got a C.

"So, it comes time to student teach. I have a great — GREAT — student teaching experience. My cooperating teacher loves me. My college observer comes one day when I happen to be teaching grammar, and not fucking *Hamlet*, and I'm on. He walks in in the middle of the class, and I already have this bunch — a really bright group of eighth-graders — all over whatever the hell I'm teaching, and they're answering questions and asking questions and 'What if this?' and 'How come that,' and one girl — I can still see her. Michelle Parker, one of three Michelles in the class, and by far the brightest. Anyway, Michelle keeps asking why. Every answer I give her, she asks another why." Mick saw Eddie push away an empty plate and take another sip of the screwdriver, another one that Mick thought was overly long. "And finally, I just turn to her and lean on the front desk and say, 'It's just the way it is, and we have to accept that as the foundation.' Or something like that.

"The class ends, and the college guy comes up to me and says, 'That's exactly how to handle that. You were just great.' And he never comes back. And my cooperating teacher tells me I sewed up an eighteen-credit A that day.

"Now, I get a letter from one of my friends who is a friend of Gretchen Fucking Van Doven, and she tells me that Gretchen spent the first two weeks of student teaching taking notes and asking questions and smiling at the principal and all of that. Then the first time her co-op puts her in front of a class, the kids start asking questions, and Gretchen flips out, screams, 'Fuck all you little mother fuckers,' and runs out of the room. Needless to say, she gets right into her car, drives back to campus and changes her major. A couple of weeks later, she breaks up with the all-American boy and takes up with a biker on the rifle team. Last I heard, she was running the concessions at some NASCAR track."

Eddie laughed and threw back his drink. "Funny. You always could tell a story, Mick."

"It's not just a story. It's my life. I was put on Earth to be a teacher. I'm a natural. I have it all over any freakin' kid you bring in."

"You left teaching once because you were put on Earth to be a journalist. Right?"

Mick smiled. "I'm extraordinarily gifted. What can I say?"

Eddie finished his drink and set it on the table, the ice cubes clinking together. "Mick, it doesn't matter. None of it matters. The federal government has decided what the qualifications are for teaching. We have a board that plans to abide by them, because it can. You want to teach? I'm sure one of the small city districts will take you. You won't face quite as much competition."

Mick knew what that meant.

"I'd be the only white guy in the place. Might be a little culture shock, for students and me alike. They might not want to deal with a white guy who drives in from the suburbs. I'd never get any teaching done. I'd spend the whole day trying to get order."

Eddie shrugged. "It depends on who you get. Lots of minority students in colleges all over the country, and they don't all come from suburban schools."

"What are the chances that the new guy gets the academic sections?"

Eddie finished the last of his fries, then took a drink. "If you were born to teach, Mick, you won't find a population in greater need. Look at the Christian missionaries. They heard the call to serve, and they chose to serve where the need was greatest, in Africa, South and Central America. The Spanish conquistadors brought priests into the Southwest to convert the Indians, right? I know you know history better than I do. Am I right about the Indians? I thought so. You want to make converts? There are schools where you can do that." He took another drink and was dangerously close to finishing.

Staring at the shallow mix in the glass, Mick clasped his hands and leaned forward. "Eddie, I'm begging you. I really, really need this job. Get me an interview." Mick unclasped his hands and opened his arms. "That's all I want. An interview. Get me in the room with this Fosburg guy and I'll knock his socks off. You have a summer school? I'll teach a class. I'll show him what I can do. Please, Eddie, please."

Eddie shook his head.

"Eddie, my kid is signing up to go to fucking Iraq cause I can't afford to send him to college. Please. Please."

Eddie spun the nearly empty glass on the table, the little bit of liquid splashing the sides.

"I'm sorry about your kid, Mick. It's the way life works, isn't it? You and I didn't go to Vietnam because we went to college. Our parents could afford to send us. All those black guys and Latino guys fought that war. There are still a lot of black and Latino guys in the service, aren't there? And some of them died in Iraq. That's where those city guys you don't want to teach are going to go. In part, because they won't have the grades to get into college. In part cause they can't afford it. And now you're in the same boat. I'm sorry for you, Mick, and I'm sorry for your kid. I hope he's okay over there.

"Mick, you screwed yourself a long time ago." Eddie counted off Mick's sins on his fingers. "First, you threw away a chance to go to a big-time college and play basketball. If you'd had a good career, you could have written your own ticket in this city in any field you wanted to pursue. And if you had wanted to go into education, you could have coached basketball, and if you were any good at it, you'd be a legend right now and never have to buy your own drink in any bar in six counties.

"Second, you coasted through college and didn't learn anything. You have nothing to show for your supposed education.

And that was okay thirty years ago, when there was a baby boom and the Twin Rivers area was begging for teachers.

"And third, you left teaching to go pursue your dream. Well, your dream blew up in your face. If you had stayed at the high school, you would be retired by now if you wanted to be, and your kid would be in whatever college his grades allowed.

"You have no one to blame but yourself."

"Is that what this is about? I abandoned the sacred calling of the classroom to do something else? Is that why — ? Is that why you people don't give me credit for what I accomplished outside the classroom? It wasn't in your little version of academia?"

Eddie laughed. "Mick, you're reaching. You just want to be a victim. Somehow." He threw down the last of the screwdriver. "That's two, Mick. Get me back to the building."

Eddie pushed back his chair and stood up. He turned to the waitress and pointed to Mick. "Give him both checks. See ya."

Mick reached into his pocket for his wallet and found a twenty. Eddie walked out as Mick waited for his change.

When Mick reached his car, he unlocked the door for Eddie to get in, then got in the driver's side.

"I gotta tell you something, Mick," Eddie said pulling the shoulder strap over and clasping it. "You're all pissed off right now because you think you've been discriminated against. You're an older guy, and you had bad grades as an undergrad and whatever else."

Mick started the car and backed up and headed for the road.

"Do you know who preceded you when you got your job at the high school?" Eddie asked.

"Some woman," Mick said, pulling onto the road and heading away from Twin Rivers. "Kids didn't like her. That's all I know."

"Lydia Kiefer. Wasn't a bad teacher, as far as I know, but, you know, she was a first-year full-time sub filling in for a woman on maternity leave. She couldn't control a classroom worth a damn. When the year ended, the administration was convinced a woman couldn't do that job. Do you know that not one woman got an interview for that job? Not one. And, I'll tell you, when they found out you wanted to teach with us, that was the end of the search. Sometimes you get the bear, and sometimes the bear gets you."

Mick had nothing to say. For a mile or so, there was no sound except the hum of the engine. Mick turned on the radio to the jazz station, but there was only news from NPR. At least the radio gave Eddie and himself something else to focus on. Each item provoked a harrumph or a short response from one of them, and that passed for conversation until Mick pulled into the school parking lot, next to Eddie's car.

Eddie opened the seatbelt. "I'm sorry I can't help you, Mick. I really am. I know you did a good job for us, but that was a long time ago. I wish the world hadn't changed so much, for your sake, anyway." Eddie got out of the car. "Good luck. I'll write you a letter of reference and send it out to you." Eddie shut the door.

"And sometimes," Mick said softly as he pulled out, "you don't even get into the fucking forest."

XVI

Mick left Eddie and drove to the Oakland area of Pittsburgh. He was starting a new course that night. The drive in took him on the Lincoln Highway, past a nice little ball field within a little stone wall he wished he could play on when he was little. Also past some asphalt basketball courts he had played on in his teens. He got onto the Parkway, drove through the Squirrel Hill tunnel, then shortly thereafter, looked at the passenger side window to see the Cathedral of Learning, the signature building on the University of Pittsburgh campus. He had grown up looking at that building, whether on school trips to the Carnegie Museum on the other side of Forbes Avenue or going to Forbes Field to watch the Pirates or just seeing it stretch spire-like over the topography from whatever direction he approached Pittsburgh. As integral a part of the cityscape as it was, Mick never took the building for granted. His father wouldn't let him. He had always told Mick how he, Mick, would go to college there, like some of his athletic heroes, and the father hoped the son would become an athletic hero, too. His dad took Mick to football games at Pitt Stadium and basketball games at the Pitt Field House. But one Saturday morning before a Pirate game, he dragged Mick into the ground floor of the Cathedral. Mick remembered being awestruck at the columns in the first-floor common area, the expanse of the common area, the openings from floors higher up looking down onto the common area. It struck Mick truly as a cathedral, more inspiring than the church he went to. His father told him that no matter how much time he spent practicing at the stadium or the field house, this was the most important building in the university. After the NFL or the NBA, in his father's view, he still would need to make a living, and Mick's dad decreed he was not to make that living in the steel mill, unless he was running it. In such an imposing setting as the Cathedral, Mick could believe that was possible. Even as a boy, Mick shared his father's faith that he would attend this college, sit in the classrooms on the upper floors and graduate to become some grand being who wore a suit and tie to work every day — after, of course, his professional sports career.

But the country changed, and Mick was among a handful of promising athletes who had eschewed what they considered the frivolity of the playing field while young men died in Vietnam and black people and women fought for rights white male Americans had been granted by law two centuries before. Mick played football and basketball in his senior year, and he led his team to the playoffs almost only on his size alone. He had had confrontations with his coach over the coach's autocracy, and he'd missed practice to participate in anti-war demonstrations — which caused further confrontations with his father. But in the playoffs, he faced superior talent and opponents who wanted the championship enough to compromise, play the coach's and society's game. An early exit followed. Still, Pitt wanted him for its less than elite basketball program. But Mick was done with basketball. He still wanted to attend Pitt as a student, but even though the mills were booming to feed the Vietnam war machine, upkeep on the house, his mother's medical needs and misplaced faith in the inevitable scholarship meant there was no money for Pitt. Mick went to a state teachers' college and played sports only in pickup games and intramural leagues. The head basketball coach saw him play in the intramural final and approached Mick about playing for the college. But Mick was adamant. One of those jobs reserved for athletes, such as checking IDs in the college dining hall or watching the door in the library would have helped, but he would play only for personal enjoyment instead of the aggrandizement of an institution. Then his dad died while Mick was in college, which cemented Mick's place in the college pecking order but did not weaken his resolve.

But as long as he was an undergrad, he felt some sort of fealty to Pitt. He tried to buy the propaganda his own admissions dean wove that his degree would be as good as any degree from any college in the country, but he had doubts. And though he had a good friend on his college's wrestling team, when his team beat Pitt, he had mixed emotions. It wasn't until he left teaching and moved into journalism that he realized that the reporters and editors who had gone to bigger, more prestigious schools had the advantage in getting jobs. More and more, he wished he had gone to Pitt.

So, when Mick lost his job at *The Sun* he took stock. No one in the industry was hiring because the economy simply fell apart for a while after the attacks of 9/11. Mick thought about how nice it would be to teach in a college, as one of his co-workers at *The Sun* had done, teaching a journalism course every semester at the local university. But he had no master's degree, and every ad he saw for a journalism instructor or professor required a master's degree or more. This struck Mick as a little ludicrous because he had worked just about every job a body could in a newsroom, and he knew that no college course would teach him anything he didn't already know. He called a journalism prof he had met at various journalism seminars and workshops over the years. After he had ascended to the head of his department, he had brought Mick there a couple of times to work with his students for a stipend. Mick asked him what he could possibly gain by getting a master's in journalism.

"Nothing," the prof said.

Mick felt vindicated.

"You have a master's in journalism," the prof said. "You earned it in every newsroom you've ever been in. You know more than most of my faculty because most of them have never touched a newsroom keyboard."

"So, hire me to teach for you."

"Can't," he said. Just that simply.

Mick didn't get it.

"It's not about what you know."

"Right," Mick said. "It's about who I know, and I know you."

"Nope," the prof said. "It's not about who you know. It's about the abbreviation behind your name. The college markets itself on the number of experts in the field and on the number of publications its faculty has."

"Does anybody care about what the students learn?"

"Sure. And don't be a smart ass. We all do. And we all think we're the best person to teach them, whether we've been in the newsroom or not. Now, I'm smart enough to know that while my faculty is a worthy repository of all the theory our students could ever need, it is short on practical knowledge. That's why I have you come visit my students every couple of years."

"So, let me get this straight," Mick said, sarcastic incredulity dripping from my lips. "You can't hire me because I don't have the right letters after my name, but you need me to visit because the people with the alphabet soup can't find their asses with both hands."

"Well," he said, "it isn't as extreme as all that. Some of these folks have worked in the trade, and the ones who haven't aren't quite as inept as you want to paint them with such a cynical brush, but your point has merit."

"It's a game," Mick said.

"And," he said, "you can't get into the game without an advanced degree."

"But not in journalism."

"Not in journalism. Political science, economics, sociology, philosophy, literature, creative non-fiction, even fiction for God's sake, though a journalist with a degree in fiction writing should not brag about that. Take your choice. Any will do. You want a master's in Asian languages? Great. I'll hire you and promise you'll never have to speak Cantonese again. But get the degree and get in the game."

Mick had a little money put aside, so he decided to get in the game, and he knew that he could go to only one place, no matter what type of degree he would take, and that was inside that Cathedral.

But the dream really cost. He had to pay out-of-state tuition, which was about twice the amount of in-state tuition. He had tried to get an assistantship, but he couldn't because his undergrad grades were too low and he was accepted only as a probationary student. Mick had tried to get a loan, but because he had no job, he needed a co-signer. No way, as a man in his fifties, was he asking someone to co-sign a loan. Besides, whom would he ask? Constance? She was the only quasi-family member he knew with any money. And the money she had was her husband's or the money Mick sent her for their sons. So, he withdrew retirement money as needed for tuition. If he lived long enough to retire, he might regret that.

Hell, he thought as he exited the elevator onto the floor of his class, he regretted it already. He thought of Sam signing up for the military. Yep. He regretted it already.

***

He strode to his classroom. He was early, as usual. A group of grad students clustered around a table. All younger than Mick. By a lot. As usual. One of them rested her elbows on the table and held her hands on the sides of her face and laughed her words out so Mick could hardly make them out.

"I don't understand why you're laughing," another one said. This one looked at Mick as though looking for an explanation. "She has no place to live," she said to Mick, although he knew neither of the women, "and she's in fits of laughter."

"No," the first one said. "It's what my pastor's wife said." Laughter. "I told her I had to stay with an old roommate one night, and I was staying with my pastor one night, well, not him, but his family, you know what I mean — " high-pitched giggling " — and my advisor's sister the next night, and she said — " turning her face away from the table, laughing uncontrollably " — she said, 'Angela, you're sleeping around.'"

The second woman snickered. Two other people in the class simply ignored the whole scene. Mick didn't get it. She looked at him.

Her elbows rested on the table, and she spread her hands out to the sides and looked at Mick in a way he was sure she thought would make him understand. He got his first good look at her. She looked familiar, like she'd been in a class before. Oh, yes, she was the tall, gorgeous one. Dark hair, roundish face, lips out of a Revlon ad, perfectly shaped eyebrows over the most soulful brown eyes God could have created. Oh, yes, Mick remembered now. He had may never have said more than hello to her once or twice when they had gone through a door together, but he could never forget those eyes. They seemed to be forever ready to crinkle into a laugh or to tear up for a sob. Even now, as she spoke through more high-pitched laughter. "My pastor's wife said I was sleeping around."

"Oh," Mick said, and he pushed out a slightly labored laugh, ever so briefly. As any middle-aged man who has worked around women since the 1990s had learned, he should never comment about a woman's sexuality or sexual encounters or sexual promiscuity, no matter how much nor how openly she talked about it. If he talked about it, it was sexual harassment. Since Mick didn't know her, he thought a simple "Oh" was innocuous, yet engaged.

He sat down. "So, you don't have a place to stay?"

"No," she said, the aftershocks of the giddiness wearing off. She crossed her arms across her chest, but still gesticulated with her right hand. "I thought I did a few weeks ago, and now my landlord, the guy I thought would be my landlord? He lost the house. I guess he didn't pay taxes or something? And they took his house? So — ." She swept her right hand back and forth in front of her.

"So," Mick said, plunging in where he would not have gone if she had been, um, not gorgeous, "you can't find a place to stay more than one night at a time?"

"No, it's just so weird. Like, my old roommate's boyfriend's family is coming in, and my pastor — ." She waved her hand to indicate how insignificant the details were.

"And you don't have anything lined up permanently?" Mick asked.

"No," she fairly squealed, leaning over the table toward Mick. Her eyes bulged, and even then, they were haunting.

"Okay. I see. Have you — ." Mick thought better of asking yet another stupid question. "If you haven't started looking for a place, I know someone in a realtor's office, and she might be able to help you."

She slapped her palm on the table. "I want to live here, not — where do you live?"

"Ohio."

"I knew you weren't from around here. I remembered — from something."

"But I was born here," Mick said. "I grew up here. I used to work here, and I'm moving back here soon, and I can give you the name of a woman who might be able to help you find a place. Unless you have it all covered."

Mick wondered what he had said to indicate he lived among the Flatlanders.

She crossed her arms again and nodded. "No. Okay. Okay."

Mick opened his notebook and wrote the name of the realtor with whom Kenny had listed his house and he wrote Ginny Crandall's name and tore the page out and handed it to her.

"I don't remember the number, but this guy's in the book, of course," Mick said, pointing to the name of the realtor who had listed Kenny's house. "Tell her, Ginny," he pointed to her name," that I suggested you call. I think she had a crush on me when we were in high school."

"And you are?"

"Mick Mackintosh."

So, she had remembered he didn't live here, but not his name. Okay.

"We were in a class once before," she said, taking the paper.

"I think so."

"Yes." She crossed her leg and looked at the sheet.

"And you are?" Mick asked.

She looked stunned for an instant. The smile disappeared.

"Angela," she said, as though he had just asked what year it was.

"Oh," Mick said. He waited for a moment, but no more came. "I see."

***

The class didn't last long, maybe an hour. First night. Maybe ninety minutes. Get the syllabus, talk about the course, do some get-to-know-each-other stuff, exchange ideas about the course material: how familiar everyone is with it, what about the course intrigued everyone to take it, blah, blah, blah. Mick didn't listen closely.

Afterward, he went to the bookstore. The book for this class would be inconceivably expensive, unless he could find it used somewhere, then it would be only outrageously expensive. When Mick was an undergrad, books were reasonably priced. They weren't cheap, but he could afford to buy all of the books in his major brand new. In grad school, having been in the work force all those years, he couldn't afford new books. What had happened in the interim? He puzzled about that walking to the store. Had the costs of production increased so much that the exorbitant prices were warranted? Had the number of textbook vendors dwindled to so few that they could charge whatever they liked? Or, as had happened in so many aspects of the economy, had the greed for profits allowed these companies to gouge students, so many of whom were at the mercy of the campus bookstore? He knew, opening the door and edging his way into the student-choked foyer, which answer he thought likely. The greed of the 1980s had reconfigured the power structure among corporations. The greed of the '90s and the first decade of this century had slashed payrolls, transferred workers from full-time to part-time and jettisoned thousands from the workforce. Mick admitted to himself that his cynicism would not permit him any answer that didn't paint corporate America in the worst colors.

Just inside the foyer, Mick encountered a table full of books intended to separate him from money he had not intended to spend. A book about the history of Pitt football. A collection of newspaper stories about the Pittsburgh Pirates down through the years. A similar book about the Steelers. A book about religion and politics. Mick wanted them all. When he was working, he might have bought a couple of them. Now, all he could do was pick them up, thumb through them, wish he could buy them. He shook his head. What the hell had happened? That was what he missed most about being out of work. Over the years, he had filled four large bookcases with books. Now, he couldn't buy any because he just didn't know how long he'd be out of work. He had to hold onto every nickel he could. Mick guessed he would buy one here and there after he finally landed something. He'd still have bills, but he could buy one here and there. Maybe one or two would come out in paperback soon.

He tore his eyes from the books that had captivated him and went downstairs to find the books he needed. He found them, took them back upstairs, said something snotty to the cashier about the lack of used books, then walked to his car.

Mick realized driving home that he had missed a lot of what had been said. He kept thinking about that woman. The young woman. Angela. She looked to be Sean's age. He couldn't remember much about her from their previous class together. Hell, he hadn't even remembered her name. Did she have one of those extraordinary minds Mick had occasionally encountered in this program? Couldn't remember. Was she one who dominated the conversation? Didn't fit. If she had been one of those, Mick would have remembered her, if only with contempt. Did she go out for beers with everyone else when the course ended? He shook his head alone in the car. Didn't remember her going. He could only vaguely remember her making a presentation in class. Couldn't remember what it was about or if it was any good or anything. Of course, they hadn't had to stand to make their presentations, and maybe she was on the same side of the table as Mick had been and he never saw her face. Who knows? Part B: So what?

Mick didn't think he'd ever heard that laugh before, so full of mirth, even at her own misfortune. He didn't get it. What else didn't he get, he thought as he turned off the interstate toward his house. Oh, that joke about sleeping around. Maybe she just laughed at everything.

Mick's mind drifted to the role he could play in her life. He imagined himself the Romantic hero, gray of goatee, the promise of youth crumbled by failures, riding to the rescue of the fair, young damsel. He imagined her devoting herself to him out of — gratitude.

No. That's not right. That's just servitude.

He imagined her buying him coffee one night after class in gratitude for Ginny's setting her up in an apartment, ending the sleeping around.

He imagined himself charming her so thoroughly that he could make those eyes crinkle into laughter on command. He imagined her insisting on discussing the class with him every night it met, and he imagined phone calls to discuss the readings and exchange ideas for papers, then reading and critiquing each other's papers. He imagined himself pointing out a crucial inconsistency in her work and suggesting the only avenue through which she could reconcile it.

He imagined her asking him what he did for a living. That wouldn't go well, so, no, he couldn't take his fantasy there.

He imagined her inviting herself to his place to cook him dinner. He imagined his place — well, he wouldn't have a job, and he'd be paying tuition and getting money for Sean's trip to Ireland and Sam's tuition to Penn State. Where the hell would he live? What the hell kind of place would he be bringing her into? No. That won't work.

He imagined accompanying her to a reading, and her asking him to walk her home. He remembered insisting on walking a girl home after a dance when he was in college, so that he would sleep well knowing she had got home okay, he had told her. He remembered that when her dorm came into view, she told him she could get in safely now, and he needn't come any farther. He remembered insisting that he would take her to the door, and he remembered her insisting that he not. He remembered the ugly timbre to her voice as she said, "Mick, this is far enough."

And he remembered saying weakly that, okay, he would just stand there and watch her walk into the dorm, make sure no one leapt out from behind the steps going up into the dorm. And he remembered the weakness. And he remembered how she scurried away. And, at that moment, in his mind, she became Angela.

What the hell, he told himself. She was the same age as his kid. What the hell was he thinking about?

XVII

From: Mick Mackintosh [mailto:mickeymack@fastconnect.com]
Sent: Wednesday, July 3, 2003 8:14 AM
To: B.D. Butterfield
Subject: Thanks for the thought, but ...

Hey, B.D..

I really appreciate your talking to Kevin about me. I should be really intrigued about interviewing with him. You have no idea how much I miss a newsroom. I even miss reporters who bury leads and don't know a percent from a percentage. Not to mention, it would be great to work for Kevin again. He always treated me well.

However, as much as I'd like a staff again, I'm committed to this graduate program. As far as I've gone, it would be a tremendous waste of money I can't afford to throw away to leave and take that job.

You know, I started this program just to learn things I didn't know. Now, I really need this degree to get a job. Unbefuckinglievable that a man with my experience can't get a job. You know, if I had any money, I'd file an age discrimination lawsuit against every newspaper in this region and some kind of lawsuit against every school district that won't hire me. Has to be some kind of discrimination. Has to be.

Of course, if I had that kind of money, I wouldn't need the job, would I? Boy, they just fuck you coming and going.

Later
Mick

XVIII

Mick swung open the door of the coffee shop and immediately saw the group of men and women he was looking for, clustered around three tables pushed together. One of the men, tall and dark-skinned, wearing an Indians cap, stood up and waved him over. As Mick neared, he heard the man say, "Fellow losers, I'd like you to meet Mick Mackintosh. He's been out of work for a couple of years. He worked with me at *The Sun* and, just like me, lost his job because of the economic downturn after 9/11. I lasted a little longer than he did, and no matter what he says, it wasn't because I had pictures of the editor and her husband's old fraternity brothers."

Now the man stuck out his hand to Mick. "Mick, I'm awfully glad you finally accepted my invitation to come out with the rest of what I like to call the White-Collar Castoffs."

Mick shook the extended hand. "Thanks, Calvin," he said. "I guess you just wore me down."

A waitress came over and handed Mick a breakfast menu, but Mick asked her to bring him only coffee, black.

Calvin instructed the group to introduce themselves to Mick, with the requisite joke about there being a quiz later. Mick tried to focus on the names, but there were probably ten people around the table, and he retained their names less easily than the circumstances of their unemployment. A few of them were former middle managers of steel plants that had survived the '80s. One was a former airline pilot. One was a former sales rep for one of the manufacturers that had gone belly up. One was a former school superintendent who had been fired when she refused to implement a curriculum that taught to the standardized tests. Mick actually had remembered reading about her and was surprised she was still out of work because that had been a number of years ago.

Eventually, Mick told his story, coming at it as part-journalist, part-teacher, which created the effect of a stand-up routine. He got a good laugh with his portrayal of Christopher Post and the Duuude. When he spoke about Sam, he lost the comedic persona, but sprinkled the story with unkind references to the president. Not all of his listeners expressed agreement with Mick's pacifism, but none of them spoke up in defense of the president. It dawned on Mick that this was about jobs and not about the war. In fact, in their introductions, no one had made any political references, not even the superintendent, who was certainly entitled, given her opposition to the mandates created by state and federal governments.

So, Mick wrapped up his story and said, "So, Calvin has told me this is a great place to commune with other people in the same fix I'm in, but what practical good are you doing yourselves?"

"Apparently," the superintendent said, "none of us has solved our problems, at least none of us sitting around this table. However, there are others who once sat here, but have moved on. Some of those came here asking for help with resumes or interviews." She waved her hand around the table. "We probably all have different techniques for our resumes or interviewing, and we've lent advice. Some has helped; some has not. We all have a tremendous amount of life experience, as you do, and we exchange the lessons that experience has given us."

"I'll give you an example," said a woman who had left a pastorate when she felt she had lost the call. "I was really scraping for money, until a guy — he was an accountant; he got a job and moved on — he explained to me I could draw down on my late husband's IRAs because he would have been older than 59-and-a-half. That hasn't solved all of my problems, but it's helped me afford to keep the lights on at night."

"I'll tell you one thing right now," Calvin said. "Just about everyone at this table and lots of those who have moved on have done consulting work. Bea — " he pointed to the ex-superintendent — "did some work for some alternative school — is that the right term? — getting that up and running, helping the teachers with all of the rules for — . Help me out, Bea."

"Helping them understand the state standards. And that came about because Phil, over there, the one who likes a little coffee with his milk, his daughter had just started working at one of those schools, and everyone was casting about to understand what was going on, even the school's director, who had come out of retirement to take the job and had already retired when the standards were implemented. So, Phil told me and I called them and offered myself as a consultant. I got a week's work out of that at pretty fair money, considering they were a non-profit.

"And," said a little guy with a trace of syrup on his golf shirt, "I used to be a construction foreman until I had to take disability. The disability isn't quite enough to take care of my wife and me and my daughter who's back home after a messy marriage and her kids, so I need to pick up a few extra dollars from time to time. These guys — " he pointed indiscriminately to the center of the table — "have let me know when someone they know needs an odd job done that I can handle. I have a bad heart, so a lot of jobs I can't do, but I can do a few things. These guys — " again the pointing — "have even tried to talk me into starting my own odd jobs business. I'm sure you've seen them around. The Honey-Do'er is one of them. Have you seen those signs? They have a bunch of guys — I don't know, maybe there are women, too — who go to your house and do stuff you can't do or don't want to do."

"What's stopping you from starting that business?" Mick asked.

"Fear, right now. I don't know if I can pull it off, if I can find enough people to do enough jobs at a price to compete and if I can make enough to give me a wage, plus pay everyone and pay back whatever loans I need to get started."

"We keep telling him there are small business grants," said the former sales rep, a man with dark hair, graying at the temples, and a graying mustache. The man flipped a cigarette lighter over and over, probably a nervous habit he developed for restaurants that prohibited smoking. Mick had noticed when the guy stood up to shake his hand that he was the only one whose clothes could be described as dressy. He wore a white Alligator shirt, black dress pants and black tasseled loafers. "He won't listen. At least, he has a chance to get back on his feet with some government help. I don't. The government won't help me a bit. I just don't fit any of their favored" — he dropped the lighter long enough to make quote marks with both of his hands as he said "favored" — "special-interest slots."

"So," the former pastor said, "can you do any consulting?"

"Actually," Mick said, "I sent out a ton of letters to newspapers all over Ohio and western Pennsylvania and western New York offering myself as a writing coach. I haven't had anyone take me up on that. And I put an ad in the paper to edit master's theses and the like. Nothing."

"Have you," Calvin said leaning in, clasping his hands on the table and staring at them, "tried to do anything with your music?"

"What music?" asked a woman who had described herself as an engineer.

"No music," Mick said.

"Mick used to be in a band," Calvin said. "He told us that."

"I never," Mick said.

Calvin chuckled. "One night we were talking about old jobs we had, and you said you were in a band. What was that name? Odd name. Wait, it had something to do with your name. What was that?"

Mick squirmed. "MickeyMack's Brass Attack," he said sheepishly.

A few of them chuckled.

"What the hell was that about?" said the man in the sweatsuit.

"Where I grew up, I had a recognizable name. From high school sports."

"Oh," the superintendent said, "you must have been a basketball player."

"Of some renown," Mick said, "so I traded on the name for the band."

"What kind of band?" the engineer asked.

"It was a brass rock band, kind of like Blood, Sweat and Tears, I tell people."

"Any of them still around?" Calvin asked.

"Aw, hell, I don't know where anyone is. Maybe one guy stayed around. Not sure."

"Form a new band," the odd jobs man said.

"Have you listened to any music lately?" Mick asked. "They aren't really playing much of that anymore."

"Hey," the engineer said, "this guy I'm dating, he takes me out to places for people our age, and we hear covers of all the old stuff.

I'll bet people would go to hear you, if you had a good band, developed a following."

"Besides," Calvin said, "One year I was at an Indians game, and they had a brass quintet do the National Anthem. Kind of a funky version. I liked it. I liked it so much, I remember going home and looking for them on the Internet. They were doing a bunch of things. They had a classical repertoire, but they also did weddings and parties, all kinds of stuff."

"It's been years since I even touched a horn," Mick said.

"What kind of horn?" the engineer asked.

"I played the trombone. I fooled around with the tuba in college, but never serious. One of the tuba guys in the band taught me a little and I taught him a little trombone. Gave the director a little flexibility if he needed a strong tuba voice in one place or a stronger trombone voice in another. That's all. But, hell, I haven't even opened my trombone case since my boys were little."

"Do your boys play?" the engineer asked.

"They both started. Neither of them stuck with it."

"Would be nice to have a family band," she said.

"Yeah, well, like I said, Sean's on his way to Ireland, if I can find the money, and Sam's on his way to Iraq if I can't."

Mick stared hard at the table at the word "Iraq" coming out of his mouth, especially in a light-hearted manner, playing with the symmetry of the sentence structure. One of the woman — he couldn't tell which — had said, "Oh, listen to you," with a smile in her voice. He felt as though he had betrayed something, his wrath, perhaps. He did not ever want to abandon that wrath, not the wrath about Christopher Post or all the part-time jobs in this economic downturn or his inability to land a teaching job where he had successfully taught or his financial disaster or, especially, his inability to keep Sam out of the Army, and the insistence of this president to send so many boys to die in Iraq.

"I'm tellin' ya, Buddy Boy," the sales rep said, flipping the cigarette lighter end over end, "that Iraq business is pretty bad. I know I wouldn't want my kid goin' over there. If I had a kid. Which I don't. And I'll tell ya another thing: I don't see the president or Big Dick or the Rummy sending their kids over there. Nope, just like Vietnam. It's just gonna be the poor kids who are gonna fight this war."

"All right, Lester, we know how you feel about the war," the superintendent said. "Let's try to keep politics out of this." Then she turned her attention back to Mick. "If you were a basketball star, you probably could help coach a team. You know, you don't have to teach in the school to coach anymore. You could be an assistant. I had lots of assistant coaches who didn't teach, mostly in baseball and football, but I know they do basketball, too."

Mick kept staring for an instant, then shook himself out of it.

"I don't do sports anymore." He looked up briefly at the superintendent, just to be polite, then he riveted his gaze back at the table. "I watch a little baseball, but, no. I left that a long time ago."

No one spoke for a minute. Then Mick heard the voice of the former pastor.

"We're trying to help, Mick. We all try to help each other. Sometimes just sitting here helps. Sometimes what you need to fix isn't strictly about jobs. Even that, we'll try to help with, if you let us. But I can tell you, because I did the same thing at first, the easiest thing in the world is to shoot down every idea we have. Let me suggest that, instead of looking for reasons you can't, you might try to look for ways that you can."

A heavy silence hung for a moment.

"Hey, I think you've said that to me," the odd jobs man said, trying to lighten the mood, Mick figured. "I have to find a way to start my business. Yep, it sounds just like you were talking to me."

Mick looked at his watch, not really caring what time it was.

"I have to run." He dug into his pocket for a couple of singles and set them on the table. "It was nice meeting all of you. Thanks for your ideas. Look, you're here every week? I'll look at my calendar and see what I'm doing next week. Well, gotta go. Later."

Mick pushed off the table to push his chair back, then pushed off it again to stand up, waiting that instant while his knees did whatever they did to get ready to move. Then he staggered a few steps until his legs were ready, then he walked more purposefully for the door.

And he wondered where all of the band members had gone.

XIX

Ginny Crandall knew where one of them was. Be-Bop Bobby Bartlett. Trumpet player. Always thought he was Miles Davis. He wasn't. Didn't have Miles' talent. Didn't have Miles' sound. Did try heroin. Still, he was a pretty fair trumpet player for that band. He had the rock idiom down. Ginny said he had never left town, and that he was sales manager at a computer store in the area.

Oh, and by the way, Ginny told Mick, she had found a place for his friend, that young woman. Lovely woman, Ginny said. You haven't lost your touch, Ginny said.

Mick chuckled at that, knowing that that young woman, Angela, — well, Mick knew he wouldn't be leaving his touch on her.

"So," Ginny said, "will you be coming back to see Bobby?"

"Don't know. Depends on whether or not he's interested."

"Well, if you do, you need to take me to lunch. No. Dinner. I got your friend an apartment and I hooked you up with Bobby. That's worth dinner, isn't it?"

"Yes, indeed, Ginny. I'll keep you posted."

So, Mick called Be-Bop Bobby.

"MickeyMack, I can't believe I'm really talking to you. Geez, how long has it been? No, don't tell me. Last time we played together was at Johnny Linelli's and they closed that hallowed venue, had to be fifteen years ago. But you left town long before that, didn't you?"

"I left town twenty-two years ago, Bobby."

"And you're back? Ginny Crandall told me you were back. Are you back?"

"I'm going to move back there soon. I'm still in Ohio."

"So, are you just catching up with the old outfit? Heck, let me think where everyone is. Betty is married and has three or four kids. Her husband directs the concert band at one of the colleges around here. And Gene is with some band that does classic rock covers, but he's lost his artistic edge. I'm afraid he's drinking, and he's had his share of tawdry affairs. You know how they always flock to those drummers. And, I don't know if you heard about Zeke. Killed in a car accident. Let me see. How long ago was that? He was still alive — ."

"Bobby, catch me up with everyone later, okay? I'm calling for a specific reason."

"You are? Oh, you should have told me. You know me. I just start in and start dominating the conversation. You were the writer, MickeyMack, but I had the gift of gab. That's how I started in sales, back when the band broke up. Because I could talk anybody into anything. And I got this computer sales gig after I almost ruined my life. I came out of rehab and had no prospects. None. Nada. Zip. Who wanted an ex-junkie? But all of these computer stores came into the area at the same time, and I went from one to another talking, talking, talking, until I wore them down, one of them anyway, and I led the store in sales for, like, five years, and they started in with me mentoring the young salespeople, and pretty soon, they needed a manager, and I applied for the job and got it."

"That's great Bobby. Listen, you could blow a mean horn in the old days. Do you still play?"

"Me? Oh, a little. Very seldom, but not like I used to. No, I can't do that anymore the way I used to."

Mick laughed.

"We all lose our chops a little. I'm sure even Maynard Ferguson lost a little before he kicked."

There was dead silence on the other end of the line.

"Ginny didn't tell you?"

"Oh, my God, Bobby, did something happen? I'm sorry. Did something happen?"

"Oh, no, Mick, I don't mean anything like that. I would have thought Ginny would have told you because it's the most important thing in my life, and I talked to her about it at length when she came shopping over here. You know, she purchased our business line for that office she works in. And I told her all about it."

"All about what?"

"I found the Lord, Mick. Or, rather, I should say He found me. I was really struggling through rehab. I wasn't sure I'd make it. Truly, all I wanted was a fix. I was willing to trade my life for a fix. Would have traded it straight up. And when I was at my lowest point, the Holy Spirit walked right into my room at the rehab center and told me God had bigger plans for me than just shooting H into my veins."

"Oh, I see." Mick knew where this was going.

"At that moment, I stopped craving smack, and the first chance I got, I went to the library and got a Bible and read it cover to cover, and I realized my destiny."

"The Bible told you to sell computers?"

"I had to make a living, Mick, so I sold computers. It's honest work. You know, there are several ministries that have a presence on line. They're saving souls every day on line."

"Some people are finding porn on line or they're joining hate groups or learning to make bombs."

"I can see you haven't found the Lord, Mick. That saddens me, my friend. Of course, every instrument of our lives can be an instrument of the Lord or an instrument of Satan."

"Even the Bible, Be-Bop."

"I don't go by 'Be-Bop' anymore. I don't like the connotations that brings with it. Too many of those be-bop guys became addicts: Bird, Miles, Red Rodney. And, yes, Mick, you're right, there are people who misuse the Bible, goaded by Satan to misread it, to abuse the Word, to take things out of context. Absolutely, Mick. Every gift that God gave us, Satan has found a way to pervert and to lead people to pervert.

"But, Mick, selling computers isn't the calling to which the Lord has brought me. There's a ministry within the sales industry. You want to know why, Mick? I'll tell you why. So many of us, in selling computers, or furniture or cars or real estate have sold our souls. We've lied to our customers, we've lied to our suppliers, we've cheated everyone just to make an extra dollar on the commission. And all we've done is cheated ourselves. And a lot of us realized that, and by the time I came out of rehab and got back into sales, this ministry was alive, and the first time I went to a sales seminar, I learned about it, and I got involved with it, and at sales seminars all over the country, I preside over worship services, prayer breakfasts — ."

"So, are you ordained?"

"No, but I'm a successful lay minister, and I can do anything except perform the Sacraments. We always find a minister in every town we go to to give us communion or to baptize someone who is just coming to the Lord.

"And in those services, I sometimes play the trumpet, only in praise of God. 'Praise him with the sounding of the trumpet,' you know. That's from Psalms, Mick."

"Yes, the hundred and fiftieth."

Be-Bop went silent for an instant.

"You knew that?"

"It's the last Psalm, Bob."

"You knew that, too?"

"I've read the Psalms, Bob. And I've heard it in church."

"What church do you go to?"

"I'm, uh, not active in any church at the moment."

"Ah, Mick, the church is the wellspring."

"Well, you know what Philip Yancey said: "There's nothing wrong with Christianity except the church."

Again, Bob was struck dumb.

"You know Philip Yancey?"

"Well, I don't know him, but I read one of his books. *The Jesus I Never Knew.*"

"You bought that book?"

"Nope. I stole it. Look, I really need money, and I thought if we could do some gigs, we could put some cash in our pockets."

"But I don't play the kind of music we used to play. It doesn't praise the Lord."

"It also doesn't revile Him or insult Him or mock Him. We played music about people loving each other."

"You're being disingenuous, Mick. We played music about all the things that lead to sex."

"And sex has led to all of us. What's the problem, Bob? I need some money. You'd be doing something for me. 'As you did it for the least of these my brethren, you did it for me.'"

"'Get thee behind me, Satan.'"

"What?!" Mick said. "What did I say? I'm quoting the Bible."

"Not an exact quote, but a good paraphrase, but you're using Scripture to try to convince me to do something I know is wrong."

"I'm not. Look, Jesus was talking about how helping the disadvantaged was the same as helping Him. Because He's in all of us. He's our Brother. Look, Bob, just help me out, huh?"

"Mick, if you need money, I'll be glad to lend you some."

"I don't want a loan," Mick said, clearly agitated. "I don't want charity. I want to earn some money. I have a talent. God gave me the talent to play music. But, good Lord, Bob, no one's going to go hear a solo trombonist at a bar, unless it's Slide Hampton, and I ain't Slide Hampton. C'mon, Bob, help me out here. I need to put together a band. You know it's the right thing to do. You know the two Great Commandments. What's the second one, Bob? 'Love your neighbor as yourself,' right?"

"Yes, but the first is: 'Love the Lord your God with all your heart, and with all your soul, and with all your mind.' And I love the Lord so much that I can't allow you to lead me astray and into bars, with all the drinking and all the men chasing women who are not their wives — and you know that's true, Mick. You and I both saw them in our day. And, we both know that you and I were among men chasing women we weren't married to. I can't go into those dens of iniquity any more. I won't do that and violate all I hold dear."

"Shit," Mick said. "I need to make some money."

"Mick, you've been tossing around the Word of the Lord since you learned that I now belong to Jesus, but you have said nothing about expressing faith in the Lord. You know, you are not supposed to be anxious about anything. Jesus told us that would do us no good. You have to put your faith in God. God will provide, Mick. Believe me. I know what I'm talking about. The Lord will provide."

"Yeah," Mick said. "Yeah. I know you're right. I know you've given me the answer."

"Repent of your sins, Mick. He will wash you clean. Give Him your burden, and He will carry it for you. Give yourself to Jesus, and the Lord will provide."

"Yes, Bob, I believe you," Mick said. "And when the college asks me for tuition for my kid's classes this fall, I'll tell them that God will write them a check."

XX

During the break of Mick's next class, Angela called to Mick as he headed for the pop machine.

"Your friend helped me find an apartment. I'm moving in next week. I really appreciate your talking to her for me."

"Sure. My pleasure." Mick surveyed the choices as he took a dollar bill out of his wallet. "Where?"

"I think it's Hoover Road."

"Yeah, but what town?" Mick said, pushing the Diet Coke button. No caffeine.

"Your friend said it was the same town you grew up in. Washington Township."

"Westinghouse Township?" Mick said. "You want a bottle of pop?"

"No, thanks. Yeah, that's it. Westinghouse."

"Both guys named George." He opened the plastic top of the bottle and took a quick swig. "Very different effects in this part of the country. One of them fell into the Allegheny River and almost drowned, then started the French and Indian War, a worldwide conflagration, single-handedly, then owned thousands of acres of land out here as a speculator. The other guy invented the airbrake and alternating electrical current. Or maybe the other one." He took another quick swig. "Or maybe he didn't invent it. Is it possible to invent an electrical current? Yeah, I don't know either. I'm out of my area of expertise here." He screwed the top back on. "I'm sure about the airbrake. He built a company and everything. Oh, I know. He invented Airbrake Avenue in Wilmerding. I think."

Angela smiled at him. "I don't know anything about history."

"Most people your age don't," Mick said, "which is why you don't know whether anything I said about either George is correct. I could be making the whole thing up."

"Well," she said, walking beside him back to the classroom, "I knew about the French and Indian War. That was at Fort Jumonville."

"Oh," Mick said. "I'm very impressed. You know there's a fort, and you know there's a Jumonville involved, and you managed to put them together. Very good. Did you grow up in western Pennsylvania?"

"Yes," she said defensively. "In fact, when I was little, I went to Camp Jumonville every year. That's a Christian camp where the battle was."

Mick rolled his eyes. "I was a Methodist," he said. "I know all about Camp Jumonville. And I know it isn't at the site of the battle, at least not the big battle. The battle was at Fort Necessity, which happened after Washington and his Indian allies killed one of the

Jumonville brothers, who was a French officer, in a whatdoyoucallit, a little battle."

"How come you aren't a Methodist anymore?" she asked, leaning her shoulder and head against the door jamb and crossing her right ankle over her left.

"Oh, good Lord, you're one of them."

She launched a short burst of a laugh. "What? One of what?"

Mick started in the door and stopped before entering the room, inches from her face. "This might not be the best time to proselytize to me." He entered the room and sat down and wrote furiously in his notebook, just nonsense. He just didn't want to invite any more discussion.

Still, as the rest of the class wore on, he found it difficult to concentrate and contribute. He knew she was trying to be nice. Why the hell did he have to be so smug about knowing things? Why did he have to take out all of his frustration on people who didn't know things he knew? He understood that the schools didn't teach what they had taught when he was a kid. How could they? He had graduated from high school more than thirty years earlier. Teachers had more than thirty years worth of literature, history, science and technology to teach than they had to teach Mick's generation. They had to teach about sexually transmitted disease, which no one talked about in any classroom Mick had ever sat in, except in the most technical — and shallow — of terms. And they still had to fit it all in in 180 days. Didn't make sense.

So, why should he expect this young woman to know things he had learned over about thirty more years of life than she had lived? His sons knew things. He made sure they knew things. He had taken the boys to Fort Necessity. And Fort Pitt, the museum and the Blockhouse. And Gettysburg. And Independence Hall, Valley Forge, Brandywine Creek, Chambersburg. And even the hill commemorating Braddock's defeat. No wonder his boys hated history. And Constance, too. He had never been to Washington, D.C., when he was a boy, and he couldn't wait for the boys to get old enough to appreciate the Lincoln Memorial and the Jefferson Memorial and all of the rest. And when the boys got old enough, they wouldn't go. They wanted to go to an amusement park — any park but Kennywood, where he had taken them many times (and where he had pointed out to them the sign about Braddock's crossing of the Monongahela to get whupped on the other side).

When the class ended, he caught up to her at the elevator and rode down with her and a handful of other people making small talk. When Angela got out on the ground floor, Mick got out, too and waited for her to drift away from the others.

"Angela, I owe you an apology," he said, just a couple of steps behind her.

She stopped and turned half toward him.

"Ya think?" she said.

"I'm sorry. I get a little full of myself sometimes," Mick said, pulling aside her.

The two of them continued toward the door. She did not look at him as she spoke. "Are you apologizing for making fun of me for not knowing all the history of a war that took place more than two hundred years ago or for making fun of my faith?"

"Oh, yes. I did do both of those things, didn't I?"

"Yes, you did," she said a loud hurt filling her voice.

"Well," Mick said, opening the door for her, "I apologize for both things. Not only do I get a little full of myself vis-à-vis my knowledge of things I think everyone should know, but I, uh. I had a, uh — . I had someone proselytizing to me not long ago, and right now, I'm not interested in being questioned about my faith's journey." Mick had picked up that term from a pastor he had known some time ago. He understood that many Christians talked in certain terms. If you used those terms, they thought you were a part of them. If you didn't, they knew you weren't.

" 'Vis-à-vis?'" she said, picking up on the wrong terminology. "Did you go to Harvard or something?"

"Hardly," he said. She started toward the library, and he just went where she was going. "Anyway, I'm sorry. Look, let me buy you a cup of coffee and make it up to you."

"Oh," she said, "I really have a lot of things to do tonight. I was going to meet some friends — ."

"Your old friends will forgive you for making a new friend, especially one so contrite as I am, so willing to get back in your good graces. After all, I helped you get your new apartment. I think you should have coffee with me and tell me all about it. You know, that's my hometown. I'll bet I could tell you a lot about it."

She sighed. "All right," she said, "but not coffee. Let's go to the Dog House."

"Great," he said sharply. The Steel City Hot Dog House. He could use a dog or two.

"Where I'm meeting my friends."

"Great," he said, less sharply.

The friends were already there, three of them, all female — one a blonde, one a brunette wearing glasses and a Steelers' T-shirt, and the third a brunette wearing a short skirt not quite covering crossed legs — all somewhere between cute and pretty. Mick went to the counter and ordered dogs and diet Cokes for him and Angela and carried them back to the table. Angela made the introductions and explained why Mick was there. He didn't know these women, so he wasn't crazy about Angela telling them he had denigrated her faith — although she didn't put it quite in those words.

As the women all chattered, Mick watched Angela deliberately lift a hot dog to her lips and take a small bite. Mick noticed how long and slender her fingers were, how perfect her nails were, each of them extending only slightly beyond the end of the finger. She used no colored polish on her nails, but they seemed to shine a bit, as though buffed, but Mick concluded she had not been to a manicurist. She was a do-it-yourself girl.

It took a while, but Mick was able to ask Angela directly about her new place to live.

"It's nice," she said. "It's on Hoover Road, like I said."

"And I still don't know where that is," Mick said.

"It's a nice quiet street. There are some kids on the street, little kids. They ride up and down the street on their bikes, but not too often. It's pretty hot this summer, so I guess they're inside playing video games. But they don't make too much noise. They don't break my concentration."

"Is it an apartment building?"

"No, it's a duplex. I have the downstairs. There's a couple upstairs. Young, married couple. They don't have any kids." Her face scrunched up in a smile, and she held back a flat-out laugh. "But they're sure working on it."

Angela let that laugh out, hard and high-pitched. One of the girls called out her name in an exclamation. The other two laughed.

"So, your bedroom is right underneath theirs, huh?"

"Yep," she said, "and they sure are busy in there." She laughed again, an embarrassed laugh she covered with her hand.

Mick couldn't resist. "So, any appeals to the Almighty? Can you hear any dirty talk?" Mick lifted his eyebrows up and down in a mock-lascivious manner.

"No, I can only hear the bedsprings. Oh my goodness."

"Well, keep me posted on that," Mick said. "I'm always interested in perversions in the human animal."

Angela laughed, the last gasp of a semi-continuous laugh that had begun with the first oblique reference to the bed. "Oh, my," she said. "And I don't have much furniture, so there's a lot of empty space, but that's okay.

"And your friend Ginny. She really likes you. You must have been really something."

"When I was younger?" Mick said it with raised eyebrows and a tone of mock hurt.

"I didn't say that," Angela said, as her friends laughed.

"Implied but not stated," Mick said. "For the record, I'm still really something."

"Really?" Angela said, leaning the side of her head on her right hand. "Exactly what are you?"

"Well," Mick said, "I'm quite tall, and I still have most of the hair Ginny fantasized about running her fingers through. Um, I, uh — I'm quite bright, and, as you've suffered, I mean, as you know from my offending you, I'm quite opinionated."

"And an atheist," Angela said. Mick felt her friends' eyes zoom in on him.

"No," Mick shook his head and gripped his Coke cup with both hands. "Not an atheist. Why is it that you people all think that if we don't accept your version of Christianity, we're all atheists?"

"'You people?'" the girl with the glasses said.

"I don't think that," Angela said, taking some offense. "I know that a lot of people who believe in God don't believe the way that I do. Jews and Muslims and Catholics, all of them."

"And mainline Protestants?" Mick said.

Angela's friends sipped their coffee and swiveled their heads back and forth between Mick and Angela.

"What does that mean?" she asked.

"You know, your Presbyterians and Methodists and Lutherans and — ."

"I'm a Methodist," said the blonde in a twangy drawl.

Mick shifted in his seat to face her, a blonde with black eyebrows, a cute nose and brown eyes set in a round face.

"And what part of the Confederacy are you from?" he asked her.

"I'm from the great state of Tennessee," she said.

"What a surprise," Mick said as dryly as he could. "And why is it that all of you Bible beaters are from the South? Did you decide that if you couldn't beat us in the war that you would subdue us with creationism and self-righteousness?"

"Bible beaters?" the girl with the glasses said with great indignation.

"I'm not from the South," Angela said, raising herself out of her relaxed posture. "I was born and raised right here in Pittsburgh."

"See," Mick said. "They're taking over one by one. Isn't that how the devil works? He insidiously invades the lives of one person after the other until he has disciples all over the world, despoiling God's children. Am I right about that?"

"Oh, you are impossible," the Methodist from Tennessee said. "I'm not listening to this." She picked up her books. "I'm not sure this was a good person for you to bring to dinner," she said to Angela. She turned and stomped out.

The others all mumbled something about having to go, and they said their good-byes to Angela. The girl in the short skirt said pointedly to Mick, "It was NOT a pleasure to meet you."

As the last of them cleared the room, Mick turned to Angela. "And don't you have somewhere to go, too?"

"Yes, I do," she said, "but I wanted to tell you privately that I have never met anyone as bigoted as you in all my life." She pushed the Coke cup away from her and scrunched up her napkin. "You don't know any of us, but you're judging all of us because we believe in God and have accepted Jesus as our Savior. Your problem is that you have no God in your life to give you the love, comfort and peace that Jesus gives us."

"No, actually, my problem is that a Bible-thumping president has started a war — a crusade, he called it — which really endeared us to all the Muslim descendants of the victims of the Crusades, and he's made it seem really appealing for young men and women to go to the Middle East and kill people who believe differently from the way we do. And, I've just had it up to my freaking eyebrows with the punitive posturing of the Christian right that wants to stone all the gays and all the pacifists and all the scientists. How the hell can you people believe that a bacterium can evolve to immunize itself against an antibiotic, but you can't believe that all of life on Earth evolved from a single cell, adapting to other forces of nature? How the hell can you believe that the planet has existed for only six thousand years? Diamonds in and of themselves have to be proof that the planet's been around longer than that. How the hell do you explain carbon-dating, by the way?"

"Well, first of all," Angela said, standing up, "I happen to believe the universe is billions of years old, like the scientists tell us, but if my God had chosen to place diamonds, fully formed, into mines in Africa, He would have the power to do that. Would yours?"

"Of course, He would."

"And I have no problem with the concept of evolution. I think my God has the power to create a universe and just let it take its own course, which, I'll have you know, is exactly what He has done with people, which is why He allowed me the choice to love Him and accept His Son as my savior, and why He gave you the choice to reject Him and demean Him."

Mick stood up as Angela started toward the garbage can with her napkin, hot dog wrapper and cup.

"I'm not rejecting God," Mick said. "I'm rejecting the people who wield Him like some weapon to beat the rest of us into submission. And I'm not rejecting Jesus. Son of God? Yes. Savior of the world? Yes. Do I pray in Jesus' name? Absolutely. Every night, when I ask God to get this lying imbecile out of the White House and keep my son from going to Iraq. It's just the dogma that doesn't come out of the Bible that gets up my — under my skin. So, you may have jumped the gun a little presupposing who I am."

"Just as you did to me."

"Good," Mick said, more calmly now. He breathed deeply. "Good. We can both admit error. We can find common ground. I'm not sure most Americans can, judging from the incessant blue-state, red-state talk. And talk radio."

"Good," she said, turning again toward the garbage can.

"So," Mick said, "can a liberal, backsliding Methodist become friends with a conservative devoted fundamentalist?"

She turned again. Mick thought her eyes seemed on the verge of crying. "I'm not a fundamentalist," she said. "I told you. I'm a Christian, but not a fundamentalist. And the president is not a lying imbecile. He's a moral man, a Christian himself."

Mick shook his head and sighed. He opened his mouth, but then closed it, took a step toward Angela and stuck out his hand.

"Can we agree to disagree about certain things and try to be friends? After, all, I helped get you the apartment that provides entertainment for you, and Ginny Crandall says I'm really something."

Angela smiled up at Mick, and the face crinkled, almost obscuring her eyes. She clasped Mick's hand and spoke while suppressing a laugh. "Ginny said you used to be something, not that you are something."

"Well," Mick said with a smile, "when Ginny becomes reacquainted with me, she'll know I still am something."

Angela broke the handshake. "You come here every week," she said. "You're not that far away. Instead of having coffee with me, you should be having dessert with her."

Mick raised his eyebrows and cocked his head.

She smiled, embarrassed. "You know what I mean, and what you're thinking isn't what I mean."

She turned around yet again toward the garbage can. "Good night, Mick Mackintosh. Drive safely."

Mick watched her dump the garbage and walk out the door, a subtle twitch to her, well, her behind. Mick even thought he detected an athletic gait.

"Good night," he called. "Welcome to Westinghouse Township."

XXI

"Well, lunch isn't dinner," Ginny said, taking the menu from the hostess, "but it's better than nothing."

"Yeah, well, maybe we can do dinner another time," Mick said. "I have class tonight, and it wouldn't be much of a dinner if I had to cut out after just a few minutes to head to Oakland."

"And, since we're going to talk about finding you a place to live," she said, "that makes it a working lunch, which means I'll pick up the check and put it on my expenses."

"I like where this is going," he said.

"Which means you can take me to dinner once you move back here," she said. "Still like where this is going?"

"That's fine," Mick said.

"Well, we have places in several areas ... ."

Mick looked her over as she went on about all the properties the real estate company had. Ginny's gray eyes darted all around the room as she talked, looking alternately at Mick, the people coming in and the people going out, the wait staff careening around Dirk's, and some brochures she pulled out of her briefcase.

When a waiter came to their table, Ginny picked up the menu and quickly turned pages with long fingers, just starting to wrinkle with age, fingernails a deep red and shaped to a somewhat rounded point. The work of a manicurist, Mick figured. Or maybe they weren't even her real nails.

Ginny ordered a salad of some description and water with a twist. Mick asked for tomato soup, half a chicken salad sandwich and iced tea.

Ginny handed her menu over to the waiter, then immediately pulled her longish light brown hair behind her left ear, from which it had escaped as she bent her head to read the menu. Her hair, curled at the bottom, framed her long, thin face, which itself showed the wear of middle age and perhaps of her unhappy marriage. She alternately leaned her slender frame back and forth in the chair, leaning in to talk quietly about "high crime" areas, then releasing backward to talk in less conspiratorial tones about houses and apartments in more, um, middle-class areas.

"Well, what about where you got Angela her place? Hoover Road? I don't even know where that is."

"Neither do I. Angela is on Herbert Road."

Mick chuckled a bit. "Angela apparently has some trouble with names."

"Well," Ginny said, "we know who Herbert Hoover was because he was still alive when we were kids, so we have some frame of reference. Angela is just a child. She doesn't know Herbert Hoover from Herb Alpert"

Mick felt a need to defend Angela. "Hey, at least I'm happy that she knows the names 'Herbert' and 'Hoover' go together."

"I suppose there's something to be said for that.

"So, what is your interest in her? Is she the daughter you never had?"

Mick looked up as the waiter brought their drinks. He tore open a packet of artificial sweetener and dumped it into his tea and poked the lemon wedge with the long-handled spoon.

"What makes you think," he said in a playful voice, "that she doesn't long for an older man, wise in the ways of the world, someone who can help her distinguish between Herbert Hoover and Herb Alpert? How do you know she doesn't find my long hair and goatee sexy? You know, I have studied anthropology enough to know that there are some ethnic groups that find a hobbling man more virile than any other man in the village, and it's entirely possible that Angela is descended from one of those groups. Isn't it?"

"Well, one thing that hasn't changed, MickeyMack, is that you remain full of shit. Seriously, do you have a romantic interest in her?"

"Well," Mick stared at his left hand twirling his glass, beaded with condensation rolling down the sides and soaking the cocktail napkin underneath, "here's the thing: I think she is a vision of beauty, and I find her very personable, very charming, and I would bet my next mortgage payment that every heterosexual man who comes in contact with her, including the most faithful husband in all of Allegheny County, has developed an instantaneous crush on her."

"And you are not the most faithful husband in Allegheny County."

"I'm not any kind of husband, except an ex-husband, so I'm free to develop crushes on anyone I wish."

"Were you faithful when you were married?"

"In deed, if not always in thought."

"Bobby told me that when you guys had the band, you used to chase women all the time."

"He's right. We did. But I wasn't married for the first few years of the band. After it became clear to me that Constance was the one I was looking for, Bobby chased women on his own."

The waiter brought their food. He ground pepper onto Ginny's salad, then scooted on to check on another table. Ginny tapped a few grains of salt onto her salad.

"So, Constance was the unfaithful one?"

"Not while we lived here," Mick said, aggressively shaking pepper into his cup of soup, "but later, after we moved to Ohio."

"I'm sorry. I know what that's like." Ginny put a small forkful of salad into her mouth.

"And you," Mick said, now attacking the chicken salad sandwich with the pepper shaker, "you married Arnie Crandall, right? Or was it his brother — what was his name? — Jack?"

"I married Arnie."

"What happened? He didn't seem the type to mess around."

"Maybe not in high school," she said before sipping her water, "but in college, he started to think a little more of himself. I was here at home going to community college, but we kept dating. I don't know if he had flings while he was away or not, but he always said he had opportunities. Eventually, that's why I gave in to him, and I got pregnant when he was a senior. I quit school. I was only going part time anyway. Then we got married after he graduated."

"Did he settle down?"

"I don't know. I was at home with the kids. A couple of times I suspected things. I don't know. Eventually, he did have an affair with a younger woman he worked with. When I found out, he asked if I wanted a divorce, kind of hopeful, I thought. I don't know. I hadn't until I heard the tone in his voice. So, what the hell? I gave it to him."

"I'm sorry," Mick said, setting onto the plate what was left of his sandwich.

"What happened to yours?" she asked. Mick thought he should talk for a while and let her eat.

"Somewhere along the line she lost interest in me. Maybe that's because I expressed more interest in my work than in her. That's my best guess, anyway. Everywhere we lived, she was deeply involved in whatever church we went to. In Ohio, she became very close to one of the lay ministers who was a local politician. He was a widower. Or maybe we just call people of both genders widows. I don't know. Anyway, this pious man of God coveted my wife, then he committed adultery with her, then she decided she didn't want to be married to me anymore. Probably I wasn't sufficiently religious because I hadn't been an adulterous lay pastor. Lay pastor. Very descriptive and apt term, right?"

"Wow," she said, tearing off a piece of a dinner roll, "you sound a little bitter."

"Let's just say I haven't felt moved to attend the annual men's Pentecostal breakfast and communion service for a while."

"So, this girl is your next conquest?"

"Despite the fact that she finds hobbling, goateed, long-haired men who prattle on endlessly about history — and, by the way insult her faith — despite the fact that she finds such a man irresistible, I just don't know if the, um, let's call it September-May thing would work."

"From what I remember, she's a lot closer to February, and if you're September, you're September in the Arctic Circle, where it's starting to be dark a lot of hours every day."

Mick smiled and twirled his glass around the soaked napkin. "You're quite the charmer yourself, there, Ms. Crandall."

"And yet, the whole way through high school, you resisted me."

And here we go, Mick thought to himself.

"If you had played your cards right," she said, pointing her index finger at him, "you could have been the first boy on the basketball team to get laid."

"Yeah, well," Mick studied the condensation on the glass. "Uh. I had a crush on Jeannie Carpenter. Real bad. I think I was in love with her. And I had principles. If I loved her, I just couldn't date anyone else. Wouldn't be right. I never could figure out why I never did anything for her."

"You know now, don't you?"

Mick looked up at her, narrowing his eyes.

"Well, she never cared for men," Ginny said.

Mick blinked a couple of times.

"She lives with a woman. Brought her to the last reunion."

"Oh," Mick said, casting his eyes downward.

The waiter came and asked if they were done, if they wanted dessert. Neither did, but Ginny asked for coffee. The waiter took the plates.

"See what you miss not attending the reunions? Everybody asks about you."

"Well, one reason we didn't come was that we never lived around here. We would have had to come for the weekend and — ."

"You were here for the ten-year reunion."

"That would have been — okay, yeah, but at that time – I was at the *Messenger* then, and I was on the Sunday staff, which meant I worked the Saturday night desk. So, I couldn't get away."

"They didn't give you vacation time at the *Messenger*?"

"Oh, well, yeah, they did."

The waiter brought Ginny's coffee and placed the check next to Mick. Ginny reached over and grabbed it before taking a sip of coffee.

"The truth is," Mick said, "Constance never wanted to go to those things. Too much drinking, and because she didn't go to school with us, she had little patience for all of the story-telling. She never liked getting together with my college friends either. She said all we did was tell stories about people she didn't know doing things she didn't care about."

"Oh." Ginny said, setting the cup down and laying her forearm on the table and dangling her hand off of it. "Well, the next reunion is just a few years away, and now that you're going to be living here, you can come. You'll enjoy it. You'll get to see the guys you played basketball with, some of the people in the band.

"And maybe by then you'll find someone to go with," she said. She smiled and sipped her coffee.

XXII

From: Mick Mackintosh [mailto:mickeymack@fastconnect.com]
Sent: Wednesday, July 17, 2003 2:22 PM
To: B.D. Butterfield
Subject: Home coming

Good afternoon, B.D.

I wanted to tell you I'm moving back home. Not to the house I grew up in. I still have no money to buy that, because, you know, in case you hadn't heard, I DON'T HAVE A FUCKING JOB!!!

But I'm renting a house, well part of a house. When I was over there for class last week, the woman who's listing the house my parents owned showed me a place on a road not far from where I grew up. Same town, different street. I was waiting to get a job so that my new employer would pay for the move, but, in case you haven't heard I DON'T HAVE A FUCKING JOB, so I have to pay for my own move. I just got tired of driving out there every week for class, and I think that once I'm there, I can respond more quickly to ads for jobs, and maybe I'll get to know people, and the editor at the Chronicle who runs the weekly regional editions says he can find me stringer work once I move back there. He's a guy I worked with when I was at the Post, and he's a pretty good guy. He likes that he doesn't have to teach me anything. And if I do well, there, maybe I can turn it into something more permanent.

I've written several things that have been published in local newspapers, but none over my signature or with my by-line. I've written them all for this group, I think I told you about, a group of Christians — real Christians, not the kind that sleep with your wife -- opposing the war. Some of them are Quakers. Others are just pacifists like me. And some just hate the president and the Iraq war, although they're okay with Afghanistan. I, of course, think they should bring everyone home and be done with it.

I did go to a march over the weekend in Pittsburgh. It was sponsored by the Christians Against the War chapter there. There were a bunch of anti-war groups. We met at the Quaker meetinghouse and marched to one of those war memorials for WW II in a little town outside Pittsburgh. Lots of speeches. I didn't write any of them, but I touched base with the local chapter leader and told him I was moving back, and I told him the kind of work I was doing for the Cleveland group. He's interested in me doing some work with them.

I don't know what that means in terms of my stringing. I might not be able to do the anti-war work. I'll have to think of the ethics of that. I'd be an independent contractor and not a staffer, and I wouldn't be covering the war or the protesters, and if there were some war-related story wherever I was stringing, I'd have to recuse myself from that story. Otherwise, maybe I could.

Anyway, I found a realtor who really likes my house. She thinks I can sell it pretty quickly and get a pretty good price. If she's wrong, I'll be in the deepest financial shit ever, trying to pay a mortgage and rent and tuition for myself and for Sean. Unfortunately, I won't be paying any tuition for Sam. He's definitely going to the service. He passed his physical. He goes at the end of September. I'm just brokenhearted about this. We have to get rid of this president and stop this war.

So, I'm moving in a couple of weeks. I'm going to rent a truck, and the boys will help me pack and move. I'm really looking forward to going home. I really wish I could hire a mover who would do all the packing then take everything to my new place and unload it and save me aggravation and my knees a lot of stress, but, In case you hadn't heard, I DON'T HAVE A FUCKING JOB.

So, catch me up on what's new with you.

Later,
MM

PS: Oh, did I tell you that my real estate agent hit on me? I think. Not the one in Ohio, but the one who got me the apartment in Westinghouse Township. We were having lunch and — did I tell you she and I went to high school together? Well, when we were kids — . Geez, this is a very long story. Sometime you call — and we can talk on your dime, I'll tell you all about it. And why am I waiting for you to call me?

BECAUSE I DON'T HAVE A FUCKING JOB!!!

In case, you know, you hadn't heard.

XXIII

"Mick?"

It was the former superintendent.

"I'm sorry," Mick said, lifting his elbow off the table in the coffee shop. "I drifted away there for a moment. It was just like I was in science class after a late night in college. You didn't teach science, did you?"

"I taught everything. I was an elementary school teacher."

"Wow. My sympathies to you. I think I need more coffee." He waved the waitress over. "I'm sorry. What did you ask?"

She smiled at him. "Oh, I just asked what had placed the dazed look on your face as you stared at your coffee cup."

Everyone else around the table laughed.

Now Mick smiled and shifted his eyes comically from side to side. "Their laughter tells me that's not what you asked. I'm guessing it was more an adult question."

"What she really asked, Mick," his friend Calvin said, "she asked — " and Calvin affected a smoky female voice " — 'And what are you wearing for me tonight, Baby?'"

Everyone laughed, including Mick.

The superintendent had laughed the least. Now she straightened up. "I asked, since you had no luck putting together a band, what other ideas you might try."

"Actually, I'm moving. That's kind of my idea."

"I hope you're moving to the Sunbelt," said the odd-jobs man.

"Nah," Mick said, staring back at the cup. "No offense if any of you is from the South, but I think I fit in best up here. I mean, after all, I have shoes and everything."

Some of them laughed. The superintendent nodded as she chuckled and crossed her arms in front of her.

"Ain't that the truth," said the odd-jobs man.

"No, I'm going home, back to where I grew up. It just makes sense since I'm going to school there, and people know me there."

"So you think your name will open some doors?" the engineer asked, twisting her napkin.

Mick winced. "Aaah, maybe not. It's been a long time since I was a basketball star. Or a musician back there." His eyes brightened a bit for the engineer. "I mean, that would be great if it did, but, you know, it would have to be somebody older. Or maybe a former student who would hire me.

"But at first, I'm going to be a stringer on a paper back there."

"What the hell's a stringer?" asked the odd-jobs man.

"A reporter who doesn't have a job with the paper, even part time, but writes stories on an as-needed basis. A contract worker, actually. You probably know guys who have worked for a construction company on just one job. No benefits, just the paycheck. The union guys don't like that much, and some places won't do it because of the union contract, but I've heard of it happening. In fact, Calvin, didn't we have independent contractors as our tech staff at *The Sun*?"

Calvin nodded.

"So, you won't be back for any more sessions?" asked the engineer.

"No." Then Mick added, "But it's been very nice being here, getting to know you."

"But we haven't been much help, have we?" Calvin asked.

"One never knows what has helped and what has hurt."

"That's all right," said the ad rep, flipping the cigarette lighter over and over, with a touch of humor in his voice, but none in his eyes Mick could see. "We never help anyone but this waitress, who's making a fortune in tips on us. It's a good thing she's efficient, cause she ain't that pretty."

No one laughed. The engineer glared at him, and the superintendent looked out the window.

"Well, Lester, maybe, in some way, coming here gave me the impetus to move back home, get me out of here, where, clearly, there is no future for me. The paper isn't going to hire anyone back, is it, Calvin?"

"I wouldn't suspect so. I don't see any more ad linage than I saw before we were given our buyouts."

"Well," said the former pastor, "we wish you good luck, and if you hear of anything that any of us might be interested, I hope you'll remember us." She looked around the table. "It's possible some of us would be willing to move in order to get a job. They don't tar and feather Browns fans out in Steeler Country, do they?"

"No," Mick said with a sly smile. "We only tar and feather fans of teams who offer us a challenge."

Mick heard some snickers, then the former pastor said, "Well, on that note, who else has something to contribute to today's session?" Silence, except for Lester's coffee slurping. "Anyone even have an interview or anything this week?"

"I didn't have an interview, really," Lester said, "but I went door to door along Market Street just trying to find something. You know there are all those furniture stores and carpet stores and flooring stores and that goddamned Bible store — " Lester waited for a laugh from his irony, but it never came " — and I just went in, dressed in my best Armani suit and Valentino shirt from when I was making professional money, and asked if anyone had any sales openings, and I got nothing. Not a goddamned thing."

"No encouragement at all?" the odd jobs man asked.

"Not so much as a 'Good luck, you poor bastard, you.'" He crossed one leg over the other and continued flipping the lighter end over end.

"Surely," the superintendent asked, "someone invited you to fill out an application."

Lester shook his head. "I'll tell ya, Sister, they take one look at me and run the other way."

"Dressed in Armani?" the engineer asked.

"Look at me," Lester said. "I have the same problem as all of you. I'm fifty-three years old. They look at me and all they see is high insurance premiums and call-offs twice a week with incontinence problems."

A couple of them snickered.

"Plus, I have a problem only a couple of the others of you have: I'm a white male with no obvious disabilities. Of course, they can't see that I'm hopped up on anti-depressants half the time, or maybe I'd be a special case. Calvin, I don't mean any offense, cause I know you're a smart guy and you earned your job, plus Mack the Knife here says you were the best editor at the paper, but, you know, every time I see an ad in the paper that says 'Equal Opportunity Employer,' I know what that really means, and that's 'No middle-aged, heterosexual white males need apply.' Hell, George," Lester pointed his lighter at the odd jobs man, "you ought to go to your next job interview carrying a cane or — hey, great idea. Rent yourself a wheelchair. Maybe you can make a deal with Jorgenson's

Drugs to rent one by the hour. You wheel yourself in in one of those babies, and you've got yourself a job."

"I think you're over-reacting," the former pastor said.

"Well," the superintendent said, trying to lighten the mood, "maybe not about the incontinence. I do notice that you go to the men's room pretty often."

Even Lester smiled. Mick figured that even though Lester saw himself as a victim — a little like he himself did, he realized — he could laugh at himself. That was a trait Mick admired, in part because he had once been that way but had grown to take himself too seriously.

"You know, Lester," Mick said, "there are economic advantages to a company for hiring minorities of all kinds."

"I'll tell you how that works with *The Sun*," Calvin said. "I was the only black man in the newsroom — now, this was maybe ten, twelve years ago, before Mick got there — and I think there was one Asian woman, and we were both on the desk, so no one even saw us. There might have been minorities in circulation, but none in advertising, at least no ethnic minorities in advertising, although we had a lot of women. None I knew of, anyway, and, hell, I didn't know everyone because they were on a different floor. Anyway, at one point, they hired a black man to be publisher. First-rate journalist. Not an affirmative action hire." Calvin turned to Mick. "You've heard of Moses Simmons, right?"

"Good man. I've heard him speak at a number of seminars. Knows his stuff."

"And," Calvin continued, "Moses looked around the newsroom and saw nothing but white faces and me and Kanami, and he called a meeting of the entire newsroom, and he said, 'Who covers the African-American community?' And this young white woman raised her hand. 'Who covers the Latino community?' Same woman raised her hand. 'Who covers the Asian community?' Same woman. And he said, 'I don't want to ghettoize the news.' That means only black reporters cover blacks and only Latinos cover Latinos. 'But how do you know what's important to all of the minority communities you cover? How do you know what bothers them about crime or the economy or the government or education?' This young woman, the woman who covered all of them, said she would just ask them. What that meant was that whenever there was a big story about the economy, the city editor would send this young white woman out to ask black people what kind of jobs they had and all of that. But, see, why should a bunch of middle-aged white men and women be making all the coverage decisions? And why should minority readers pick up a paper that doesn't even employ minorities in important positions? You know, Lester, if you ran a grocery store in a predominantly black neighborhood, would you know what inventory to stock?"

"Sure, chitlins." Lester said, a little defensively.

"And do you even know what chitlins are?"

"No."

"They're the insides of a pig, intestines. And if you think that's all you need to stock, you'll go broke, my man. The economy has become diverse, and what I mean by that is that when we were kids, white folks had most of the disposable income. Now, it's all over. Blacks, Latinos, Asians, women — all of them make a lot more spending decisions than they made thirty — even twenty — years ago. A newspaper has to have serious discussions about how to get that money into their coffers, and so do furniture stores and carpet stores and Bible stores. Did you look closely at the Bible store? Did they carry the Koran?"

"I don't know," Lester said, with some resentment. "They didn't have any jobs for me, so I wasn't going to spend my money there."

"Calvin's right," the superintendent said. "I hired minority teachers, in part, because they related better to minority students. And the students, some of them, at least, performed better in class because they could identify with people who looked like them. Plus, they got to see, if they didn't see it in their own families or neighborhoods, that minority men and women could become professionals, could be authority figures, could drive nice cars without selling drugs."

"Okay," said the engineer, "but did you ever hire a minority teacher who was less qualified than a white candidate."

"Occasionally, I did — if you mean 'qualified' only in an academic sense. In other words, did the white candidate have a better grade point average than the minority candidate? Sure, sometimes. But, hiring is subjective, and it has to be, and — especially for teachers — you can't hire based only on college achievement. I know, Mick, this has frustrated you. I sympathize. In addition to some of the other demands No Child Left Behind put on me, that caused me to resign, I felt like my hands were tied in hiring. A good superintendent — any good hirer — has to be free to go with his or her gut in making choices. Sometimes, a situation called for a minority hire even if that person didn't have the academic achievement of a white candidate. 'Qualification' is kind of a subjective word.

"I sympathize with you, too, Lester. The age thing is definitely against us all. You might very well have a legitimate concern that you've been passed over because you're a white male. That might not be fair. On the other hand, look at the world white males have brought us. It might be time for a change."

"Well, all I know, Sister, is that while you all try to change the world, my wife is the only breadwinner in the family, and we're starting to run out of money. Pretty soon, we're going to start missing mortgage payments, cause we bought a house that fit the salary I made when I was a top salesman for a Fortune 500 company.

"And now I have to take another piss, but that doesn't make me incontinent. It just means I have a small bladder. Which was never a problem when I was making enough money to buy Armani."

XXIV

From: Mick Mackintosh [mailto:mickeymack@fastconnect.com]
Sent: Saturday, July 26, 2003 9:22 AM
To: B.D. Butterfield
Subject: Did you see this?

Saw this in the paper this a.m. (Online, of course, which means for free. How can the newspaper industry give this stuff away and expect people to subscribe? No wonder the newspapers aren't making any money.)

Anyway, it seems that a bunch of nuns who had been protesting at some missile silo somewhere out west were sent to prison. Don't know what that says about the First Amendment. Or maybe it says something about the courts. Or the Bush Administration. Or the mood of the country. And I wonder if the judge who delivered the sentence is one of those guys who protested the war in Vietnam when he got his draft card but now is all for the war or for missiles or for mutual assured destruction.

Well, whatever, but it seems that a bunch of other protesters picked up where the nuns left off and have started their own protests. Maybe there's hope for the country yet.

MM

XXV

Mick saw the people cluster at street level as he approached the microphone. He had to wind his way through four or five people looking over typed sheets of paper or chatting together. The men and women in his way parted for him. One petite redhead looked up at Mick and smiled. Mick smiled back. He recognized her. She would be speaking today. She was a Democratic state senator hoping to become a candidate for the U.S. House in 2004. Mick slipped the microphone into the stand just at the top of the steps leading from the courthouse down to the sidewalk. He turned it on, ready to say those immortal words: "Check, one two," but he did not.

From his perspective, he could see a couple of police

officers on the edge of the gathering crowd, which now spread maybe forty feet along the sidewalk. The ages of the protesters reached from high school kids to senior citizens. Black, white, Asian, Latino. One man, probably Mick's age, but paunchy in a short-sleeved white dress shirt gapping between the buttons, carried a sign that said: "Impeach Bush" on one side and "Bring home the troops and send Dick to Iraq" on the other side. A thin, gray-haired woman wore a white T-shirt with blue piping around the crew neck and blue stripes an inch below the neck and an inch above her belt. In between, in red, were the names of those killed in Iraq. Two young women, one blonde-ish and the other brunette, both dressed in mini-skirts and sleeveless tops, sipped from large bottles of water and talked between themselves. One pointed at the blonde female reporter from the ABC affiliate, who cradled a microphone and chatted with her cameraman.

It was different now, Mick thought. During the Vietnam War protests, all the young women wore jeans and tie-dyed shirts, their hair hanging straight on either side from a part in the middle. And in those days, all the women were young. His father's generation did not start to oppose the war until late in the going, and few of them showed up, at least at the demonstrations Mick had attended. He figured some of the older folks gathering on the sidewalk had marched against Johnson's war. They would know the drill.

In the sixties and seventies, Mick could always recognize the battalion of print journalists, and every TV station in the market sent a crew. Even some radio stations showed up. Now, Mick saw no one from *The Sun* whom he knew. He didn't know many of the reporters from the Cleveland paper, but he could see that no one wandered around with a notebook under his armpit, clicking a pen against his teeth. Mick looked in vain for other TV crews. This would not resonate much in the community.

"Check, check," Mick said, even though he knew already that the microphone worked. A part of him wanted the podium. He had given some speeches during college protests during Vietnam. He felt something welling up inside himself, the old words echoed in his head, his hands shook as the adrenaline surged through him. But he had to suppress it. The leadership of Christians Against the War would be speaking today. An Episcopalian priest, a college professor, the mother of a man killed in combat — they would be the speakers, too, along with a Democratic member of the U.S. House and the petite state senator who had smiled at Mick. Mick stepped away from the microphone and told the priest, who would be the master of ceremonies, that it was ready whenever he was.

While the priest called the gathering to order, Mick hobbled down the far side of the courthouse steps and leaned against one of the thick, round, steel gray pillars, perhaps the only place a man of his size could be inconspicuous. The priest offered a prayer, and Mick bowed his head and folded his hands together in front of him. The priest said, "In Jesus' blessed Name, Amen," and Mick looked up to see a number of people, but not everyone make the sign of the cross. He noticed old men wearing yarmulkes and a couple of women wearing saris. A truly catholic crowd.

The priest started the oratory with words about the immorality of an unjust pre-emptive war. His voice was a little tinny to Mick's ear, but quivered with passion. He introduced the remainder of the speakers. As he mentioned each speaker, he gestured to him or her behind him, and each rose in turn from a row of folding chairs just back of the podium. The priest said each of them would speak for five minutes, "even the politicians," the priest said with a practiced smile. The House member bent his head and smiled and shook his head, taking the joke on himself good-naturedly, also practiced, Mick thought. Mick wondered if a politician blasting the president of the opposition party could stop at just five minutes.

Then the priest introduced a couple of students, one male, one female, from the local college. The young woman played guitar and young man sang the old Chicago song "It Better End Soon." Mick was surprised how relevant those words, almost thirty-five years old, remained for this bloodletting in Iraq. Then they played one the woman said she had written about oil and war. Not bad, Mick thought.

The House member spoke next, a young guy Mick would never have voted for, blown-dried reddish blonde hair; long, thin face, a smirk instead of a smile. An opportunist at best, Mick thought, even if he was blasting the war and the president. He talked about the need to take back both houses of Congress in '04 and take the war out of the president's hands. Of course, Mick knew that the Dems had given the president the go-ahead, the contemporary version of a declaration of war, as much as the GOP in Congress had. Mick guessed this guy would count on voters' short memories.

The college professor, perhaps a couple of years older than Mick, made comparisons between the war in Iraq and the war in Vietnam. As the prof ticked them off, Mick thought most of them were valid, but that some were a stretch. At about the fourth comparison, a heavy-set man with glasses, maybe in his mid-thirties, wearing a white shirt and blue-and-red striped tie and dark blue suit in the late July heat, yelled, "Bullshit." The professor went on unfazed. A couple of points later, the guy yelled, "That one's bullshit, too." Mick figured he was a conservative businessman. This part of Ohio was pretty well split politically between right and left. Again, the professor continued. At another point, the guy yelled, "Don't you pinheads ever do any research? Nothing you've said is accurate."

Mick saw a police officer move closer to the man. Mick didn't know if the cop would try to shut him up or protect him if necessary. The cop spoke calmly to the man. The man answered in earnest, spreading his hand and shaking his head, gesturing to the speaker to make his point. The cop, a little guy in a white shirt and blue baseball-style cap, put his hand on the small of the man's back and continued to talk to him. The man and the cop continued their conversation through the brief remainder of the professor's speech. The professor had not given any indication he had even heard the man. The man in the suit moved away from the cop, shaking his head. Mick watched the cop watch him for a while, until the priest introduced the redhead. Mick walked over to the cop and leaned down to speak directly into his ear over the high-pitched voice of the senator.

"I don't know whether you're on our side or not," Mick said, "and I don't care. I just want to thank you for talking to that guy. Whatever you said made him move on, and I appreciate that."

"He don't mean no harm," the cop said. "Well," the cop said crossing his arms in front of him, "he don't wish you no good, but he just don't agree with you. He's just a Bush guy. I know what you guys are saying, and I respect that, but, like this guy said, them A-rabs bombed us, and Bush is just givin' it back to them, like he said we would. That's all."

Mick wanted to argue with him, but he realized that his conciliatory opening had made that impossible.

"Well, there's no evidence that Saddam had anything to do with the attacks on Nine-Eleven," Mick said, "but I just wanted to thank you for talking to the guy." Mick offered his hand, and the cop took it, then Mick moved back to his pillars.

Mick had missed much of the state senator's speech. He leaned against the pillars again as the mother of the dead soldier started her speech. She began by describing her son as a patriot. He loved this country, she said, and he wanted to protect it. He wanted to go to Afghanistan, she told the crowd, after the attacks on New York City and Washington, after the crash of Flight 93 in Pennsylvania. But when the president started talking about attacking Iraq, a country that had done nothing to us, she said, her son objected. He did not want that mission. He did not want to kill innocent people. But he was a soldier, she said, so he went. A soldier does his or her duty, she said.

She recounted the details of his death, a couple of weeks after the president's self-congratulatory "Mission Accomplished" spectacle aboard the *USS Abraham Lincoln*. His platoon leader had written to her, saying that her son's last words were about his parents. The platoon leader had written that none of them in the platoon believed in the war, believed in the president.

"Bullshit!! Total bullshit!!" Mick looked for the voice. It was on the other side of the crowd from him, on the fringe. Several men and women tried to shout him down. Mick saw the cop scurry over there.

"You're makin' it up, lady! You're dishonoring your son's memory with this fiction. What's wrong with you? You're perverting your son for your own selfish needs."

The woman stared at the man in the blue suit. The cop tried to pull him away. Mick tried to get over there, but he had to go behind the crowd and into the street to do it. The man broke free of the cop and ran back to the crowd.

"If that's all true, your son was no patriot and neither was his platoon leader."

The woman tried to resume her speech. Mick closed in on the man, whom the cop — now joined by another officer — had by the arm.

"Do you even have a son that was killed in Iraq, or are you making that up, too?"

Mick got within a couple of feet of the man in the suit. He stared into his eyes, dark brown, angry. Mick could make out drops of sweat rolling down a puffy face and settling onto thick lips. Mick noted the sagging ring of fat, also sweaty, folding over the collar of his dress shirt. The man stared back and started to yell something at Mick, but the police dragged him away. Mick followed them to the corner of the city block and watched the officers take the man to the far corner of the next block. They let go of his arm and talked to him. Mick saw the man answer, gesticulating, pointing back to the protest. The cop Mick had talked to shook his head and pointed in the far direction, apparently, Mick figured, directing the man to move on, to stay away from the protest. He wouldn't be arrested, Mick figured. That's probably best. Mick was a free speech absolutist. Of course, speaking freely could have consequences, and anyone who indulged in it should recognize that and be ready and willing to pay those consequences, the way the civil rights advocates in the South had. Mick lamented that one of the consequences he had been ready to deliver was a punch in the face. Mick walked back to the courthouse steps and thought about the limits of his own pacifism.

    He settled in at the back of the crowd, actually standing on the street, just off the curb, to listen to the woman finish her speech. He thought about the man's accusations and recalled all the zealots he had read about or, more importantly, had met as a reporter and an editor. In those days, his own bullshit meter was always on. Thinking back, he wondered how much of the woman's speech was true and how much was bullshit.

XXVI

Mick walked into the real estate office and asked for Ginny. The receptionist picked up the receiver for her phone and dialed a four-digit number.

"Mr. Mackintosh is here," she said.

In an instant, Ginny appeared out of a hallway. "Come on back," she said.

Mick followed her back to an office, wood-paneled on two sides, with one window looking out into the hallway and another window, framed by white curtains, looking out onto the parking lot where Mick had parked. Pictures of houses and pictures of Ginny with happy customers — including one of her clutching the arm of a politician from the next county over — looked out from the walls onto the office.

Ginny closed the door behind them, then went behind the desk and opened the top middle drawer. "Did you ever see pictures of my children?" she asked reaching into the drawer. "Did I show them to you when we had lunch?"

"No," Mick said.

She palmed a key with one of those orange tags attached to a string tied to the key, then picked a pair of picture frames connected by a hinge off her desk and handed it to Mick. "Mindy is my daughter and Arnie is my son."

"She's just as pretty as her mom, but Arnie looks nothing like his dad. You sure he doesn't belong to the mailman?" Mick chuckled.

"I wish," she said, handing him the key. "You didn't show me pictures of your kids when we had lunch."

"Oh, right," Mick said reaching into his hip pocket for his wallet. He opened the part with the photo sleeves and pointed to the pictures of Sean and Sam, in facing sleeves, as Ginny leaned across the desk to see, showing Mick more cleavage than he cared to see.

"This is Sean. He's the one in college. Sammy is the one headed to the service."

"They must look like their mother."

"Thank goodness," Mick said, snapping the wallet shut and sliding it back into his hip pocket.

"So, where should we go for coffee?" Ginny asked.

"Sorry. I have to cancel. Gotta run to class."

Ginny glanced at her watch. "What time does class start? It's not even four o'clock."

"I know, but, for some reason, the afternoon traffic going into town is just as bad as it is coming out. I even stopped taking the Parkway. It seems all of those idiots taking the bends on the Parkway at seventy-five miles per hour have to crawl through the Squirrel Hill Tunnel. I go through Braddock and out Braddock Avenue."

"Through all those little towns?"

"All those little towns."

"No wonder it takes forever."

"No longer than sitting in traffic on the Parkway," Mick said. "I'd better be going."

"Where is your class?" Ginny said.

"Pitt."

"I know that, silly. What building?"

"The Cathedral of Learning," he said, walking toward the door of her office.

"What time will you be done?"

"Oh, eight-thirty, or thereabouts."

"You'll be hungry after. How about if I meet you and we'll find someplace for a late dinner?"

"Oh, I don't know, Ginny. I'd still have to drive back, which puts me home at ten o'clock at best. If we eat, that's an hour at least, and I won't get home 'til eleven."

"You could stay the night."

Mick took the door knob in his hand and looked at her over his glasses.

"The kids are gone," Ginny said. "I have two extra bedrooms in the house, so — ."

"Ah. Okay. Look, I'm on the fifth floor of the Cathedral. When you come out of the elevator, you'll see a warren of offices — ."

"A warren?"

"There's a door with a bunch of offices on one end, and there's, uh, at the other end is this room with what looks like a check-in counter of a motel."

"A motel?" Ginny said.

"Or, I don't know, the office at the high school, okay?"

Ginny tried to restrain a smirk.

"There's a table in the — I don't know — lobby of that room. You can sit down there. Oh, it's room five-oh-one. That's the one you want. I'll meet you there at about eight-thirty. We'll think of someplace quick to go, then I can hit the road."

"So, you're not staying the night."

"Nah, I wouldn't be comfortable. Not right. What would your neighbors think when I left? What if your kids found out? I don't want anyone thinking — ."

"Mick, I'm not exactly the neighborhood whore, and in the twenty-first century, who cares who comes of out whose house at what time?"

"Well — ." Mick shook his head.

Ginny came around the desk and met Mick at the door and patted him on the shoulder.

"But it's very kind of you to care about that for my sake," she said.

***

Mick was eager to tell Angela about his new place, that they would be neighbors, but she came in just a bit after the professor. During the break, she got up to walk toward him, smiling that sweet smile Mick loved so much, and Mick stood up to meet her, but one of the other women in the class took her by the arm and dragged her off to talk about a presentation the two of them were to make the next week. Angela looked over her shoulder and smiled again at Mick, who waved.

As the class neared its end, Mick saw Ginny standing in the hall just outside of the doors. She waved to Mick, and Mick smiled at her. Mick thought she was hemming him in.

When the professor said good night and the class members started closing notebooks and gathering belongings, Ginny slipped into the room, caught Angela's eye, and walked toward her. She put her hand on Angela's forearm and squeezed as she passed her on her way to Mick, who sat at the opposite end of the big table from Angela. Angela smiled and said hello to the back of Ginny's head as Ginny passed the younger woman.

Mick stood up and Ginny walked right up to him.

"I've been building my appetite," she said. "Where should we go?"

Mick watched Angela pack up her stuff and thought he'd take a shot.

"Do you like hot dogs?" Mick said.

"The Dog House?" she said.

"It's quick, so I can get out of town."

"Do they have anything other than hot dogs?"

"Oh, yeah, you can get other stuff, too."

"Good. Are we ready to go?"

Mick stacked his textbook on top of his notebook and tucked them under his arm. "We're ready to go," he said.

Angela waggled fingers at him, then turned for the door. Ginny saw him look after her.

"She has a positively electric smile, doesn't she?" Ginny said.

"She lights up every room she walks into," he said.

"So, how was class?" she asked as they left the room.

Mick saw the question as an opportunity to launch into a story and eliminate what could be awkward silence as they walked to the restaurant. Usually, Mick took charge of asking the questions, like any good reporter, avoiding the yes-and-no questions in favor of those that evoked longer, more detailed responses. This evening, though, Ginny had beaten him to it, so he told all about the class and his role in it and Angela's and whatever funny thing had happened and blah, blah, blah, down the elevator and out onto Forbes Avenue. As they walked past the Schenley Hotel, he launched into a dissertation about how all the visiting National League teams had stayed there when the Pirates played in Forbes Field and how that hotel was now the student union, and how the old home plate from Forbes Field was inset in the floor of that building whose name Mick could never remember and how it was supposed to be in the exact place where home plate was at Forbes

Field before that building took its place, but it wasn't because that would have been in the ladies room or something.

And by then, Mick was happy to note, they had reached the Dog House. Mick ordered a couple of dogs with mustard and "lots of onion" and iced tea. Ginny said she would just have half a vegetarian hoagie and a diet Coke. They walked to a table on the other side of the restaurant, and Ginny asked if Mick wasn't having some of those famous fries.

"Too greasy this late at night," Mick said. Only partially true, Mick thought. Every order of fries was huge and would take longer to eat than Mick wanted to stick around.

Several long tables something like picnic tables, awaited them, but none was empty. Mick found one with just a lone young man wearing a Notre Dame hat askew reading at the end of the long table near the wall and asked the man if they could sit down. He barely looked up from his book and wordlessly waved them over.

"Is Angela enjoying her new place?" Ginny asked as they sat down.

Mick shrugged as he pushed his long legs, throbbing slightly from the two-block walk, under the table. "Haven't had much of a chance to talk to her. She's finishing up this summer, so she's putting the last touches on her thesis and meeting with her advisor and working on her projects for this class, and interviewing for jobs. I don't see her as often as I'd like."

"I see," Ginny said. "How does she like the idea of you moving in next door?"

"She doesn't know yet. I was going to tell her tonight, but the fates conspired against me."

"Well, you'll move in next week, right?" Mick nodded as he chewed. "It will be a nice surprise for her."

Mick nodded, then drew on the straw sticking up out of his iced tea.

They ate in silence for a while, then Mick asked her how her day had gone. It had gone just fine, Ginny said. Mick heard her go on about something having to do with, um, well, he knew it had something to do with either selling a house or buying a house. Or maybe both. Mick tried to follow it all, but, he admitted to himself, he had no interest in any of it, and as she chattered on, he realized he had no interest in anything that had to do with real estate. Not exactly true, he told himself, lifting the second dog to his lips. He did like to look at houses. But the whole listing price, selling price, housing market up or down or neither, or whatever else, he simply had no interest in.

"Am I right?" Mick was suddenly aware that Ginny had asked him a question.

"About ... ?"

"About your reaction when I told you you could sleep over at my place."

"Uh, what do you mean?"

"You weren't listening."

Good lord, Mick told himself, that was one of Constance's favorite accusations.

"Well, it wasn't that I wasn't listening, exactly. It's that I drifted off just a little bit because I was interested in these two people up at the French fry counter." Ginny turned to look. "Oh, they're gone now. I could have sworn one of them was a guy in drag."

"And a guy in drag trumps my inviting you to come home with me?"

Mick shrugged. "What can I say? It's the voyeur in all of us. So, what was your question?"

"I was saying that you act like a guy who hadn't dated at all since you and your wife broke up."

Mick shrugged.

"I tried," he said. "My heart wasn't in it."

"How come?"

"I think I loved my wife. It didn't matter that she didn't love me anymore. I think a person loves whom he loves. Or she loves. I think it's not really a conscious decision, like I'm going to wear a red shirt on Tuesday.

"So, I tried, but when I realized I was trying just to try," Mick shook his head, "I just quit."

"So, nothing intimate in all this time?"

"Nothing."

"No friends with benefits, no hot one-night stand?"

Mick shook his head. "I just never met anyone who, I don't know, made me think about permanency."

"Mick, it's the twenty-first century. Who cares about permanency?"

"Second time you've mentioned that I'm a little behind the times." Mick gazed at his right hand as it spun his iced tea cup around by its base. "I'm not a fuddy-duddy. I'm not a Luddite. I can embrace new technology. I'm all for increasing diversity in our society. I like a lot of changes — evolutions — our society has made. I can even accept that the Dodgers have been gone from Brooklyn for almost fifty years. But if ESPN Classic runs an old Kinescope of a Yankees-Brooklyn World Series, I'm going to allow myself to watch Jackie Robinson and Roy Campanella and Allie Reynolds and Phil Rizzuto."

"I don't know any of those names except Robinson," Ginny said.

Mick leaned forward.

"Kids embrace what's new," Mick said. "It's all they have." He shook his head and knitted his brow. "That's not right. It's all they own. We did the same thing. We didn't want Tony Bennett or even Frank Sinatra. We wanted the Temptations or Blood, Sweat & Tears or the Stones or the Beatles. They were ours, and our parents most decidedly did not want them. But now, as long as we've lived, we have a choice. We can choose what was ours, what is our kids'. Hell, we can even choose what was our parents'. Like the Brooklyn Dodgers or Lana Turner or Benny Goodman.

"Maybe it's different for you, because you have clearly prospered, despite losing Arnie, but for me, the older I've gotten, the worse life has treated me. It's natural for me to find sanctuary in old values, like monogamy."

"Except now," Ginny said, "you're interested in a girl young enough to be your daughter."

"Oh," Mick said, staring at the empty plate in front of him, "I don't know if I'm interested in her the way you think. Besides, even if I were, that's a perfectly natural and time-honored way for an aging man to act, isn't it?"

Suddenly, Mick's became conscious of his face brightening and he raised his eyes above Ginny's head to the fry counter. "Speaking of which."

Angela had just turned the corner and burst into a smile as she saw Mick. The friends Mick had met on his first trip to the Dog House with Angela trailed behind her, glaring.

"Mick. And Ginny. How nice to see you," Angela said. She turned to her friends. "You remember Mick, don't you?"

The blonde Methodist from Tennessee folded her arms across her chest and turned her head.

"And," Angela went on, "this is Ginny, the real estate person who helped me find my apartment. Hey, it's great to see you." Angela's eyes sparkled, and her perfect lips drew back into a perfect smile over her perfect teeth. "So," Angela said a little suggestively, "what's up with you two?" Then she winked surreptitiously at Mick.

"Just a quick bite after class," Mick said. "Just catching up. It's great to see you. We didn't have a chance to chat this evening at all."

"I know," Angela said. "Every time I headed your way, I was interrupted."

"We're going to find a table," the blonde said, laying her hand on Angela's forearm. "We'll save you a seat."

"They still love me, don't they?" Mick said.

Angela giggled. "You leave an indelible impression."

Mick turned to Ginny. "They're not big fans. It seems the night I met them — ."

"Oh, I'm sorry, Mick," Ginny said, gathering up her purse, "but it is getting late. I have an early staff meeting in the morning." She pushed her chair back. "Would you walk me to my car? I'm not very confident about this neighborhood."

"Yeah," Mick said, standing up, holding on to the table for balance. "Sure. Angela, it seems we don't have the chance to talk yet again tonight. But we'll talk soon. Okay?"

Angela briefly hugged Mick. "It was nice to see you again," she said to Ginny, offering her hand. "Maybe I'll see you after class another night when you can stay longer."

Ginny shook Angela's hand. "That would be very nice," she said.

Ginny turned and walked around the corner, toward the door, Mick a step behind her. When they reached the sidewalk, Ginny apologized for interrupting any chat Mick might have had with Angela.

"Oh, that's okay," Mick said. "I can e-mail her tomorrow. Or maybe I won't. I could tell her we'll be neighbors in an e-mail. Or maybe I'll keep that as a surprise."

"You know you have no shot with her," Ginny said.

Mick instinctively thought that was a little mean, but then he revised his thoughts.

"You think I feel something that I don't," he said.

"I'll bet," Ginny said as they neared the old Schenley Hotel. "Well, you don't look to me like a mentor advising a mentee. Maybe you would if she weren't so charming and so beautiful."

"Aaah," Mick said. "She's half my age."

"Less than half," Ginny said.

They walked a couple of steps in silence.

"So," Mick said, "where'd you park?"

XXVII

Mick picked up the phone on the first ring.

"Mick." It was Constance. "Have you come up with the money for Sean to go to Ireland?"

"'She asked, knowing the answer,'" Mick said into the phone.

"So, how is Sean supposed to finish his degree?"

"I can point him in the direction of a very nice bank that will make him a loan. He has two semesters before he finishes, right? A year's worth of student loan is not going to cripple him for life, unless, of course, he's not appointed the U.S. ambassador to Ireland a week after he graduates, but then Sean's stepfather is a good, God-fearing Republican, maybe even one of the president's Pioneers, so, come to think of it, a post in Dublin is not out of the question, is it?"

"You could dip into your own retirement fund, couldn't you?" she asked.

"I could, but I still have a mortgage to pay and my own tuition, and I'll be moving back to Pittsburgh soon. And the judge, in her infinite wisdom, decided I had to pay child support out of my retirement, which has taken a considerable chunk out of it. Oh, and I might want to retire someday myself."

"Don't you think it was awfully selfish of you to go to grad school while you had two sons ready to go to college?"

"I can always tell when you've been watching a 'Law & Order' marathon. You make me feel like that prosecutor has me on the stand. And, yeah, I guess it was pretty selfish, except that it was pretty clear that I had to get an advanced degree to get a job. Your president's economy has dried up and your president's war isn't creating any jobs, and your president's No Child Left Behind is depriving students of my considerable talents. So, unless I go to grad school, I'll never have another job. And here's another news flash for you, Sweetheart, I no longer have non-IRA mutual funds in my retirement account, which means that I'm paying a helluva penalty on what I withdraw, not to mention that everything I take out of there is taxed as income, and I don't have an income to pay the government what I owe it. Now, Sean has other options for paying for these next two semesters other than my retirement fund, so would you please ask him to access one of those options? And now I've just used 'access' as a verb, which shows you what you're pestering has done to me."

"Well, if you can't support the children you brought into this world, I guess Carl will write the check for the Ireland trip and everything else. Sean is not his son, and Sean won't let Carl treat him like a son, except in this instance, because his own father won't or can't live up to his own paternal responsibilities. Carl will fill in for you."

"Good. And that means you get to throw something else in my face. I didn't walk out on you, Sweetheart. You walked out on me.

We could still have been a family, and your income as a teacher would have kept us going, but now you've married a big-time — at least in his small mind and in his small town — politico whose Protestant ethic won't allow his wife to work, although it did not prohibit his adultery. You made all these choices, and I have to suffer from them, not only losing my family, but also suffering the indignities you are certain to throw in my face every chance you get. Nice. Are you loving, honoring and cherishing me now? Oh, I'm sorry. That vow has been abrogated by your adulterous relationship with a member of the Moral Majority. Thanks a lot, bitch."

Mick slammed down the phone.

He had never called her any sort of derogatory name before. He ran his hand over his face and through his hair and down the back of his head.

All things considered, he couldn't figure out why he'd waited so long.

XXVIII

From: Mick Mackintosh [mailto:mickeymack@fastconnect.com]
Sent: Saturday, July 26, 2003 12:09 PM
To: B.D. Butterfield
Subject: Bank error — not in my favor

I'm ready to take a life.

I just got my mail, and my bank statement had come, and I opened it up, although — I may have told you this before — I never reconcile my check book. I have no patience for that kind of shit. So, I'm off a penny or two here or there. I don't know why the hell I even opened it, but it's a good thing I did. I found that they've been taking $35 out of my checking account every month since February for being overdrawn. Every fucking month. Naturally, the bank was closed by the time I called. I can't fucking believe this. And because I didn't know they were taking this money out, I've probably been overdrawn every fucking month.

I CANNOT FUCKING BELIEVE THIS.

MM

XXIX

Mick pulled the truck onto Herbert Street and looked at his watch.

"A little after nine," he said. "We're getting a good, early start.

Sam, on the bench seat beside him, asked, "How far is this from where you grew up?"

"Coupla miles. That big empty lot we passed on the way up here?"

"At the bottom of the hill?"

"Yeah. That used to be Westinghouse Shopping Plaza. Man, it was the coolest thing. Used to walk there from Grandma's house."

Mick checked the number on the lease.

"Seven-twenty-one. Seven-twenty-one. Let's see this side is odd. Seven-fifteen, seven-seventeen, seven-nineteen. Seven-twenty-one-A. That's it." He turned to Sam. "It was so cool. It had an underground mall. First enclosed shopping center in the area. National Record Mart was downstairs." He searched Sam's face. He made a circle with his index finger. "Records were little round things with a hole in them. Music came off of them."

Sam laughed and clapped his hands. "I know what records are. They're what you and Mom used to put on after Sean and me went to bed, and then you'd make out."

"Apparently you didn't go to bed."

Sam laughed. "So are you upstairs or downstairs?"

"Downstairs. I told Ginny, the way my knees are, I can't do stairs the way I used to."

Mick climbed down from the cab and landed with a wince. He rubbed his knees. Sean and his girlfriend, Heather, got out of Mick's car, which he had parked behind the truck, blocking in the driveway between the house where Mick's apartment was and seven-nineteen — maybe Angela's apartment.

"So, are you upstairs or downstairs?" Sean asked.

"Upstairs," Mick said, hands on hips, gazing up at the building. "And the stairs turn halfway up. I figured you and Sam could carry the big desk up there, right?"

"Aw, geez, Dad," Sean said.

"Good lord, Son, you're a big lad." Mick said. "Don't men in Gaelic studies do manual labor? I'm sure that generations of Irish men have carried heavy objects up many flights of stairs. Aren't you of that stripe? Maybe your little brother can help you, even if he was too much of a wimp to be a wrestler." He smiled to be taking a shot at both sons in one remark.

Sean ignored him. "The big desk upstairs? You have like three desks. Can't you leave one in storage or something?"

"Asshole," Sam said, pushing him lightly. "He's downstairs. He's yankin' your wanger." He turned to Heather. "You don't mind, do you?"

"Fuck you," she said wearily, staring at the ground through her sunglasses and scratching her thigh just below the cuff of her short shorts.

"Yes, you're a charming bunch," Mick said. "I can't wait to take you to the Duquesne Club."

Heather turned back toward the car, and Mick supposed she was rolling her eyes, although he could not see through the shades. "I'll get the suitcase out of the trunk." She turned back. "Sean, keys?" She shifted her weight to one leg and held out her hand. Sean tossed her the car keys.

"Gorgeous girl, Sean, but what a freakin' attitude," Mick said. Mick always tried his best not to curse in front of the boys, even as old as they were, even though he knew their mouths were as profane as his. It just wasn't right.

"She just doesn't like being yanked around. Oh, and, like most of the rest of the world, she thinks Sam's as funny as a rabid Doberman."

"Well," Mick said, walking toward the door of the duplex lettered "721 A" and pulling out his own key chain. "I hope to hell she doesn't use that mouth in front of your mother and Carl. No, on second thought, I hope she does. At church. In front of Pastor Peter Paul Pervert."

He fitted the key into the lock and turned while he held the door knob, which he turned after the lock tripped. He pushed the door open; it opened right onto the living room, four plaster walls, white, interrupted by windows on three sides. The fourth side had a four foot-by-four foot opening cut into the plaster, giving a view of a small kitchen. The living room led to a small dining area. Mick stood looking at it, hands on hips. The boys squeezed in around him.

"I don't think the big desk is gonna fit in here, Dad."

"It'll fit. It'll all fit. There are two bedrooms off the dining room."

They walked back toward the bedrooms. Heather joined them, lugging the suitcase that Mick's parents had bought him when he went to college and a travel bag, both full of clothes.

"Where do you want this?" she asked.

Mick pointed to the room on the left, the bigger of the two. "In there."

Heather took it into the room, also four walls of white plaster, a small window on each of two walls. It was the larger of the two bedrooms, but not very large.

"Would you please put that into the closet, Heather?" Mick said as she began to set it down against the near wall. "We'll need to put furniture against that wall. Bookcases, I think, since there's no window. And we'll put a dresser under each window, and the bed coming out from this wall here." Mick gestured to the wall to the right of the door.

Mick heard a knock on the door and turned to look, but Sam was in his way.

"Dad, some chick's at the door."

Mick walked to the door and looked out the window to see a brunette woman standing there with her back toward him. He reached for the handle, and she turned to face him.

"Mick?"

"Surprise!" Mick said, stepping onto the stoop.

"Mick!" Angela broke into a wide smile, showing her white, perfect teeth, crinkling her eyes. She stepped forward to hug him. "I had no idea. You said you were moving here near where you grew up, but you didn't say you were moving to Herbert Street."

Mick broke the hug and looked at her. He stepped back toward the door, but the boys shoved the door open into his back and went past him to start unloading furniture. He gestured weakly toward the boys, and Heather, who followed.

"My boys, and my oldest boy's girlfriend." Mick fixed the screen door to stand open. "I'll introduce you.

"No, Angela, you said you lived on Hoover Street, not Herbert Street. Remember? I told you I didn't know where Hoover Street was. In fact, I didn't even know there was a Hoover Street. And, it turns out there isn't. Ginny asked if I wanted to live next door to you, and I said yes."

She giggled and crossed her arms.

"That's so funny. Cause my mom came to visit last week, and she got lost looking for Hoover Street, and when she got here and knocked on the door, she wasn't sure this was my place. Some guy at a gas station had mentioned maybe it was Herbert Street. Well, you know, they both start with 'H' and have two syllables."

"And," Mick said, "knowing how well you know your history, I wonder if maybe in the back of your mind you might half remember reading about or hearing about a president named Herbert Hoover."

She snapped her fingers. "Oh, yeah, that's right. Herbert Hoover. And there was another Hoover, wasn't there?"

"Sure the guy who invented the vacuum sweeper," Mick said.

"No." She smiled. "Really? Would I have heard about him in history class?"

"Well, I'm wondering what, if anything, you've ever heard about in history class, but no, you're thinking of J. Edgar Hoover, head of the FBI. I guess I'm lucky you didn't tell me you lived on Edgar Street. Of course, there is an Edgar Street, but I'd be surprised if you lived there, because that's not in the township, but in Twin Rivers, and that's where the, uh, houses of ill repute were when I was a kid."

"Dad, did you go to whorehouses?" Sam asked, walking past Mick, carrying one end of a bookcase, while Sean handled the other.

"You know, boys, when I bought that bookcase I carried it into the house all by myself, and here it takes two of you to carry it in. Just remember, no matter how long it takes, I'm not paying you by the hour." Mick had to shout to make them hear him as he saw them disappear into the bedroom.

"You're paying us?" Sean asked, coming out of the house on his way back to the truck.

"No, I'm paying your tuition."

"I thought Carl was paying it."

"Carl is paying for Ireland. I'm paying the tuition."

"Am I getting paid?" Sam asked.

Mick stared after him, but said nothing. Angela seemed to notice the change in Mick's demeanor and looked after Sam, then studied Mick's face. Sam climbed up into the truck after Sean.

"Uh, Sam's going to the Army," Mick said softly. "I'm not happy about it. He's going 'cause he thinks I can't afford tuition."

Angela crossed her arms in front of her chest and twisted back to look at the truck, then back at Mick. "How could you not afford his tuition if you can afford tuition for yourself at Pitt?"

"Long story," Mick said, head down. He lifted his head. "So, since you didn't know I was moving in, this isn't a welcome."

"Well, why didn't you tell me?" she asked.

"Never got a chance to talk to you last week, remember?"

"Oh, yes," she said. "Because you were on your date with Ginny."

"You're dating someone, Dad?" Sam asked breezing past.

"No. Definitely not. So, Angela, what's up?"

"Oh," she said, dropping her arms and shooting her left arm to her left at the driveway. "I was going to tell you that you blocked me into the driveway and I was going to ask you to move. Not the truck. The car. But that was just to make sure I wasn't setting a bad precedent by letting some stranger block me in. But, you know, it's you, so go ahead. I'm not going anywhere. How long do you think you'll be?"

"Oh, I don't know," Mick said, stepping aside to let Heather move past him with a desk chair. "Four of us. Shouldn't take long."

"Hey, I can help," Angela said.

And she turned toward the truck, subtly swiveling her hips. She wore a pink tank top and blue shorts. Not hot pants, but well above the knee. Mick watched her. Exquisite legs, he told himself.

As she climbed up the ramp into the back of the truck, she called out, "Hi, I'm Angela. I'm in a class with your dad."

Just exquisite.

A little before noon, once Sam had assembled the dining room table and Heather had set the chairs around it, Mick called for everyone to take a break for lunch.

"What's the best pizza place around?" Mick asked Angela. "That delivers."

"I found this place Gianinni's, out on the highway," she said. "They're pretty good. I don't know if they deliver this early."

"Used to be a Mr. Gianinni taught social studies when I was a student here. Do they deliver pop, too?

"I don't know. I don't ever have them do that."

"Let's find out," Mick said. "I'm guessing you have them on speed-dial on your cell phone, right?"

"No, of course not. You make me sound like all I do is eat pizza."

"You don't look like you eat a lot of pizza," Sam said, still sitting cross-legged on the floor.

"Forgive my son. He has the manners of — well, not a gentleman."

"No," she said. "It's all right. It's a nice compliment. I'll go call and see if they're open. What should I order?"

"Two large," Mick said, studying the group. "What do we want on them? I'm good no matter what."

The boys and Heather debated. Mick walked to the far end of the dining room and looked out the window, leaning on the window sill. Below him, over the hill, he could see the cracked asphalt surrounding the crater in the middle of what had been the parking lot of the former Plaza. Mick wondered when they had torn it down and what they were going to do with the land.

He heard Sam say, "Go ahead. He's not listening. He's reliving his childhood or something. Order one with pepperoni and sausage and one with mushrooms and peppers. He likes both of those."

Mick turned around to see Angela looking at him for a decision.

"Yeah, Sam's right. Hey, remember to have them deliver it here and not to your place. And get a couple of liters of pop. At least one liter diet. Both if you want. Will that be enough? Nah, get three liters, at least one not diet."

Angela left to phone in the order and Sam got off the floor. Sean and Heather sat snuggled together on the couch in the living room.

"Geez, Dad," Sam said, "there's not much space here. You're gonna be pretty cramped."

"Oh, just temporarily. As soon as I get a job, a full-time job, I'll be able to move out of here and buy myself a house. Maybe not as big as the one back home. I mean in Ohio. I mean, what do I need four bedrooms for, right? But three. That would be fine. One room for you guys to visit. One room for books. And I could put a cot in there if need be."

"And," Sean said, "do you envision anyone else, uh, staying over?" Sean nodded his head toward the house where Angela lived.

"Seriously?" Mick said. "She's your age."

A shadow fell across the room from the front door. Sean looked up to see the telephone man.

"Dad. Guy at the door," he said.

Mick let him in and reminded him that he needed two lines, one for his phone and one for his computer.

"You're better off going with a cell phone, Dad," Sean told him. "Saves you the cost of a land line."

"Maybe another day," Mick said. "I seem to remember you having some pretty hefty cell phone bills. I'll stick with what I know. After I get a job, maybe I'll have a boss who requires a cell phone. That will make it deductible as a business expense."

"You have every angle figured, don't you, Mr. Mackintosh?" Heather said.

Mick moved to the door and looked out. "Does this look like the home of someone who has every angle figured?" He turned and glanced into the room before turning his gaze back to the yard. "And Sam would be going to Penn State instead of Fort Dix, or wherever the hell he's going."

Angela returned to say that lunch would arrive in about twenty minutes. She brought a pitcher of lemonade and a plastic container full of ice cubes. She said they could have lemonade now and pop when the pizza arrived. Everyone had a glass of lemonade, then resumed bringing in the last of the furniture from the truck, as the phone guy left.

Angela was in the kitchen unpacking dishes and glasses and such, and Sean was hooking up Mick's radio-CD player-cassette player and Sam and Mick were emptying boxes when the pizza arrived. They all stopped what they were doing. The women looked in the kitchen boxes for plates and glasses, while Mick paid the deliveryman and brought the pizza to the dining room table. The boys washed up.

When everyone was settled into the dining room, Sean poured pop into all the glasses. As Sam lifted a glass to drink from, Mick interrupted.

"Wait. I want to make a toast."

"With Diet Pepsi?" Sam asked. "How fu- . How freakin' lame can you get?"

"Up, up, up. No, Heather, just your glass. Have a seat. To MickeyMack's return home, where everything will fall into place."

They clinked glasses of pop and drank, then Mick ran his hand over his face and back over his head as everyone else reached for pizza.

"It just occurred to me," Mick said. "Anyone ever read *Portnoy's Complaint*?"

"Never heard of it," Sean said.

"It came out when I was in college. Or maybe high school. I read it in college. Over a weekend. Everyone else had gone home, and I had nothing to do but read. Funniest book I ever read, but sad, too. It's about this guy, Jewish guy — telling his shrink about his life, starting out when he's a kid, in New York, who doesn't fit in, and he thinks it's because of the *goyim*, the gentiles. Nothing works for him, and eventually, he decides that he needs to be in Israel. Israel is the Promised Land, of course, and when he's in Israel, everything will work out. If I remember correctly, he meets this woman on the plane, a major in the Israeli Army, and they get cozy, and they decide to have, um, an assignation when they land."

"They're gonna knock one off," Sam said, turning to Heather. "I thought you might need help with the big words."

"And they get together," Mick said, glaring at his son, "and Portnoy is just elated to be in the Promised Land, and he goes on his date with this woman, and he can't — well, it doesn't work out."

"Can't get it up, huh?" Sam says.

"It's a tough life," Mick said.

"Okay," Angela said, "but you're not like that guy. You have a plan beyond living in a certain place. When you have a master's, that will open a number of doors for you, plus, everyone knows you here. That has to help. I'll bet you have a job in no time, maybe not exactly the job of your dreams, but that's okay. You're just between lives. Your next life will be way better. You know, it'll all work out."

While they ate and drank, Angela asked the boys about Mick as a father, and they chattered away. Even Heather told a couple of stories. Mick tried to spin some of what the boys said to his advantage.

"But the most god- ." Sam stopped himself then said, "Cool, Mom's not here. I can say 'goddamned.' The most goddamned annoying thing — ."

"I wish you wouldn't take the Lord's name in vain," Angela said.

Sam shook his head and put up his hands in a defensive posture. "Geez, where do these people come from?" Mick felt slightly proud. At least part of him had rubbed off on one of his sons.

"The most annoying thing about my father is that he obsesses about Pittsburgh. Best city in the world. Franco Harris. Roberto Clemente. Terry Bradshaw. Mario Lemieux. And he doesn't even like hockey. And steel mills. All the times he brought us back to see ball games, I never saw a freakin' steel mill in my life. The toughest thing for my dad moving back here is gonna be for him to live in the twenty-first century."

"Who are all of those people?" Angela asked. "Wait. I know who Franco Harris is. He's a football player."

"WAS a football player." Sam said. "WAS. And Clemente's dead. And Bradshaw is some bullshit football announcer. And Lemieux retired as a player and just owns the team. No, wait, he did come back, didn't he? Okay, so there's one thing that my dad talks about all the time that still exists. This shopping center, best shopping center in the whole world, but when we pulled up, it's this hole in the ground over the hill that *used* to be the shopping center. You gotta come into the twenty-first century, Dad."

"That was a shopping center?" Angela said, leaning her head on her hand, "No way. I've been wondering what that was."

Sam got up from the table. "I gotta see if there's something in the truck we forgot." He went outside, carrying a glass of pop, ice cubes clinking together.

"That used to be," Mick said as he turned around in his chair and looked out the window, "the coolest shopping center around. Westinghouse Shopping Plaza. Great stores. Gimbels, Sears, Penney's, Woolworth's, like, five shoe stores, National Record Mart, two grocery stores, a bank, Sun Drugs. Wow, it was great, and my buddy Tony and I used to come up here every Saturday and run around and meet girls and buy records and have cherry Cokes at Sun Drugs. Oh, and there was even a movie theater. My mother brought me there to see 'My Fair Lady,' and Tony and I saw 'Shenandoah' there one Labor Day. Jimmy Stewart movie. Anti-war. Great flick."

"My dad does a terrible Jimmy Stewart impression," Sean said.

Angela smiled.

"It was just a great place," Mick said, avoiding the possibility Angela would ask for the impression.

"What happened to it?" Angela asked.

Mick leaned back in his chair.

"The world changed. See, this isn't a main highway out here." Mick waved out the window toward the four-lane road a quarter mile away that the empty lot faced. "Not anymore. Not like the Lincoln Highway. When I was a little kid, this was just a two-lane road. It ran between East Pittsburgh and Twin Rivers. This area grew up after the war, World War II. A lot of people moved here from all the mill towns surrounding it: Twin Rivers, Braddock, East Pittsburgh, Wilmerding, Turtle Creek. Lots of people moved in. Enough that someone had the idea to build the Plaza. And it flourished. You know, people were starting families, buying new furniture and refrigerators and clothes for the kids. You name it. It had the right demographic, and it had all the traffic between Twin Rivers and East Pittsburgh. Of course, Twin Rivers had a couple or three — wait — four steel mills off the top of my head, and, of course, East Pittsburgh had Westinghouse Electric, and right down Turtle Creek, Wilmerding had Westinghouse Airbrake."

"I had no idea," Angela said.

"Oh," Sean said, "he just loves having an empty tablet to fill up."

"Yes, I do, Son. Anyway. When the Plaza took off, the towns died. And there were other malls that grew up in other suburbs. Each one was more modern than the one before, and the towns all died. No business. Oh, Twin Rivers tried lots of stuff. They blocked off Fifth Avenue and made it just a mall, and they painted some design on the cement, right over the streetcar tracks, which they hadn't pulled up yet. That didn't work. Then someone figured out that the malls didn't make you pay for parking, so Twin Rivers took out its parking meters. But it was too late. The Sears and Penney's and some of the other stores, the shoe stores, that moved to the Plaza had left the city to do so. And pretty soon, the towns' commercial districts dried up. All you'd find down there were bargain stores. Even the movie theaters shut down, and when I was a kid, Twin Rivers had three of them. Of course, when my dad was a kid, there were seven, I think he said.

"So, the Plaza did really well until the early eighties. The steel mills died out. Just like that."

"What happened?" Angela asked.

"Lots of stuff. Many different factors. Anyway, it was like one day there was a steel mill everywhere you looked, and the next day they were all shut down. Steel was so deeply ingrained in our beings that the steelworkers who had lost their jobs wouldn't take other jobs for half what they were making. First, they were insulted by the money. Second, they kept saying the mills would come back. Some of them said that right up until the wrecking ball took them out. Jones and Laughlin, National Works, even the Homestead Works went down. A few years later, Westinghouse Electric moved out of East Pittsburgh. Okay, now, not only has the demographic aged, so no one buys new furniture and whatnot, they've all retired, or some of the retired people moved out, and the people who moved in didn't make the kind of money people made in the mills, and pretty soon, there was no traffic moving past the Plaza. No disposable income, no traffic. And what's next was predictable. All the big-box discount stores moved in in other townships, and what was left of the Plaza, on life-support with discount book stores and a flea market every weekend, just gasped its last."

"So," Angela said, "the Plaza had killed the cities, and then the discount stores killed the Plaza."

"It is," Mick said, "what all of us secular humanists like to refer to as 'evolution.' Not only do organisms evolve, but businesses, industries, cities — they all evolve. Car makers switched to fiberglass or plastic for some parts of the cars, aluminum for others. Foreign countries subsidized steel production, and the U.S. companies, which didn't modernize their plants cause they didn't want to spend the money, couldn't compete, especially since they'd given away the store to the union, which meant their labor costs were through the roof. They laid people off, they restructured their companies, they de-emphasized steel, they — .

"Long story short — ."

"Yeah," Sean said, "that ship's sailed."

" — the world changed, Angela, and a whole class of workers disappeared from this city. And Pittsburgh has moved away from steel quite nicely, thank you very much, with health care and medical research and software and education. Of course, those jobs aren't nearly as numerous, and they don't pay as well, for most of the people who work in them, anyway, and not quite as many people live here as used to, which means this whole region needs fewer teachers and fewer newspaper reporters and editors and ad salesmen."

"No ad salespeople?" Angela asked.

"Who the hell do they sell ads to? Of course, supermarkets that used to do a lot of advertising every Wednesday now send their fliers through the mail, and people who used to buy classified ads now place ads on the Internet — and what the hell did I come back here for?"

Mick turned and looked out the window.

"But you have an education," Angela said. "My dad always said education gives people an advantage."

"Used to," Mick said. "Used to."

Mick couldn't see so much as a pigeon in the huge empty lot over the hill.

XXX

"All this Steinbeck," Angela said, kneeling on the floor of the back bedroom, taking Mick's books out of one of the boxes and placing them in piles, fiction behind her, sports books to her right, politics on her left, etc. "Is Steinbeck your favorite author?"

Sam, Sean and Heather had taken the truck back to Ohio, and Angela had offered to help Mick unpack.

"Oh, I don't know," Mick said, polishing the shelves of the bookcases that now lined one of the walls. "Maybe. I like Philip Roth, too. And, some guys who write primarily sports. Roger Kahn."

"And apparently this guy W.P. Kinsella. You have — " Angela scanned the pile she had created — "three of his. They all have baseball players on the cover."

"Oh," Mick turned and looked at what she had done. "Those are fiction. They go in the fiction pile. Don't you know who he is?"

"Well," she said, looking at the spines of the books, "he's the author of *Shoeless Joe, The Iowa Baseball Confederacy* and *The Dixie Cornbelt League*." Mick was not looking at her, but he could hear the smile in her words. "See, I know who he is."

"Then," he said, polishing the bottom shelf on one bookcase, "you know which major motion picture grew out of which of those books."

"Um, I never heard of any of these as a movie. But I know who Shoeless Joe is. My granddad always talked about him."

"*Shoeless Joe* was made into *Field of Dreams*."

"With Kevin Costner. I saw that. It made me cry."

"It makes everybody cry," Mick said.

"I wish I could have a catch with my dad," Angela said softly.

Mick heard the change in her voice and looked up at her. "Is he dead?"

"I don't know," Angela said. "He left. I was seven, and he left the day after Thanksgiving."

Mick stood up, straightening slowly because of his knees. "I'm sorry. And you've never heard from him?"

"No." Angela was turned away bent over books, but Mick imagined the look of pain and the tears welling in her eyes.

"Were you close, I mean when you were really little?" Mick went into the kitchen and took the pitcher of lemonade out of the refrigerator, calling into the bedroom, "Want something to drink?"

"No, thank you, not right now.

"You don't know. You have sons. Little girls think their dads are the greatest men in the world. I thought my dad was the most handsome man God had ever created. And he was, really, very handsome. And he was a good athlete. That's where I get my sports talent."

"Oh? You're an athlete?" Mick carried the lemonade pitcher into the bedroom.

"Well, I could have been. I was always the best in my gym class, but I couldn't stay for practices or anything. But anyway, when I was little, he played in a baseball league. Not softball, baseball. My mother said it was a semi-pro league. We went to see him at the high school field. He was a shortstop. And we had a hoop over the garage. I watched him shoot a basketball into that hoop many nights. He tried to teach me how, but I was too little to even hold the ball. My hands were so tiny. My mother said he was a basketball star."

"In high school?" Mick asked, thinking Angela's dad must have been near his age.

"Yeah."

"Really? What was his name?" Mick poured himself some lemonade.

"Paul Catanzaro."

Mick took a drink from the glass and stared off. "Name's familiar. Do you know what high school he went to?"

"North Union," Angela said. "He and my mother were high school sweethearts."

"Paul Catanzaro," Mick said. "Yeah. I know the name. We didn't play North Union, but, yeah. Guard. He was a guard. In fact, I think he and I played in an all-star game together. You know, here in Pittsburgh they do, or at least they used to do, this all-star game for high school seniors: the best Pennsylvania players against the best players in the country, you know, the other forty-nine states. And they had a preliminary game for the local district — District 7, we are here — against kids from a different district, and when I was a senior, I was on the District 7 team, and your dad was on the — what is that, District 9? No. Yeah, it's just over the District 7 line."

"Holy shit, I played basketball against your dad."

Angela showed a look of amazement. "You knew my dad?"

"I didn't know him, I mean we shook hands after the game, and I probably fouled him or something, but I didn't know him. Not like you mean.

"What happened to him?" Mick asked. "Did he play in college?"

"I think he started somewhere but quit college after his first year. He just went home and married my mother and started having kids. I was the last. An accident, they tell me."

"What did he do for a living?"

"Worked for PennDOT. Nothing important, but after he left, every time I drove past a road crew, I looked for him. I still do.

"But that's so cool that you knew him," she added

"Why did he leave?"

"I guess he had a girlfriend." Angela reached for another box of books and didn't look at Mick. "That's what my mother said. I didn't understand. He always said I was his girlfriend. Me and my sisters."

Mick could hear her voice choking. Angela stood up and looked around. "Do you have any tissues?"

Mick looked around. "Ah. Um, I guess they're packed somewhere." He reached into his hip pocket and pulled out his handkerchief. He held it out for her. She shook her head no and reached instead for one for the unused napkins from lunch. She blew her nose into it, then grabbed another napkin and wiped her eyes.

"I'm sorry," she said. "I really loved him."

"Oedipal," Mick said. "You were at that age."

"I guess," she said, "but I still love him. I've Googled his name. I never come up with anything. I mean, I can find lots of Paul Catanzaros. One sells real estate in Arizona, but he's younger than my dad. You know how their pictures are on their web sites. And one is a lawyer in Boston, and there's one who is a councilman somewhere in Nevada. But I haven't found anyone who seems to be him. He probably just works on some road crew in some other part of the state."

"Maybe you'll finally see him sometime, somewhere," Mick said.

Angela closed her eyes for an instant, then shook the thought out of her head. "I doubt it."

"Well, let me ask you," Mick said, "if you saw him running a backhoe on Interstate 80 outside, I don't know, State College, would you stop and jump out and talk to him?"

Angela thought for a minute, then she smiled, though her eyes were still tearing. "I might. I don't know." She got back down on the floor and settled back on her haunches. "I might. I'd still love to have a dad."

"You're not bitter?"

Angela made a backhand wave of her hand. "No, not at all. Jesus won't let me be bitter."

"But Jesus allows you to be sad?"

"Yeah, that's okay, but if I were bitter, it would mean I had not forgiven him in my heart, and I have. Because I love him. He's my dad, and I'll always love him."

"How would your life have been different if he had stayed with you?"

Angela wiped tears out of her eyes with her fingers, then wiped her fingers on her jeans. "Oh, I don't know. Well, I would have played sports in high school. My mother just didn't have the time to get me to and from practices, and she had no interest in sports anyway. I don't have much to do with my mother anymore. And maybe, if he had been a good dad, I would have felt more at ease with men."

"Oh?"

"Yeah, I had one brother, but he was a lot older than me, and we didn't have much contact. I had one female friend in college who grew up with three brothers, and, of course, there were all kinds of guys in and out of her house all the time, and she can just sit down among any group of guys and fit right in. I can't."

"How come? I mean, when you see a group of guys, what do you think, or why won't you go near them? I mean, apart from not feeling comfortable. Let me put it another way: What about them makes you feel uncomfortable? See, I used to be a reporter, so it only took me three attempts to ask the question properly."

Angela smiled, and Mick was glad to have made that happen.

"I don't know. I guess I don't know what to expect from them. Or what they expect from me. My mother just taught me that all men wanted was sex."

"Is that why you were so cold to me when we met? I mean, you know, when you were 'sleeping around?'"

She smiled again. "Was I cold? Gee, I'm sorry. I didn't know I was cold."

"You didn't tell me your last name. I had to listen for it when the prof called the roll."

"Oh," she giggled a little. "Well, I don't know. I probably didn't look at you and decide immediately that you were going to try to take away my virginity, but I guess I have this — what's the word — reflexive defense that I throw up around men.

"Plus, you're old enough to be my father."

Mick felt a little sting, but he tried to disguise it. "You mean," he said playfully, "that you weren't fooled about my age by my boyish good looks? My long, flowing blonde locks? My youthful gait?"

Angela's eyes crinkled into that smile Mick was growing to love. "The guys my age all have shaved heads or really short hair. Only you hippies have all that long hair. And I learned that in a man your age, your hair is not blonde, but ash."

Mick clutched his chest. "Oooh, that hurts. Really, really hurts."

"And," she hurried to add, "you can hardly walk. Your youthful gait is like a rusty gate."

"Ouch," Mick cried in mock pain. "You have cut me to the quick. I believe my quick is bleeding. I may need you to nurse me back to health."

Angela looked at him out of the corner of her eye and put up her hand in resistance. "I don't want anything to do with your quick, whatever that is."

Mick let a beat pass, then asked, "Is that what your friend with all the brothers would have said?"

"I don't know. Maybe not. She might have said something about a quick-ectomy."

"Hey, that's good," Mick said approvingly.

"Or, maybe she would have. Being comfortable doesn't always mean that she's flirting or something. Maybe I've grown more comfortable this summer. And this afternoon."

She bent over a stack of books and lined up the spines. "Are you ever going to put any of these books on the shelves," she asked, "or are you going to leave them in these piles on the floor? Aren't you done polishing those shelves?"

"Yeah, I think I'm done. Give me, uh, let's start with the sports books. We'll put them on the top shelf of this one."

Angela reached up a stack of books, and Mick reached down. Her eyes widened as they looked upward to find Mick's, so far up there. Mick took the books from her and kept his eyes on her for just an instant. It was not difficult for him to imagine how she looked as a little girl, as her eyes looked up at his.

Mick turned and set the stack on the top shelf and moved one book here and another there, alphabetizing them by author. His back was to her, but her image burned through and imprinted itself on the spines of the books Mick examined.

"I never told another man about my dad," she said.

Mick turned to look at her as she reached another stack of books up to him. "I've told my girlfriends," she said, "but never another man."

"Maybe you really have grown more comfortable with me."

Mick turned and set more books on the shelf and starting moving them around again, alphabetically. Angela stood up and reached down to pick up another stack. She carried them to Mick.

XXXI

"May I speak to Jeff Burleigh?"

"..."

"This is Mick Mackintosh."

"..."

"Oh, when is he due back?"

"..."

"Well, I talked to Jeff last month, and he said that he would have some stringing for me to do, that I could cover some of the townships and cities for your zoned editions."

"..."

"I'm living east of the city."

"..."

"Well, Jeff told me there would be opportunities to string, covering meetings and such."

" ... "

"Well, there must be some misunderstanding. You said he comes back next week?"

" ... "

"Would you ask him to call me please?"

" ... "

"Thank you."

XXXII

From: Mick Mackintosh [mailto:mickeymack@fastconnect.com]
Sent: Monday, August 11, 2003 10:03 AM
To: B.D. Butterfield
Subject: Lots o' stuff

Hey, B.D., congratulations on the piece about the kid's surgery. I'll bet it was a nice break to get away from the environment for a while. It really was a good piece. I feel for that kid. Of course, in large part, that's because of the outstanding picture you painted of him. This is award-worthy.

I have a lot to tell you. Sorry I haven't talked to you for a while. I've finished my summer session, and it took me a while to finish the paper for it. It wasn't great — well, it wasn't awful. My new friend Angela, the woman I told you about, gave me a lot of suggestions for it. She's an academic. I never will be. I just don't think that way, but I'm grateful that she does. She helped me a lot and helped bring it up to the level it needed to be at. (My mother would shoot me if she knew I had just used a preposition to end a sentence. With.)

Anyway, since Angela is right next door, this is pretty nice. We took the bus in to Pitt together and came out together and talked the whole time. It's neat that we just never have nothing to say to each other. And on nights we didn't have class, we often got together and just read and discussed what we were reading. It sharpened me for the classes and really helped me. And since she's not seeing anyone — what the fuck is wrong with the guys around here? — and since she is a HUGE movie fan, we've been watching lots of movies together. We just stay away from the histories. Not her thing.

And, geez, B.D., she loves sports. One night we went over to the elementary school and just shot hoops. She has a nice shot. And then some kids came along to play, and she played. I tried, but I mostly stood at the high post and passed off because of my knees, but she did just fine with the guys who were playing. She handles the ball pretty nicely. She had trouble winning rebounds, but she threw a few elbows. Oh, yeah, she accounted for herself pretty well. She says she plays racquetball and softball, too. I can't do anything but hobble on the racquetball court anymore, but I would have loved playing her when I was younger. She was so quick on the basketball court, I'll bet she's just all over the racquetball court.

She's young, B.D. Two years older than Sean. Geez. And I know I'm old, and I have NO CHANCE with her. And I probably don't want one. I mean, she's gorgeous. High cheekbones, lively, expressive eyes, luxurious hair. And legs. Exquisite. It's the only word that fits. But, you know, she's young. And we have different interests. She's not interested in talking about sports or watching ball games, and she has no interest in history or politics, except to vote straight Republican. Boy, have these kids been brainwashed. But she's really a nice person, and very nice to be with. Just to be with.

Geez.

I hooked up with the local chapter of Christians Against the War. I've done a couple of op-eds for them. Still not signing them myself. And I've been to a couple of rallies around Pittsburgh. And I hear the FBI is attending these things. There were lots of people taking pictures at the last one I attended. I thought they were all journalists. Now I'm hearing from people in the group that several were FBI agents. I'm not comfortable with this. I mean, I don't need to get on some list that will prohibit me from ever getting a job, that's true, but I'm less comfortable with the idea that the FBI is keeping track of people who disagree with the administration. I thought J. Edgar Hoover was dead. I guess the Ashcroft Justice Department has never heard of probable cause.

Oh, I meant to tell you: Remember the charge I had from the bank back in Ohio from an overdrawn account? You'll love this. They told me that I had deposited a check and then started writing checks out of my account before it cleared, and some of the people I had written checks to had cashed them before the deposit had cleared, which meant there was no money in the account to pay the bills. The bank, because it is kind and generous and providing a service to me, went ahead and paid the payees, then charged me for the overdraft.

So, I asked how long it takes for a check to clear, and they said three days for a local check and five days for an out-of-state check. And I asked why in the age of computers and instant movement of money from one account to another it would take that long to verify the money existed in the account the check had come from. This woman, a very arrogant woman who was personally offended to find out that reconciling my check book was NOT my favorite form of entertainment, gave me some jibber-jabber that, when all is said and done, blah, blah, blah, all of which means, I think, that if they cleared a check instantly, they wouldn't be able to charge $35 dollars for overdrafts.

So, I ask her where this check had come from, and she says she doesn't know. My account doesn't show that, and she says that she can have a copy of the check mailed to me so I can find out. Okay, so I have the copy mailed to me, and I opened it up and looked at it and just about blew a gasket. So, I got in the car and drove all the way back to Ohio and sat down at her desk and said, "How long does an out-of-state check take to clear?" And she said, "Five days." And I said, "How long to clear an in-state check?" and she said, "Three days." And I laid the copy of the check on her desk, and I said, "And how many days does it take for one of your own checks take to clear."

They had held a check from a CD from their own bank for five days. Can you fucking believe that? I had cashed it so Sean could write a tuition check. Can you fucking believe that? Their own fucking check. And this woman snaps it up and looks at it, and I say, "Is there something I should know about the solvency of this bank?"

And all she could do was say that it was all my fault because I didn't reconcile my statements and my checkbook, and all of that utter HORSESHIT. Anyway, they restored to my account all the money they had stolen, and I closed my accounts and moved everything back here. I found a bank with an officer I went to high school with, and she set me up with as sweet a deal as she possibly could to minimize the fees and the waiting period for checks to clear and all of that.

But here's the thing. The teller who held the check and this arrogant bitch who gave me such a hard time about everything: They both have jobs, and I still don't.

MM

XXXIII

"Jeff. Mick Mackintosh. Welcome back from your vacation. I called last week, and whoever I talked to said you would call me whenever you got back. I guess things really piled up while you were away."

" ... "

"Well, I wanted you to know that I'm all moved out here, and I'm ready to start stringing for you whenev — ."

" ... "

"But you said — ."

" ... "

"Well, what happened? You said — ."

" ... "

"But   I   don't   understand   why   —   ."

"…"

"Yeah. Thanks a lot."

XXXIV

Mick had just sat down with a bowl of soup to watch a movie when he heard Angela yelling his name as she crossed the driveway. He could hear her kicking up gravel, and he knew she was running. She passed in front of his living room window in a blur. Mick struggled to his feet and set the bowl down on the coffee table, then he hobbled to the door as quickly as he could.

"What's wrong?" he said, opening the door.

She leapt into his arms, and Mick quickly wrapped her up.

"Nothing's wrong," she said, breathing heavily. "Everything's right." She let go of Mick and plopped down in the easy chair next to the couch. "Mick, I got a job."

"You did?" Mick said. "What kind of job? Where?"

She sat forward and put her left hand on her chest. "Oh, I'm sorry, you're eating lunch. I'm interrupting." She stood up. "I'll come back."

Mick leaned forward on the couch and waved off the bowl. "It's soup. Sit down." He smiled broadly. "Tell me, tell me. What kind of job?"

"I'll be teaching."

"Really?" Mick felt his enthusiasm soften by a few degrees. "Where?"

"Right here. Eastern Valley High."

Mick sat silently for a moment.

"English?"

"Yes, silly. English. What else? I interviewed a couple of weeks ago with a guy named Mr. Webb."

"Eddie Webb," Mick said softly, looking at his hands.

"Yeah, well, he introduced himself as Ed, and all the secretaries and a janitor who came into the office called him Mr. Webb. Do you know him?"

Mick continued to look at his hands.

"Didn't I tell you I used to teach over there?" he said. "Eddie was a science teacher. Taught biology." He lifted his eyes and met hers. "Evolution. He's an evolutionist. You're going to work for an evolutionist."

Angela's eyes crinkled into laughter.

"Who cares? I have a job. I have orientation the twentieth and twenty-first, and then we have in-service the twenty-second. That's a Friday, right? And the kids start the twenty-fifth. Isn't that great? I can't wait."

Mick stared straight ahead.

"You ever taught before?" he asked.

"No. Well, I tutored. When I was an undergrad. So, yeah, I taught."

"You taught college students."

"Yeah. Freshmen mostly. Athletes."

"College students."

"Yeah."

"All of whom had some motivation to be there."

"Well," Angela crinkled her eyes into a smile, making them simply shine, "some had more motivation than others. But if they wanted to play football or basketball or whatever, they were motivated. So what?"

"You've never taught high school, where teenagers are warehoused because the state says they have to attend, and the kids have no other reason to be there. They hate everything you're trying to do. They hate your very existence. They won't sit still and daydream, so they use all of their energy to make a mockery of what you're trying to do. They do nothing but disrupt. They make teaching impossible. You've never done that, have you?"

Angela smiled again. "I did student teaching. It's not all that bad. There are some students who want to learn, and they'll like me. I'll be fine. Is that the kind of experience you had? Where everyone wanted to disrupt?"

It was not, Mick told himself. He was the one who had made the hard cases take an interest in something. Maybe not all of them, but he ignored none of them. None of them came into his classroom thinking they could sit and stare off into space and leave forty-five minutes later unaffected by what had gone on.

"It's very difficult for women," Mick said, "especially first-year women. And the district has changed since I was there. A lot of high-income people have moved out. The kids who go there now aren't — . They just don't care."

Angela leaned forward in her chair and folded her hands, interlocking her fingers.

"Mick," she said, "it sounds as though you're trying to talk me out of taking this job. Are you?"

Mick got up and picked up the soup bowl and walked it into the kitchen. He set it down and leaned on the kitchen counter and put his hand on his hip and shook his head.

"No," he said. "I mean, I don't think so. I'm just — . You know, you want to know what you're getting yourself into. It won't be a picnic." He wiped his hand over his face and back over his head, through his hair. "I mean, if I were you, I don't know if I'd be celebrating so much. It's, uh, it's a tremendous responsibility."

"I know it is," she said. "Don't you think I'm up to it?" Her eyes widened and Mick thought he saw them moisten.

"No, I mean, I don't mean I don't think you're up to it." Mick shifted his weight from one foot to another. "I mean, in some ways, a high school is not even a safe place to be. Look at Columbine. And there are lots of other schools where — . I remember hearing about a school where I used to live, where a kid took a knife to three different girls' throats and raped them. You're an attractive woman. You know, I mean, you'll be a target."

Mick saw Angela's eyes darken, definitely moistening now. She took a tissue from the box on Mick's coffee table. "You can't scare me out of this job," she said. "I can do this job, and I can take care of myself. I'm not some prissy little thing. If they hit, I can hit back."

"No, I know," Mick said. "Still — . Look, Angela, I'm not trying to talk you out of it." He felt awful, like he had betrayed her, lied to her. He watched her interlock her fingers, as though praying, tightening them, then loosening them and so on. "Look, congratulations. I know you've needed a job. We all need jobs, right?" Mick tried a smile, but feared it was unconvincing. "Hey, if I had any money, I'd take you out to celebrate. A nice dinner."

"I don't feel like dinner with you right now," she said.

Angela gave him one last look and wiped tears from her eyes. Then she got up and left.

"Good luck," Mick said as the screen door clicked shut.

Mick walked into the living room and looked out the window for her, but she had already disappeared into the house. Or somewhere.

He turned back to the room and dragged himself to the couch.

So, Eddie Webb had hired a woman who had no experience instead of hiring him. Eddie Webb had hired a woman who, maybe was a whiz at English, but who probably could never put anything she taught into any sort of historic context. A woman who was young and unproven. How fucking unfair could this all become? And a friend. Mick told himself that Eddie probably knew Angela lived right next door to him and had hired her just to rub it in his face.

No, that wasn't it, Mick knew. He was just a failure. He was Twin Rivers: stripped of purpose, but unable to die. Nothing substantive lived within him anymore, he told himself. It was just that his pulse continued, though he knew that was easy enough to stop. His father still had a purpose in his fifties. He still went to the mill every day. Had his father lived to see the mills close, he would have had his pension, and he probably would have plowed the ground behind the house and planted tomatoes and peppers and onions and carrots and kohlrabies and who knew what else. He would have kept himself busy. He would have had a purpose.

What purpose did he have, Mick asked himself.

Well, he had the responsibility to put his kids through school. And he had failed. One kid had bailed him out financially by going to the Army, and the other was going to school on his stepfather's largesse. He was never going to have a relationship with another woman. He would never have other children. He would never own property. The house he grew up in, his parents' home, sat on the market, and he was unable to buy it. He was stuck here in this stupid little apartment.

Mick got off the couch and hobbled to the kitchen. He looked at the soup, now cold, the crackers he'd broken up in there all soggy. He poured it into the sink and ran the water until soup and crackers had all disappeared down the drain. Then he set the bowl into the sink and ran water into it.

He knew he was just feeling sorry for himself. Deep inside himself, he knew he had a chance to turn things around. He could have another career if he earned a master's degree. The master's, he assumed, would pre-empt the poor undergraduate grades. Wouldn't they? He might even get to teach journalism at a college. Who knew? The degree might open doors he had never recognized before.

Maybe.

What if this was another lie? He had told himself when he had left *The Sun* that another paper would be only too happy to have a man of his experience. None had. He assumed, given his experience with the written word, that he would have his choice of schools in which to teach kids to write. Wrong again. What if he finished this degree, spending maybe twenty thousand dollars, investing who knew how many years of his life, denying his sons money they could have used for college — and still came up empty? What the hell could he do? Well, he wasn't quite old enough to be a greeter at Sprawl-Mart. Then again, he might be, depending upon how long it took him to get his degree.

He remembered the steelworkers he had talked to in the early '80s. They wouldn't take a job painting or washing walls or whatever because it didn't pay what they had been used to. Could he stoop to working at Sprawl-Mart for minimum wage? Mick remembered the story he'd heard about one guy who had gone into a bar in Twin Rivers, set a twenty on the bar and quietly drunk beer after beer. The men around him cursed the owners of the mills, cursed the president, predicted the always imminent war with the Soviets that would prove to everyone how much they needed the steel mills, how much they needed the steelworkers. This guy never said a word, just kept drinking until he stood up and walked toward the door. The bartender had called after him to, for God's sake, pick up your change so you can get smokes in the morning. The guy had turned around and looked at the change and said, "Where I'm goin,' I won't need no smokes." A few days later, his body washed up on the shore of the Monongahela, gashes opened by rocks, pieces bitten from his fingers.

Is that what happens to me, Mick thought, walking back to the couch. No one in his family, as far as he knew, had ever killed himself. His father had come through the months when the mills were down to one or two days of work a week, and he had not killed himself. Of course, his dad had a wife to support him and a son to look after. Mick had no wife, and he was already a failure in looking after Sean and Sam. He didn't even have a dog to take care of. And, now that Angela had gotten this job, he had lost his only friend, at least his only friend in the area.

The job. That's what it all came down to. Mick knew that in this society, a person was only as good as his job. You meet a new person, and what does he want to know? What do you do for a living? Even when he was a journalist, a thing he knew the great unwashed hated because they thought all journalists were the same as the sensationalists in the tabloids or some muckraker like Geraldo Rivera, even then, he could feel at least a grudging respect. "Oh, I never could write," the person would say. Or, "I'll bet you've met some interesting people." Anyone, especially a man without a job, felt nothing but scorn from the rest of society. He remembered that between the time he had left teaching and caught on to his first newspaper, he had tried to freelance, and one of his retired neighbors, noticing that Mick had never left the house, asked how come he wasn't working. Mick had told the man he was writing, and the man had said, "No, I mean a real job." Mick had defended writing as a job, but the old man had just sniffed and walked away, muttering something about welfare.

Should he get a job at a convenience store? Everywhere he went, those places were looking for someone to work the overnight shift. Of course, Mick told himself. Overnight is when these guys get robbed and killed. Maybe he should just go to work at McDonald's. That what everyone else did. The whole damned country was in a McDonald's economy. Nobody made steel anymore, and hardly anybody made cars, but everybody made hamburgers. How much worse could he demean himself than by flipping burgers or stuffing fries into a bag and handing them out a window?

"FUCK!" Mick screamed at the top of his lungs.

All he knew was that in the years since the *Sun* editors had recruited him to help them revive their newspaper, he had gone from someone prized to someone inconsequential.

XXXV

The knock on the screen door interrupted Mick's reading. A new semester had started, so Mick was back to the grind of reading his weekends away, lying on his bed, a fan cooling what would probably be one of the last truly hot days of the year.

"Mick," he heard Angela call.

Mick closed his eyes and laid the book on his chest. He hadn't seen or spoken to Angela since the day she got the job.

"Mick," she called more loudly.

"Yeah," he yelled back. "Coming." He stuck a bookmark in the book and pushed it aside. He pulled himself to a sitting position and reached for a T-shirt, which he pulled over his head as he walked to the living room. He rubbed his hand over his face and felt the beard. He hadn't shaved all week, and he could hardly tell where his week's growth left off and his goatee began. He smoothed his hair. It felt a little greasy to him. He hadn't been in a shower since going to the bank to cash the latest check he got out of his retirement fund.

Mick padded his way to the door, knees not entirely cooperative, bare feet digging into the carpet. He unlocked the screen door and opened it for her.

"Hey, Stranger," she said, stepping in, carrying a bowl with plastic wrap stretched across it. A smile crinkled her eyes. Mick looked into them and saw them glisten. He hoped that was from joy and not from a pending tear. With Angela, it was hard to tell.

"I haven't seen you all week," she said.

"Busy."

"Uh-huh," she said. "What are you busy with?"

"Reading," Mick said. He pointed to a bowl in her left hand. "What do you have there?"

"Well," she said, marching into the kitchen, "I bought that salad stuff in a bag? And it always goes bad before I can finish it up." She set the bowl down and opened Mick's cupboard and found two salad bowls. "I think this will survive in my fridge for another day, two at the most, so I threw it all into a salad bowl, and cut up a tomato." She turned to Mick and stood still for a moment, holding the bowls. "You like tomatoes, don't you? Yeah, I've seen you order them on a hamburger." She set the bowls down. "And some onion, which I know you like. You have salad dressing? I forgot to bring some, but I have a couple of different bottles at my house. Good. Oh, and cucumber."

She went into Mick's silverware drawer and rooted around for a serving fork and a serving spoon and tossed the salad. "Mick, would you get a couple of forks? Oh, and I'd like a knife to cut up my lettuce a little more."

Mick got the forks and knives and set napkins on the dining table next to the fat free Italian dressing he had pulled from the refrigerator, salt and pepper, bread and margarine.

"What are you reading?" she asked, setting the bowl on the table.

"Book for class."

"Oh, class. How's that going? Is it as much fun as the summer class?" She put some salad into his bowl.

"You're not in it."

"So, it's not as much fun, right?" she smiled; again the eyes glistened; again Mick wondered to what outcome.

"It's not as much fun." Mick doused his salad with dressing. "All you have to do this semester is your thesis, right?"

"Right. It's going to be hard, with all the time I'll need preparing for class, you know, to teach."

Mick didn't say anything for a minute as he stabbed at tiny tomato wedges and cucumber slices, then he forced out, "How's that going?" but he did not look up at her.

Mick was vaguely aware that she was nodding her head. "It's okay. Kids have been fine, so far. No one has put a knife to my throat." Mick looked up to see her with a slight smile. "And I went to the football game last night with one of the other teachers." Mick wondered if she had gone with a man or a woman, but he didn't ask. "I asked Mr. Webb if he remembered you. He does. He said you were a really good teacher. And he said to wish you good luck finding a job. Are you looking for a job?"

"I'm out of work," Mick said. "What do you want to drink? I have iced tea and I have lemonade mix I can make."

"Iced tea. So, are you looking for a teaching job? He seemed to think you were looking for a teaching job. He said he knew there was an English opening at Twin Rivers High. Are you looking for a job in Twin Rivers?"

"No." Mick put ice cubes into two glasses.

"How did he know you were looking for a job?"

"I talked to him about it a while back." Mick poured the tea.

"Did you apply to Eastern?"

Mick set a glass near Angela. "There's artificial sweetener of some kind on the counter," he said.

"Did you apply to Eastern?" She kept looking at him, holding her fork above her bowl.

"Yes, I did."

"For my job."

"It wasn't your job when I applied."

"For the job I got."

"Yes."

"Why didn't they hire you?"

"Personal failings. This is good. I really appreciate your feeding me."

"What kind of personal failings?"

"I'm not a very nice person."

"No, that's not it," she said. "In fact, you know Celia Breidinger?"

Mick nodded. "She still there?"

"She's head of the department. She said she knew you. She said you were really nice, and that the kids loved you. So, why didn't you get the job?"

"It doesn't matter. You have it. Enjoy it. Maybe you'll have a nice, long career teaching gerundal phrases to kids whose only aspiration is to write good flows for 50 Cent, in which case, as we all know, all he has to be able to do is conjugate the word 'fuck.'"

Angela set her fork in the bowl and crossed her arms across her chest. "This is why you didn't want to congratulate me when I told you about the job."

"Angela, forgive me for saying this, but I know ten times what you know. I just never took the Praxis test so I could prove it."

"I scored in, like, the 87th percentile."

"Nice, very nice. If I had taken it, I probably would have scored in the 98th percentile. I know this stuff."

"Then why didn't they hire you? Did you do something to a kid once or something?"

Mick stared at her, then he chuckled. "Is that what you think? You think I molested a kid? Are you serious? Jesus — . It's my undergraduate grades. That's all. I didn't go to class back in the '70s. I got a lot of Cs. You thought I molested a kid? Good lord." Mick pushed his food away. He saw her eyes moisten.

"How come you didn't tell me you applied for that job?"

He shook his head. "No point."

"No, no point. Instead you walk away from me. Like my dad did. You stop talking to me. You resent me for something I had no control over. You couldn't be happy for me for something good that happened to me. You're just pre-occupied with your own bitterness. Everything is all about you. You know this and you know that, and you did this and you should own the world, but you don't, and that's everyone's fault but yours. It's my fault I got a job, the job you wanted."

She stood up.

"My first impression of you was right. You're a real jerk."

She turned and walked out.

Mick just watched her.

"Of course. Leave," he said to the empty room. "Makes my life easier anyway. I don't have to have anything to do with you. I don't have to listen to you talk about your fucking boyfriend. If you have a fucking boyfriend. Or whenever you get a fucking boyfriend.

"Fuck."

XXXVI

Mick slept fitfully that night, replaying in his busy head the conversation he had had with Angela, thinking about her at the football game with a faceless man, thinking about himself in front of a classroom, thinking about himself running a newsroom, thinking about his parents' house that he couldn't buy and his ugly encounter with the woman who owned it, thinking about Christopher Post and the Twin Rivers *Independent*, thinking about all the unfulfilled expectations since he left *The Sun*. He finally drifted off sometime after four a.m. At least the last time he remembered seeing on the digital clock was 3:51. His clock radio went off at seven a.m., with the start of a radio program about media practices. He still considered himself part of the media, so a part of him thought he was working to some degree. Some small degree. He lay in bed and stretched as the hosts talked about a series of reports on the war, then an ad campaign by some software company he had never heard of. At the first local station break, reminding him that he was not a member supporting the jazz, news and NPR, he dragged himself out of bed, slowly testing the strength of his knees, and he unbent his long frame from the side of the bed.

    He walked to the dresser under the window that looked out onto Angela's duplex. No movement. As he unscrewed the caps on the anti-inflammatory medicine for the arthritis and the collection of pills for his diabetes, he checked to see if there was a strange car in the driveway, even though he knew that Angela was a virgin and a virtuous woman. Still, he didn't trust them. Constance had taught him not to trust them, and no woman he'd known since had disabused him of that lesson.

    He hobbled into the bathroom for a glass of water, pills deep in the palm of his right fist. He threw the pills down and gazed at himself in the mirror. His beard was heavy, gray pushing through the blonde. Red lines meandered through the whites of his eyes. Below, the skin, dark from sleeplessness, sagged to his cheeks. He ran his hand through his hair and found it greasy and stringy. He had to clean up.

    He rubbed shaving cream into his face, thinking about his project for the day. He had to set up microphones, speakers, a lectern and chairs for a rally at a United Presbyterian church in Pittsburgh. Christians Against the War had organized a march emanating from every church in the downtown to the biggest United Presbyterian church in the city. Mick envisioned people streaming out of various doors in the downtown, down the broad steps leading to street level and organizing on the sidewalk. Some churches beyond the downtown would come out of the doors and descend their steps to get onto buses that would bring them to various points in the city to start their marches. The idea was to have streams of people all over the city, showing themselves to Steeler Nation on the way to Heinz Field for a morning of tailgating before the first game of the season; showing themselves to merchants getting ready for a Sunday of business; showing themselves to street people and cops and bus drivers and taxi drivers and hotel guests and joggers and anyone else anywhere in the downtown — perhaps picking up people on the way to its destination. The church groups would walk the streets singing "Abide with Me," "How Great Thou Art," "I Heard the Voice of Jesus Say," and other hymns whose lyrics sped through Mick's head as he shaved. Lots of hymns all the way to the rally. Lots of hymns, but not "Onward Christian Soldiers." Mick smiled to himself as he splashed water on his face to wash off the leftover shaving cream. Wrong message, Mick thought to himself. No crusaders or messages of crusading in a peace march. Let the president stick his foot into his mouth about a crusade. Opponents to the war — pacifists all — would not want to conjure the image of an armed battalion of Christians storming Muslim battlements.

Shortly before arriving at the church, each group would launch into "Just As I Am," which Mick personally hated because of the slow tempo and the six verses. The organizers hoped that the groups would converge on the church in something like unity. Mick was skeptical. They all would gather in the churchyard behind the church, where crews, even as Mick set down his toothbrush and stepped into the shower, were assembling risers, one for speakers and one for a Peace and Unity Choir that had been rehearsing special music, some of it written by various choir directors with composing talent.

As Mick let hot water stream over him and rubbed soap onto his body, he hoped there would be lots of reporters there, print and broadcast. It would be a pretty cool spectacle, Mick thought, marchers coming from all over, a huge choir thundering through the morning air. He hoped that Pennsylvania's right-wing U.S. senator would get the message, that Christ's message was peace and not punishment.

He toweled off and dressed, flush with the old fire from the anti-war days of his youth. He could feel the adrenaline surge through him as he stepped into the driver's seat of the car and pulled out of the driveway. He felt it a little ironic that he felt himself going to war in the cause of peace. Maybe that's how the president felt, he conceded to himself. The difference in Mick's view was that George Bush had exercised — indeed, abused — his power to send Americans to die, and all Mick had in his arsenal was a little know-how about sound systems and a deep conviction that this was the wrong war at the wrong time.

As Mick pulled away from the house, he saw Angela step onto her front stoop and turn to lock her door. She wore a white top, cut lower than Mick thought a Christian woman should wear — he even glimpsed a bit of cleavage, reluctantly, he felt rather than thought — a sky-blue skirt, maybe denim, of which Mick did not approve for church, just above her knees and black shoes with a little heel. Church, he figured. He wondered where Angela went to church and whether she might end up at the rally today. Mick watched her, but, even though he knew she had to have heard the car or seen the motion even peripherally, she did not look up or look in his direction at all as she walked to her own car.

Fine. If that's how she wanted it. Mick sped past her, kicking up stones as he spun out of the driveway, without acknowledging her, and as he did, he felt stupid, like an aggrieved 16-year-old showing off for the girl who had spurned him.

When he arrived at the church, he parked on the street across from the building, thrilled to park on a downtown street without feeding the meter. The doors were open to accommodate the growing heat and humidity of the second Sunday morning in September, and Mick heard the choir practicing for the service and perhaps for the rally. Mick crossed the street and walked along the narrow concrete walk to the back of the church, where the rally would take place in the sprawling churchyard, probably the only one in the downtown that could accommodate all the people the organizers expected. He greeted a couple of other men from Christians Against the War who were checking the junctures of the risers. They pointed Mick to the truck with the sound equipment to be set up and connected. Mick went to work, listening to tunes he had learned in church as a child.

As he worked, he sang the lyrics that he knew and hummed along when the choir went to the third or fourth verses of some of the songs. He remembered singing in the choir as a young man, until he decided, with the influence of some of the college players with whom he sometimes played pickup basketball, that the whole church thing was a scam. He hadn't changed his mind about that. He felt himself to be a spiritual person, a believer in Christ, without attending a church. He occasionally picked up his Bible and read from it. He would occasionally linger — for a couple of minutes, anyway — when his remote control surfed its way to one of the televangelists. Now, hearing the music, seeing congregants walk through the churchyard on the way to the building, he missed it a little. Or maybe, he told himself, he missed the magic of belonging to a new congregation struggling to establish itself, meeting in a fire hall, on its own crusade to raise money for a building. Maybe he missed the vibrant youth organization he belonged to or maybe it was just the pretty auburn-haired girl, a few years older than Mick and quite sophisticated, who sat in front of him in the choir.

As the start of services drew near and Mick tested the microphone, he saw a familiar face, a little puffy, a little jowly. He couldn't quite place the face, as the heavy-set man strolled through the yard, just looking over the set up. He wore a blue suit and white shirt and striped tie, white on burgundy. Mick watched him for maybe a minute. He was younger than Mick. Mick couldn't place him, but knowing he knew him, he tossed out a "How ya doin'?" The man turned and looked at Mick, and without acknowledging Mick, the man turned away and hurried back along the concrete walk toward the front of the church. Mick shook his head, still trying to figure out where he knew the guy from.

Mick finished the electrical work and helped set up chairs on the risers, then wandered back out to the front of the church. Maybe, he thought, the guy would still be outside, roaming around, maybe having a smoke before entering the building, maybe just communing with other congregants. If he looked at the guy long enough, he might remember. But the man wasn't there. Probably he was inside the church, Mick figured.

So Mick walked around the downtown. He enjoyed looking at the architecture that soared above the city and the grit that clung to the streets and to the occasional person, men mostly, who lay against the wall of a building or in a doorway. He liked the sounds of the buses accelerating and decelerating along the city streets. He sat down on a bench he found after his knee had started to throb. He rubbed his knee and reveled in the relative calm and quiet of what was usually a loud, busy city.

After a while, he finally heard voices raised in Christian music. He swiveled his head to see if he could home in on the sound. He determined it was coming from behind him and to the right. The volume grew stronger, and presently he saw a photographer run around the corner and crouch just into the street to set himself up for the shot of the vanguard of the group turning the corner. A man, possibly the pastor, Mick thought, led the people turning the corner, with another man walking backwards waving his arms, presumably the choir director. The force of the voices turning the corner suggested to Mick that the choir made up the first of the parade, although they didn't wear robes — typical of some churches between Memorial Day and Labor Day. Within seconds, "What a Friend We Have in Jesus" overwhelmed Mick, and the congregation threatened to sweep him off his bench. He got up and jogged as much he could off the sidewalk and onto the street to watch the singers pass. He heard the waves pass: the choir, full of powerful voices — particularly the male voices — then pockets of good singers as the congregants passed by, mixed with children's voices and weaker, less melodious voices. After they passed, Mick followed them, able to keep up with them because some of the older people hung to the rear and moved slowly themselves.

The nearer they moved to church, the more different groups Mick could hear. He could tell that some of them had broken into "Just As I Am." Perhaps they had started prematurely; perhaps the group he followed was late. As Mick turned onto the block where the church stood, he heard a cacophony of voices, the dissonance abusing his ears. While Mick had been gone, the police had set up wooden horses as blockades for the street to allow the people to gather without contending with traffic. Various groups had to wait as others streamed back along the concrete walk. Mick could hear all of the congregations, black, white and mixed race, trying to get to the same lyrics at the same time. A tall woman wearing a blue robe with a gold stole climbed the front steps of the church and sang out over the crowd, forcefully attempting to get everyone together. Group by group, most people in dress clothes, some of the men in shirtsleeves, some men and women wearing jeans, some choirs adorned in robe and stole combinations — they all turned to watch her direction and try to pick up where she was, and pretty soon all of the groups sang in unison as they waited for their turns to walk back to the church yard.

As they ran out of verses, the woman on the steps started "Holy, Holy, Holy." Then another group would round the corner, singing "Just As I Am" and figure out soon enough what was going on. Mick knew he should be in the churchyard, making sure everything was ready for the speakers, but he could not tear himself away from the convergence of people, all of whom, he assumed, opposed the war, and he wondered where the president thought he had the mandate for this war. If every major city was like this one — of course, Mick realized the cities in the so-called red states might not oppose the war, might never be able to deliver such a coming together. And he figured that some of the local evangelical churches might not participate in an anti-war rally. Still, the sight Mick beheld as hundreds of worshipers sang together shot a current of joy through his system.

When the last of the groups cleared the street, a couple of police officers trailed the people back to the churchyard, and Mick followed them back. The Peace and Unity Choir was all gathered on three tiers of risers to the left of the speakers' riser, along one of the long sides of the churchyard. They sang "Nearer My God to Thee." Mick stood and admired the sight and the sound and figured that even the people living in the Gateway Towers and the lofts, those who weren't already here, could hear the power of these purposeful people praising God and pleading for peace, and Mick believed deeply that none of the Christians like Constance and Carl would go near a place like this. And Mick remembered what one of his Sunday school teachers had taught him: "If you have to tell everyone you're a Christian, that might be because you're not living like a Christian." These people, at least today, were living like Christians.

Mick looked quickly around the churchyard and saw TV cameramen and –women from each of the three predominant local stations. He saw two still photographers, one from each of the Pittsburgh dailies, Mick assumed. He knew they would feed the Associated Press. He couldn't pick out any TV reporters, no one standing around with microphones, although he saw mikes with the local station logos had been added to what he had put together earlier. He assumed reporters from the two dailies were here, but he didn't see anyone with a notebook.

The choir director, the woman who had mounted the front steps to bring the voices together, checked the speaker's dais every few bars until Mick saw one of the pastors stand up. The director brought her charges to the end of their song and motioned for them to sit down.

The master of ceremonies was the pastor of host church, and he walked to the lectern to welcome the crowd and express how gratified he was that so many people had turned out. Arrayed behind him were the usual politicians, pastors and parents of servicemen and –women killed in the war.

Mick listened for a short while, then zoned them out. He'd heard it all before. He started wishing he had a little radio with earphones so he could listen to the Pirates or the Steelers. Then he scanned the crowd — some seated, some standing — to see if he recognized anyone, particularly Angela. But partway through his scan, he thought he saw the guy in the blue suit standing near the corner of the building on the concrete walkway. From where Mick stood, he could see the man at best from the side and at worst only the back of his head, so Mick wasn't sure this was the guy he had seen earlier. He moved around until he could see the guy's face and study it. He tried to identify what he felt when he saw the guy, where he might be able to place the guy. This was familiar. Putting the guy in this type of situation was like getting the little ball into the little hole in those plastic hand-held games from his childhood.

Then the man shook his head, and Mick knew. The man called out, "Lies. All you're doing is telling lies."

He was the guy from the rally in Ohio. Why was he here? Did he live here or in Ohio? Was he acting on his own, or was he part of some group that assigned him to rotate from one rally to another to disrupt the speeches. But Mick had only seen him at these two, and no one else had disrupted any other rallies Mick had attended.

The speaker ignored the man. A police officer sidled up to the man and talked to him. The man gestured to the speaker and seemed to tick off point after point on his fingers. The cop spoke some more, and the man shook his head. The cop touched the man's arm, and the man nodded his head yes, and the cop moved away. The man left the yard.

Another speaker took the lectern and raised question after question about the president's motivation for starting the war. Then from the alley that ran behind the churchyard, Mick heard the man's voice again.

"He didn't start the war! He responded to violence with violence! He's protecting America!"

Another cop strode to where the man stood and talked to him. Mick could see the man pointing to the street, then pointing to the church yard. He shook his head no. The cop put her hand on the man's arm, gently, and seemed to speak forcefully. The man continued to shake his head. He crossed his arms across his chest and made his body rigid. The cop spoke into her radio on her shoulder, and the man moved away again.

Mick felt his ire rising. He walked out to the front street and stood on the sidewalk, hands on hips, scowling and looked up and down the street. Mick knew that the man would be back. He didn't see him. A cop came out and told him to come back to the rally. Mick opened his mouth to speak, but he realized that saying anything that the cop could interpret as Mick being a bouncer of any sort would get him into trouble. He closed his mouth and moved back down the walkway to the churchyard and to the rally.

Mick crossed his arms and peered into the crowd. He would find the guy.

Another pastor took the lectern and recalled the immorality of the Vietnam War and talked about the quagmire that had resulted. She pointed out the number of Americans who had been killed since the "Mission Accomplished" sign had appeared on the *Lincoln*. She said that nothing had been accomplished and that this war would wear on and on the way Vietnam had.

Then Mick saw him. He had taken off his jacket, maybe put it in his car, parked nearby, Mick thought. The man was walking in a small, tight circle near the fence beyond the choir, occasionally shaking his head, moving his mouth. Mick started moving toward him, arms still folded. He knew that a man his height would attract attention, so he moved slowly, intermittently. Mick could see no cops between himself and the man. He noted that the man was close enough to the back of the property to run out if he had to. Mick aimed to cut off his escape route. It took him a couple of minutes to get into position. He was behind the man, but close enough to hear him mumbling. Mick picked up the words "lies" and "liberal propaganda."

Another speaker opened up, talking about presidents who had worked for peace instead of war: Theodore Roosevelt, Jimmy Carter, Ronald Reagan, Bill Clinton. He mentioned the limited warfare of George H.W. Bush, the reluctant warfare of Woodrow Wilson, and he compared all of them to George W. Bush and his pre-emptive war.

The man erupted and shouted, "You're not for peace, you're for capitulation." Mick closed in on him and put his arm around the man's shoulders, trying to calm him. "You all hate America," he yelled. Mick tried to pull him away, but the man twisted out of Mick's grasp and stiffed-armed Mick. Mick could see both police officers running his way.

"You love Al Qaeda," the man yelled. "You're just encouraging another 9-11."

Now members of the crowd noticed the fracas and ran toward Mick and the man. Mick lunged for the man and grabbed his shirt, which tore at the seam across the top of his shoulder. The man turned and shoved Mick, and just as the police arrived. Mick yelled, "Hey, jerk," and shoved the man, knocking him down. Mick moved in on him, enraged, and the male officer pushed him away. Mick felt people tugging at his arms, trying to get him away from the man. Mick pushed the cop's arm away. He heard someone yell about getting the maniac out of there. A woman yelled that they were about stopping the fighting, not fighting among themselves. The male cop pushed him away again, shouting something Mick couldn't make out over all the tumult. He felt a tug on his elbow and heard a female voice say, "Mick, leave him alone. Mick, let's go. Stop it." And suddenly, Mick realized the voice belonged to Angela, and he turned to face her.

"Mick," she said pulling him away, "come on. They'll throw you in jail."

Mick looked back at the man, pinned against the fence by the female cop's nightstick. "C'mon," Angela cried. He yielded to her. She dragged him away, out the alley behind the churchyard.

"C'mon," she cried, pulling him along, trying to run, but unable to drag Mick into anything more than a feeble trot. Mick heard an approaching siren.

"Ow, ow," Mick said, limping on his right leg. "My knee. Angela, let me go. My knee." He reached down and rubbed the knee.

"C'mon, you have to get out of here."

"My car," Mick said. "It's out front." He turned to go that way.

The wailing cop car pulled up behind the church, and Mick heard another pull to the front. Angela pulled him away, around the corner. They walked arm in arm for a block, two blocks, neither of them speaking, until Mick saw an open coffee shop.

"We have to stop," he said. "My knee is killing me."

They took a booth in the back, Mick's back to the door. A waitress came over, and Mick and Angela both ordered coffee. Mick dropped his face into his hands.

"Mick, what happened?" she asked.

Mick shook his head, leaving his hands hiding his face. "I don't know," he said through his hands. "I just lost it."

"Why didn't you just leave him alone? The police were there."

"He was in Ohio."

"What?"

"At a rally I attended there. He did the same thing. Yelled, called everyone liars." He pulled his hands down from his face, slumped on the bench and stared at the ceiling. "I'm on edge. I guess my emotions are just shot. Nothing goes right." He ran his hands back over his face. "The bastard keeps killing our kids, and Sam is next. Shit." He stared at the table as the coffee arrived. "And this bastard — . Why couldn't he just let them talk? Why the hell did he have to be there?"

He looked Angela square in the face for the first time since he recognized her voice in the churchyard. She looked over the rim of the cup as she sipped her coffee.

"I'll tell ya why he had to be there," Mick erupted. "Because they're sending these bastards out to disrupt these things, these rallies. That's what's happening."

Angela put down her cup and crinkled her eyes into that smile Mick loved. "Who? Hillary's vast right-wing conspiracy?" She giggled.

"You think that's funny. Well, she was right."

Mick slouched in the booth and crossed his arms over his chest.

"Really?" Angela asked, with a tiny smile. "I wonder where they held the meetings. I could have invited them to meet at my place, if I'd only known who they were."

Mick frowned.

"Oh, come on. 'A vast right-wing conspiracy?' Really? I wonder if they designed that robe with the gold stripes that Supreme Court justice wore."

Mick allowed himself to smile at her.

"Okay," he said. "Yeah, I thought she was a little — what's the word? — histrionic, when she said that." Mick stirred his coffee. "But, seriously, then these guys, this outfit gets into office, and all of a sudden, she looks pretty sane to me. Why else would a guy be at one rally in Ohio and another in Pittsburgh? Can you explain that?"

"You were," Angela said, dropping a few grains of sugar into her coffee, looking up at Mick playfully from under her eyebrows.

"Yeah, but I moved. I mean, I used to live there, and now I live here."

"Maybe he did, too."

Mick shook his head. "Nah. Too much coincidence. No. Somebody sent him."

She crossed her legs and set her hands in her lap. "I don't know, Mick. After the first time he yelled, I looked for him, and at the end, I saw him. He was too, I don't know, emotional." She took her right hand out of her lap and tapped the nail of her index finger on the table to emphasize her words. "Don't you think that if someone had sent him, if he had been assigned this job, he would have been a little more — what's the word? — programmed? And if he were programmed like that, don't you think he would have been a lot more under control? Did you see him just walking around in a circle? He looked like he was taxiing for a takeoff."

Mick leaned back and shook his head.

"No. Someone sent him. Had to. Had to."

"That's not logical," Angela said. She sipped her coffee. He let his coffee sit.

"Jesus," he said, turning in the booth and throwing his arm over the back of the bench.

He avoided her gaze, looked at the other side of the coffee shop. He turned back toward her, but watched himself rotate the creamer pitcher around and around.

"I thought you were really pissed at me," he said. "I mean yesterday."

"I was. And I am."

"So, why didn't you just let me be?" he asked, meeting her eyes. "They might be after you, too."

"I know you," she said. Now it was Angela's turn to avoid Mick's gaze. "I like you. I want us to be friends." She paused and smiled at him. It's like I found my dad running a backhoe on I-80 and I jumped out of my car to talk to him. Even though I'm upset with you, I don't want you to go to jail. I said mean things to you yesterday, and I shouldn't have. I should have been more understanding. I'm sorry, and I hope you'll forgive me. Aren't you angry at me?"

"Yeah, a little." He stared at the coffee. "No. Not at you. I'm mad at the world. You just happen to be in it. You're the best part of it, and I have to be more — selfless, I guess. And, of course, I forgive you. I'm really sorry I couldn't be happy for you getting that job. I should have — . If I were a better human being — .

"I really needed that job, Angela." He slumped in the booth. "I so needed that — freaking job."

"So did I," she said. "I have student loans. I have a car payment. You're not the only one."

"I know," he said. "I know. It's still not fair."

She shook her head. "I can't do anything about it. I'm not resigning."

"I don't expect you to. I don't want you to. I want them to have hired me based on what I've accomplished, which is a lot. Some of it for them, for the kids in that school district. Hell, you'll be teaching at some college in a few years. You'll leave them. In a few years, I'll just be a few years older."

They sat in silence another few minutes. She opened her purse and fished out a couple of dollars and called to the waitress. Mick straightened up on the bench and stuck his hand into his pocket. "No, I have this."

"No," she said, handing the waitress the money. "I'll see you later."

She stood up.

Mick put out his hand, just short of touching her. "Don't be mad at me."

"I'm not," she said. She took a step toward the door, then a step back. "I feel bad for you, Mick. I pray for you every day. You and my dad."

She walked out.

Mick sighed and tried to follow her, then sank back into the booth and rubbed his knee. He shook his head.

XXXVII

"Hello?"
"..."
"Yes, this is he."
"..."
"I'm sorry, what district?"
"..."
"Okay. Yes, I did."
"..."
"Oh, I'm sorry to hear that."
"..."
"Yes, more than twenty years at various newspapers, as a reporter, editor. You name it, I did it in a newsroom."
"..."

"That would be great. And what grade?"

"..."

"Yes, I did, years ago, at Eastern Valley."

"..."

"Tomorrow would be fine. What time?"

"..."

"At the district office or the high school?"

"..."

"I'll be there."

"..."

"Thank you. Bye."

XXXVIII

Sam pushed his dad up to the door of the school, then spun the wheelchair around so his dad faced the parking lot. He opened the door and propped it open with his right foot as he pulled the chair through the doorway. He pulled the wheelchair backward toward the door of the central office, then turned around to reach for the door only to find a student holding it open. Sam and Mick both thanked the student, and Sam pulled his dad through.

A woman stood behind the counter and smiled broadly as she looked down at Mick. "Good morning," she said. "May I help you with something?"

"I'm Michael Mackintosh. I have a nine o'clock appointment with Dr. St. Joseph." Mick carried a folder with his resume, references and other information — things he knew the district had, and didn't need to bring — which he held on his lap over the tiny hole in his big blue suit.

"Um. Oh," she said, shoving a pen behind her left ear, under short black hair done in a way that was stylish when Mick was in high school. She was tall and so slender as to be without contours, even in a rather tight, sleeveless flower-print dress, Mick thought. "Welcome to West Suburban Area High School. Dr. St. Joseph will be with you in a minute." She began to motion toward a chair. "Would you have a — . I mean, um, may I get you a cup of coffee?"

"That would be very nice," Mick said. "This is my son Sam. Is it all right if he waits out here? He's my chauffer today."

"Oh, certainly," she said. "Would you like some coffee, too, Sam?"

"No, Ma'am. Thank you.

"Mr. Mackintosh, would you like cream and sugar?"

"No, thank you. Black is fine." Mick rubbed his knees. "Black is fine."

Sam maneuvered Mick's chair against the counter facing the opening that led behind the counter. Mick checked the folder then watched the woman duck her head into a door beyond the counter and to the right. She seemed to hang her head in there longer than Mick figured it would take to announce his presence, then she disappeared down a hallway. Mick turned his eyes toward Sam, sitting in one of the chairs, right ankle sitting on his left thigh, foot flexing up and down. In his shorts, T-shirt and tennis shoes, Sam looked like he belonged in a school, not a platoon.

The woman returned, carrying a white mug of coffee lettered with the words "Fighting Scots" in a tartan font in her left hand and a clipboard in her right hand.

"Here," she said, handing Mick the clipboard. "This was the sturdiest thing I could find back in the break room for you to set your coffee on. Is that all right?"

"Yes, thank you," Mick said, setting the clipboard on top of his folder. "That's very kind. That will be fine."

After Mick took a couple of sips of coffee, a stocky woman in a brownish business suit emerged from the doorway into which the secretary had ducked her head and walked to the counter, then around it to the other side.

"Mr. Mackintosh?" She extended her right hand. "I'm Loretta St. Joseph. Thank you for coming in today. I'm the building principal. Our superintendent is out of town on business, so I'll interview you. He said he would embrace any recommendation I would make."

Mick reached his right hand up to take hers. "Thank you for inviting me. Please call me Mick." He nodded to Sam. "This is my son Sam. He's my chauffer today."

She reached her right hand out to Sam, who stood up and accepted it as they exchanged how-do-you-do's.

"Well, Mr. Mackintosh, would you join me in my — ." She turned toward the door and seemed to size it up, then turned back to size up the chair. "Uh, I'll tell you what, uh, the, uh, cafeteria is just down the hall. A short walk. May I wheel — ? May I push — ? May I help you down there?"

"Sure, that's fine. May I take my coffee with me?"

"Of course," she said. "I'll be right with you." She left Mick and went into her office, then returned with a manila folder. She stuck it under her arm as she took the handles of the wheelchair.

Sam opened the door to the general office, and the principal pushed the chair through and turned right. Reaching the cafeteria door, she stopped, not quite sure how to proceed.

"The best way," Mick said, smiling up at her, "is to turn me around, open the door and just pull me through."

"Oh. Yes. Of course."

She did so, and they entered a large rectangular room with a stage at the front and bleachers in the rear, clearly a combination cafeteria/auditorium. She pushed Mick to a table at the far end, sat on a stool extending from the bottom of the table and opened the folder where Mick assumed his resume was. Mick took the coffee cup off of the clipboard and set it on the table, then set the clipboard next to it.

"So, Mr. Mackintosh, are you not working now?"

"I am not," he said. "I'm in a master's program at Pitt."

"So, you're a full-time student."

"Uh, no, part-time. I don't have the money to go full-time. I scrape together enough for a semester at a time and hope I can get a job that reimburses me for tuition. It hasn't happened yet." Mick reached for the cup and took a sip.

"Why do you think that is?"

Mick shook his head.

"You know, I always come up short, I guess. Just short. I mean, I don't really understand it. I have teaching experience, I have newspaper experience. I've written a book."

"Yes, I see that," she said, looking at the resume. "You're uh, undergraduate grades weren't very good."

"I know, but I've learned a great deal since then. If you had a Praxis test sitting right here, I'd take it, and I'd bet I'd score higher than anyone else on your staff."

She chuckled. "You might be right, Mr. Mackintosh. You might be right."

She paged through the folder. Mick couldn't figure what she could have been looking for.

"Has your, um, have districts been unwilling to hire a man in a wheelchair?"

"Oh," Mick said, "this is relatively recent. Actually, this is the first interview I've had in this."

"Um," she said, gazing at the wheelchair, a look of puzzlement on her face.

"I suspect," Mick said, pushing the coffee cup away from him and laying his eyes directly on hers, "that you're not allowed to ask the question that's on your mind. Well, I'll tell you. I'm very upfront about it. I believe in confronting things. I have arthritis. I have diabetes. Neither of those things affects what I know about writing, literature, grammar or public speaking. Neither of those things affects my ability to convey what I know to my students. Neither of those things has the slightest effect on the presence I bring into a classroom. I can engage a group of students as easily as I ever could. They will recognize me as an authority in my subject matter and an authority in the classroom." Mick gave his head a quick shake and closed his eyes for half a moment. "I will not have problems."

"You're a very brave man, Mr. Mackintosh."

"Not at all. The brave men — and women — are in Iraq and Afghanistan. I'm in a cafetorium in a suburban high school outside of the greatest city on the world."

Dr. St. Joseph closed the folder and set her hands on it, interlocking her fingers.

"As I told you on the phone, the young woman who had this job is moving to Philadelphia to care for her mother, who had a stroke. Tragic. She was the newspaper advisor, and she taught a journalism course that was quite popular here. You might not know that our school newspaper has won the Pennsylvania competition for high school papers three of the last four years. We're very proud of that."

"Was this woman a journalist?"

"Actually, no. She had attended some workshops on high school newspapers, and she had very talented students, and she studied very hard to come up to speed about newspapers. She had guest speakers in here from the Pittsburgh newspapers all the time. She was just excellent.

"We would like for that to continue, and that's why we invited you in here to interview. The other two candidates do not have any sort of journalism background, but they have outstanding undergraduate grades. If one of them is hired, I'll give the newspaper to another person on staff who is interested, although she is also not very well versed in journalism."

"What are the other courses I would teach if I were hired?"

"Three sections of composition to sophomores and three sections of American lit to juniors. This is a fairly small school. All of our teachers have multiple preps — uh, preparations, but you know that." She smiled briefly. "No one gets to teach the same thing all day long."

"I wouldn't like that anyway," Mick said. "Switching off keeps me fresh and energized."

Dr. St. Joseph had a series of questions about his teaching experiences, philosophies, what he had learned since leaving teaching that would contribute to his lessons, etc. Mick answered them all smoothly. At her invitation, Mick asked a couple of questions about the percentage of students who go on to college, the percentage of students on free or reduced-cost lunches, involvement of parents — trying to get a sense of the demographic of the area.

"Anything else?" she asked.

Mick lifted his hands off his lap as if he were a pastor offering a benediction. "I think that's everything."

"Then let me take you back to your son."

"Very well."

Dr. St. Joseph took the handles and pushed him out of the cafeteria, into the hall.

"Oh, when do you anticipate making a decision?" Mick asked.

"As soon as possible. The interviews will be over tomorrow, and the board has advertised a special meeting to effect the hire. The thing is that Ms. Daley has already left, so we have a substitute teaching the class now, but, you know, she's retired and really has no wish to stay in the classroom all year. If I can't make a hire quickly, I will have to find a permanent sub to replace the sub I have there now. Oh, this is just so difficult right after school has started. Terrible timing."

"Of course," Mick said, as they pulled up to the door of the general office. "You want to get the students settled and into a routine as soon as possible instead of giving them any indication that this is a chaotic situation. They'll respond to whatever message you send them."

"Exactly," she said, coming around the back of the chair. She opened the door to the office and leaned her head in. "Stan? It's Stan, right? Oh, Sam. I'm so sorry. Sam, I think your dad's ready to go."

Sam came out of the office and took his spot behind the chair.

"Mr. Mackintosh," the principal said extending her right hand, "it was truly a pleasure to meet you, and I will be in touch with you as soon as we make a decision. Thank you very much for coming." Mick shook her hand and expressed his appreciation for the interview. Then the principal extended her hand to Sam and expressed a "Nice-to-meet-you." Sam said the same, then wheeled his dad out to the van.

XXXIX

From: Mick Mackintosh [mailto:mickeymack@fastconnect.com]
Sent: Monday, September 10, 2003 9:37 AM
To: B.D. Butterfield
Subject: Finally

B.D., I had resigned myself to thinking that this day would never come, but I just hung up from accepting that job I told you about. I'm a little stunned. I just had no confidence that — .

Well, actually I didn't just hang up. The first thing I did was go on line and see if my parents' house was still for sale. It isn't. Shit.

That's a huge disappointment, but everything else looks good. Later on, I'm going to the nearest bookstore and buy every book on the list I've been compiling since I lost my job at The Sun. Then I'm going to call Angela and beg her to have dinner with me. I feel like such an ass getting pissed off at her because she got a job and I did not. She kept telling me I'd get one, but I didn't believe her. I just needed the right situation. Now, I need to beg her forgiveness and invite her to dinner.

Then I'm going to call my broker and take enough money out of my retirement to pay back my ex's husband for what he paid to let Sean go to Ireland. Then I'm going to sit down with Sam and see if I can talk him into backing out of the enlistment. If it's not too late. I don't know if it is or not. Now that I can pay his tuition, he doesn't have to go to the Army. He can go to Penn State. It would be very nice if he started at the local branch. He could stay with me to avoid housing costs. Of course, he'd have to wait at least a semester. I guess. Maybe a year. I don't know. Whenever he can go, he can go. If he has to wait, I can save a little money.

B.D., do you know what this means? No more Sprawl-Mart!

Oh, you know what just occurred to me? I have to get a new suit. The old one — . I need a new suit. Just as soon as I leave the bookstore. My credit card is gonna get a workout like it hasn't had in a looong time.

Wish me luck. Duuude!

Mick

XL

Mick got out of the car and slammed the car door shut. He set his briefcase on the top of the car and slipped on his new suit coat. Blue pinstripe. He looked at his reflection in the driver's side window to check his tie. Red power tie. Striking.

He pulled the briefcase off the top of the car and strode from the faculty parking lot to the building. He barely felt the pain in his knees. Along the way, he tossed off a confident, "Good morning" to a couple of students meandering their way up the walk. Early birds, Mick thought. That's wonderful. Great attitude.

He yanked open the door with a controlled power, crossed the hall and opened the door to the general office. The woman who had greeted him on the day of his interview sat behind a desk, neatly organized, and looked up. Her eyes widened.

"Good morning, Mr. Mackintosh," she said in wonderment.

"Good morning," Mick answered. "You know, when I interviewed, you never told me your name, but I think it's Gwen. Am I right? When I accepted the job, Dr. St. Joseph said I had to see Gwen to sign some papers today and that I should come in a little early. So, are you Gwen?"

She stood slowly, straightening her top over the waistband of her skirt, and walked to the counter, head slightly cocked, almost, Mick thought, like a dog who hears a sound he doesn't understand. She reached the counter and stood behind it wordlessly.

"Do you have the papers you want me to sign?" Mick asked.

"Oh, yes," she said, sticking her pen behind her ear and wincing. "Where's my head?"

She scampered back to her desk for a handful of papers clipped together, then brought them to the counter. Mick flipped through them, counting seven different sheets.

"Is there somewhere I can sit down to do this?" he asked.

"Um, well, have a seat," she said, pointing to the chair Sam had sat in during Mick's interview, "and I can get you a clipboard."

Mick smiled. "That would be fine. I'll just sit right out here, then."

Gwen got the clipboard and handed it to Mick, who moved to one of the chairs and sat down. He bent over the papers, reading, filling out, signing.

About halfway through his stack, the general office door opened. Mick looked up to see Dr. St. Joseph walk in.

"Good morning," he said, standing up and extending his right hand.

Dr. St. Joseph took it, looking up at him, mouth agape.

"I can't wait to get started," he said.

"Of course," she said, eyes narrowing. She spun around and stomped to her office, stopping to unlock the door. She pulled it open with so much force, Mick thought she might clobber herself in the forehead. She glanced at Mick, then entered the room.

Mick sat back down and returned to his paperwork. After a minute, he heard the principal ask Gwen to get her coffee, then he heard her heels digging into the carpet as she walked deliberately to the counter.

"Mr. Mackintosh," she said, "may I see you in my office?"

"Sure," Mick said, pushing himself up out of the chair, wincing a bit, carrying the clipboard and briefcase with him.

He went past her and into the office. Dr. St. Joseph closed the door behind them. She walked around to her captain's chair behind the desk and sat down.

"Please sit down, Mr. Mackintosh."

Mick sat down. "Please call me Mick."

"Mr. Mackintosh," she said, leaning forward, elbows on the desk, hands clasped in front of her face, "how are you?"

"Fine, thank you. How are you?"

"Have you recovered from your diabetes and your arthritis?"

Mick shook his head. "No. As far as I know, no one recovers from either of those things, although I have to tell you, I'm so excited about teaching, starting here, that I've pushed all of that to the back of my mind. I'll probably overdo it, and they'll have to carry me out of here by the end of the day, but for the moment, I feel great."

"Well," she said, looking briefly at the desk, then back at Mick, "if your knees start to bother you, maybe you can call Sam and he'll bring the wheelchair over."

"Oh, Sam's back with his mother. They live in the northwestern part of the state. I'll be fine."

"How long were you in your wheelchair?" she asked.

"Not long."

"Miracle recovery? Did you go to Lourdes?"

"I don't understand," Mick said.

The principal lifted herself powerfully out of the chair and walked to the window, hands on hips. When she turned around, she appeared to Mick as though she were biting her lip.

"Mr. Mackintosh, please do not be disingenuous with me. Was the wheelchair just a prop?"

"A prop? What are you saying?" Mick saw her part her lips to speak and jumped in. "Are you saying that you hired me only because I was in a wheelchair?"

She crossed her arms and walked toward him, head down. Mick knew that she was weighing her words, thinking about how they would sound in court.

"When we make a hire, Mr. Mackintosh, we hire the totality of the person. Some candidates have great charisma, and I'm certain they could hold a class, but they might not have the grades. Others have grades, and they might not have any sort of spark. They don't show any potential for magnetism, or even commanding a room. Some of them have unusual life experiences that make them desirable. They will bring to our students an awareness of certain life conditions that they would not otherwise experience."

"Like living in a wheelchair?"

"I said there was a totality. What you are now presenting to us is — . What you are suggesting to me is that I cannot trust you."

"What can't you trust me about?"

"You came in here for your interview and portrayed yourself as a person in a wheelchair, and now you walk in here perfectly healthy. You lied to me."

"I never lied to you. I never said one thing that was a lie, not one thing that was inaccurate in the least. You asked if I had failed to get jobs because I'd been in a wheelchair. I said no because I had been using it only a short time, which was true.

"You know, Dr. St. Joseph, sometimes people incur injuries that require they spend short amounts of time in wheelchairs. Sometimes they have a chronic condition that worsens for a short time and then improves."

"You said nothing to imply that you had a recent injury or that you had a temporary condition."

"I also didn't say I would be in the wheelchair for life. And I don't know why that's important. You know, you aren't even permitted to ask questions in an interview about my health. I volunteered the information that nothing about my condition would keep me from doing the job I was interviewing for.

"You know, all this time I've been looking for a job, I've been told it's all about qualifications. I lacked qualifications, you said and others have said, because thirty years ago — thirty years ago — I was an indifferent student. I've accomplished a great deal since then, but all some districts cared about was what I did thirty years ago, completely disregarding the possibility that I could have evolved, that I could have mastered my subject area. Thirty years ago, the Berlin Wall was stopping people from achieving freedom. Thirty years ago, I could get a box seat in Three Rivers Stadium for five bucks. Thirty years ago, you couldn't throw a stone in Allegheny County without hitting a steel mill. Things change, people change.

"But from the time you saw me in a wheelchair, that 'D' in basic physical geography I got thirty years ago disappeared. I don't know if it was because you have some liberal guilt that makes you give preference to people in certain minorities or if you were afraid of a discrimination lawsuit if you didn't hire me — I don't know, but you hired me, and you're stuck with me because if you fire me now, I will damned sure file a lawsuit, and I'll look forward to your explaining why my employment depends on my being in a wheelchair. I strongly suggest you allow me to do my job, and you may find that I am a damned fine teacher who knows more about my subject matter than anybody else you have on staff."

Dr. St. Joseph stomped back behind her desk. She leaned on it, placing all of her weight on her fingers.

"I'm not going to do anything right now, Mr. Mackintosh," she said. "But know for a certainty that I will keep a very close eye on you, and that any lapse, the most minor lapse, and you will be gone.

Glance at the bosom of any woman in this building, student or staff, and you will be gone. Touch any student in any way beyond a handshake, and you will be gone. If you so much as misspell Shakespeare's name on the blackboard, I will start proceedings to have you removed.

"You have perpetrated a fraud on this school district, and I will see that you do not profit from it."

"I don't think so, Ma'am," Mick said. "I think you made a decision based on something you misunderstood and maybe applied to a flawed value system. If there's anything fraudulent, it's the system. You allowed a president who hasn't read a book past Dick and Jane to sell you a set of educational standards that has nothing to do with education and everything to do with punishment. Now, is it all right with you if I finish filling out these forms and Gwen shows me to my new classroom?"

XLI

Mick had just finished putting a half gallon of milk and a can of sliced peaches into the refrigerator when the doorbell rang. From the kitchen, he could see what he thought was a police officer on the front stoop. When he got to the door, he saw there were two, both men.

One of them was the Pittsburgh cop who had tried to hold him away from the guy disrupting the rally.

"Are you Michael P. Mackintosh?" asked the one Mick recognized.

Mick shaded his eyes from the glaring afternoon sun just over the rise across the street. He knitted his brow at the sight of the blue uniform trousers and blue pants of the two officers. The one who spoke was tall and reedy, older than Mick and the hair showing beneath his hat was completely gray. His nose was red and bulbous, which Mick had not noticed that Sunday, his lips thin and set. His blue eyes darted from side to side and inside to see Mick and look beyond him. The other was short, broad and thick, young and dark, with a black mustache. He rested his right hand on his hip, which he cocked to the right. He stared at the ground.

"Yes," Mick said.

The young one pulled handcuffs off the back of his belt. The other said, "Step out of the house, Sir."

Mick hesitated. "What's this about?"

"You're under arrest, Sir, please step out of the house."

"What am I charged with?" stepping onto the stoop.

In an instant, he felt the sweat moistening his long-sleeved white shirt, tie loosened.

"Put your hands behind your back, Sir."

Mick did as he was told. The younger officer cuffed him. The older one turned him around and pushed him against the brick facing of the house right next to the door and kicked his feet open to a spread position.

"Mick?" A female voice came from next door. "Mick, what's going on? Are you all right?" Then to the officers. "What are you doing to him?"

Mick said nothing. He glanced at her and instantly locked into his brain the picture he would carry with him. She wore the Eastern Valley Area High School T-shirt. Mick knew that, even though she had crossed her arms across the logo that bent over her breasts. She had on those jeans shorts, Mick always thought not quite appropriate for her, revealing the exquisite legs he had always admired. Her feet were bare, and she lifted one of them off the stoop, heated through the day by the sun, and she stepped onto the grass. The officers ignored her.

"Misdemeanor assault two on, I can't remember," the older cop said. "What's the guy's name?"

The other officer finished cuffing Mick, spun him around to face them both, then pulled the warrant out of his pocket. "Albert Stanley Wyckoff."

"Albert Stanley Wyckoff," the older cop said. "It took us a while to track you down. We thought you lived in Ohio."

"Wait, wait," Mick said, as he tried to maintain his balance on his wobbly knees. "Who the hell is Albert Stanley Wyckoff?"

"He's the guy you beat up at a peace rally downtown," the older cop said. "The one I tried to keep you from hitting."

"I believe you were one of the peace people," the younger one said with a slight chuckle and a decided leer.

The younger one frisked Mick, reaching up to the shoulders of his six-foot, seven-inch frame, reaching up under his shaggy hair that rested on his shoulders, below the collar of the back of his golf shirt, across his broad shoulders, then around the front of and down the back of his abdomen, and finally down the legs of his slacks, roughly feeling every inch of him. There was no need for this, Mick thought, because he was already cuffed, but assumed the cop enjoyed pushing people around. He reached into Mick's pockets and pulled everything out. He picked the Swiss Army knife out of a handful of change and a set of keys. He stuck that in his pocket.

The younger officer turned to the woman next door and yelled, "You stay right there, lady. Don't even go in the house until we pull away, or we'll draw down on you, swear to God."

"Where are you taking him? Mick, I'll call a lawyer. Where are you taking him?"

"Don't worry about a lawyer, Angela. I'll get a public defender."

The officers ignored the exchange as the older one jerked him away from the brick facing of the house and dragged him to the car. He dug his fingers into Mick's shoulder, and Mick felt the nails dig into his arm. The younger one walked along, reading Mick the Miranda card.

"Could I at least lock up my house? Jesus!"

The older cop walked to the door.

"You'll need the keys," Mick said over his shoulder. Then to the younger cop, "Did you put them back in my pocket?"

The cop said nothing, but dug back into Mick's pocket for the keys.

"You took the knife didn't you?" Mick asked.

"Yeah. A little Swiss Army Knife. Were you in the Swiss Army, pal?"

"I'm going to want that back, pal." Mick returned the sneer and the tone the young cop had given him.

The younger cop yanked his elbow, and Mick winced as his shoulder seemed to slip a little out of the socket.

Mick heard his own door slam behind him and glanced over to see Angela still standing on the grass. The older cop took Mick by his left elbow, and the two cops walked him to the car.

On the other side of the car, the younger officer opened the back door of the squad car. Mick stepped in with his left leg. The officer pushed his head down and shoved him inside, but left the door open. As soon as Mick was seated, looking forward at the grillwork between the front and back seats, the younger officer got into the driver's seat. Mick heard the engine turn over, then a hum and saw the front driver's side window slide down. The older cop got into the back seat on the passenger side. "Okay, Louie Lou-I, let's get this guy downtown."

The instant the door slammed shut, the driver stomped on the gas and pulled the car away from the asphalt lip abutting the grass of his property.

Mick looked out the window to see Angela standing on her front stoop, arms across her chest. The car moved past her property, and Mick twisted his neck to see her as the car passed her by, then she dashed into her house.

"Will I have a chance to get a lawyer?"

"Our job is just to get you to the lockup," the older man said. "After that it's out of our hands."

Mick settled back and closed his eyes and mumbled, "I can't fucking believe it. I barely touched that guy."

"Well," the younger cop said, "he filed charges, and we had two officers on the scene, including Louie Lou-I, here, and they were witnesses to the assault, so that's that."

The car left the neighborhood and turned onto the Lincoln Highway, taking the familiar route to the Parkway the main route into Pittsburgh from the eastern part of the county. This was how Mick had gone to the ballgame all his life, whether it was his dad driving him to Forbes Field in Oakland in the used car of the year or himself driving his wife and boys to Three Rivers Stadium in that Satellite he and Constance had bought new or himself driving alone to PNC Park in the scratched and dented Neon that burned so much oil. Now, the police car sped along Ardmore Boulevard past the little strip mall and past the tidy shopping district with bakeries and craft shops, past the park, where the pre-adolescent Mick just wanted to play baseball on the little field, where now kids played only soccer. They barely slowed down for the traffic lights through the residential section of Forest Hills, stone houses perched on terraced slopes, stone houses Mick always wanted to live in. Then they zoomed onto the Parkway, steadily speeding up on the acceleration lane, which the younger officer entered without so much as a glance into the side-view mirror. Mick thought of how afraid he always was to enter the highway there, with traffic from Churchill and Monroeville thundering down on him on a highway that his dad always told him was obsolete the day it opened. The officer pulled immediately into the fast lane, never slowing from his leap onto the highway for the traffic slowing in front of him for the entrance into the tunnel.

How could he be going to jail? This couldn't be happening.

The officer sighed as he finally had to brake for the traffic stacked up in front of the dark tunnel entrance.

"Fuckin' people can't drive through tunnels," he mumbled. He glanced into the rearview mirror. "You all right with him, Lou?"

The older one shifted in his seat and cracked his knuckles. "No problem, Frank."

Finally, the car crept into the tunnel, and the traffic sped up past the tiled walls, and soon the early evening light loomed just ahead. Suddenly, the car shot out of the tunnel, past the Squirrel Hill exit, where the school buses had once left the highway, taking Mick and the other Little League boys to Saturday afternoon knothole games at Forbes Field to see Vernon Law or Curt Raydon or Bennie Daniels pitch, seemingly always against the Milwaukee Braves. Now Mick was in the back seat of a police car speeding past the exit on his way to jail, and Forbes Field was gone and Law, Raydon and Daniels were decrepit old men, and the Braves were in Atlanta, and nothing was the same, and Mick was on his way to jail.

Mick turned to the older one. "Did you grow up around here? I mean, maybe you've heard of me. Mickey Mackintosh. From the sixties. Eastern Valley Area High School. MickeyMack. We won Section 2 when I was a senior and played Donora in the WPIAL quarterfinals. We got killed, but I scored twenty points and Pitt brought me in to play forward."

"You that guy?" the younger officer asked, shifting his eyes up to the mirror and back down to the Parkway.

"Yeah. Hell, I taught at Eastern Valley Area."

"How the mighty have fallen," the younger one said, then chuckled to himself.

"I'll give you a word of advice," Louie said softly into the back of the front seat. "Don't be going on about MickeyMack and Donora and all that when you get inside. Nobody wants your goddamn resume."

Mick took a deep breath and let it out and dropped his head back, but he was too tall for it to reach the back of the seat. "Jesus. Jesus, please help me."

They got off the Parkway at Second Avenue and made quick turns on brick streets until they entered a garage and pulled into a space designated for car 402.

"Okay, MickeyMack," the younger one said, mockingly running both names together as he got out of the car, "this is your stop."

The older cop got out of the car and reached inside to take Mick by his elbow to drag him toward the open door. Mick scooted along the seat, knees bumping the back of the front seat. He stepped out with his left foot and pushed off as the officer lifted him by his elbow. Mick wobbled on one leg and dragged his right leg out of the car, falling against the door.

"Stand up, MickeyMack," the younger one said. "You didn't score no twenty points with that kind of balance."

"Arthritis," Mick said. "Both knees."

"You should tell your new friends that," Frank said. "The pimps and the rapists, they'll take pity on you for that."

Lou led Mick toward an elevator, and in a short succession, the door opened and they all got in and the elevator jerked away from inertia and up a few floors, then the door slid open, and Lou led Mick along a hallway and through double doors, reinforced steel with a wire-embedded window the size of a metropolitan phone book. Lou led him to a counter. Another cop, fat as a sumo wrestler, lifted himself out of a captain's chair and walked toward the counter.

"Wha' cha got, there, Frank?"

"Mackintosh, Michael P. Warrant from Judge North," Frank read off a pink copy. He handed the copy to the fat cop.

The fat cop pulled a manila mailing envelope from under the counter and slapped it on the desk. "Empty your pockets and put everything on the counter. You may have to uncuff him there, Lou."

"No, he's fine, Buck," Lou said. "I have his keys right here," he said, tossing them onto the counter. Lou patted his left front pocket and found it empty, then patted his back pocket and reached in for his wallet and handed it to Buck.

"Okay, let's see," Buck said opening the wallet, "no bills, a MasterCard, lots of business cards, a few pictures, lots of little pieces of paper I don't know what they are."

Mick considered telling him what the pieces of paper were, addresses and phone numbers of friends, a note Constance had given him when they dated, the boys' Social Security numbers — the skeleton of his life.

Buck pulled every piece of paper out of the wallet, every piece of plastic and identified them as he listed them on an inventory. Mick watched every movement he made.

Mick felt Frank dig into his right front pocket and pull out change and a few bills of various designations and a couple of receipts. Frank unfolded a receipt. "You bought wine this afternoon, there, MickeyMack. Big date tonight? Well, you might still have a big date tonight if you play your cards right." All three of the cops laughed.

Frank tossed the change, bills and receipt onto the counter. Buck orally identified each and added them all to his inventory. Frank found a handkerchief, blindingly white and perfectly folded in his back right pocket, and he dropped that on top of the change. He pulled Mick's belt out of his pants and set that down, too. Lou untied his tie and pulled that out from under Mick's collar and handed that to Buck.

"I guess we'll have to uncuff him to get the watch off, Lou," Frank said.

"And he'll have to sign for givin' me this stuff," Buck said.

"You want to put my Swiss Army knife on the counter?" Mick said, as Lou opened the cuffs.

"You got a Swiss Army knife?" the fat cop asked.

"He's delusional, Buck," Frank said, and turned to Mick. "Now, I told you in the car to shut up." Buck looked at Lou as he put everything into the envelope. Frank turned back to Buck. "Wouldn't shut up the whole time down here. Big-time basketball hero back in the day. Gave us play by play of every fuckin' basket he ever made."

"He has my knife, damn it," Mick said. "I want it back when I get out of here. It was a gift from one of my sons. I don't sign anything until I see that knife go into that envelope and onto the inventory."

Buck held his hand out to the younger cop. "Frank." He wiggled his fingers back toward himself.

Frank dug into his pocket and handed it to Buck. "Fucking crybaby. I'm just fuckin' with you, asshole. Wait 'til the boys in lockup get at you. They'll have lots of jokes for you."

Mick saw a woman in the corner close her eyes briefly, which Mick took as a sign of disgust at the language. "Can't wait 'til he tries that shit with the pimps and rapists," Frank said to Buck.

"That's good," Mick said. "Don't ever change winning material." Then to Buck. "He used that image on the way down." Lou took off the cuffs, and Mick signed the inventory.

"Image?" Buck said picking the pink piece of paper up and looking it over.

"Line. Same line, is what I meant."

"Shut up, you crusty old fart. Buck, you'd better get this guy in holding before he starts to piss me off. Wish I could be here when you do the strip search. Scum of the earth, these guys, and they think they get to hold court."

"Strip search?" Mick said, feeling the fear well up in him. "You're going to strip search me?"

"Procedure," Louie said softly. "Everybody who comes in goes through one."

"Come on, Mr. Mackintosh," Buck said, moving toward the opening between counter and wall and motioning Mick along.

"We're timin' out, Buck," Frank said. "We need a shower after dealin' with this fucker."

Mick twisted away from Buck's reach as he got to the end of the counter. "I figured you were hot to shower with Lou," he said. "I'm a little surprised Lou's into that."

Frank rushed at Mick but Lou caught him by the arm and dragged him out the door.

"You don't make friends easy, do ya, Mac?" Buck said, grabbing his arm.

Buck took him through another steel door and led him down a short hall. "I didn't talk about myself the whole way," Mick said. "All I did was — . Fuck. That little puke wants to play, I'll play, but he doesn't seem to like it when other people play rough, too."

"Frank's old man is the mayor's driver. Wrong man to fuck with, buddy." Buck knocked on yet another steel door, and another cop, a barrel-chested man about Mick's age, opened it.

"Do I get to make a phone call?" Mick asked.

"Later," Buck said as he pushed the door open.

"New one for ya, Moses," Buck said, handing Moses the pink sheet. "Let me frisk him."

Buck gently pushed Mick against the wall, pulled his front pockets inside-out and quickly frisked him, the same way Frank had frisked him at the house. "All yours, Moses."

Moses took Mick a few steps into a small room with two desks, and a second man at one of them. "Mackintosh, Michael P," Moses said. The other man wrote the name on the white sheet of paper in front of him.

"Okay, Buddy, take 'em off," Moses said.

"Take what off?" Mick asked.

"Jesus Christ, Lonnie, we got us a virgin." Then to Mick, "Undress, mister. Everything."

Mick painfully unbuttoned his shirt, his hands shaking, knees quivering. He handed the shirt to Moses, then he kicked off his loafers. He leaned against the wall to pull off his socks. It hurt to bend his knees that way. He stood in only his briefs. He looked at Moses, as though appealing to some sense of decency, some extension of mercy.

"Shorts, too. C'mon."

Mick pulled down his shorts and felt himself blushing. Moses put on latex gloves and turned Mick around by the shoulder, just looking at him.

"Okay, bend over."

Mick did as he was told.

"Spread your cheeks."

Again, Mick obeyed.

"More."

Mick pulled his buttocks as far apart as he could.

"You'd be surprised what people put up there, mister," Moses said. "Now, grab hold of your balls and shift them all the way to the right. Okay, now all the way to the left. Okay."

Moses tossed him his clothes, and Mick quickly dressed, except for his socks, which he put into his pocket. Moses pulled a key on an elastic lead from his pants and turned the key on another steel door. "In here," he said, pulling Mick in by his elbow. A cage loomed before Mick, big enough for only two guys to stand. No chairs. A third guy wouldn't have fit, Mick decided. Moses pulled a different key from what Mick guessed must have been an elastic ball attached to his belt. He opened the cage and shoved Mick in.

"Now, what?" Mick said.

Moses turned away from him and closed the steel door behind him.

Mick still faced the steel door, but turned his head to examine the other man, who was of average height and weight with dark hair and dark complexion, maybe in his late twenties. The man leaned his face against the bars and stared at the floor. Mick looked down to see if something was moving there that the man as watching. Nothing. It was just bare cement. Not even a spider creeping across it. Mick looked behind him at the walls. Steel gray.

"Not much décor," Mick said. The other man said nothing.

"So, are we the only two guys in the jail?" Mick asked.

"You'll get moved. You'll see more guys."

"You been here before?"

"You haven't?" the other man said, moving his face from the bars and looking up at Mick.

"No. And they got me on a bullshit charge. There's nothing to this." Mick stopped and looked down. "I'm sorry. I guess everyone says that."

"Not me."

"Oh." Mick looked up. "Is it rude to ask why you're here?"

"I beat the shit out of my father."

"You beat up your dad?"

"He was lookin' at my girlfriend like he wanted to fuck her."

"Ah," Mick said.

A blonde-haired officer, whistling something Mick couldn't recognize, and a dumpy cop with a shaved head came through a door to Mick's left. Mick got a glimpse of what was on the other side. He saw another cell; this one seemed to be bigger in the brief look he had. He saw maybe a handful of guys before the door shut. The blonde guy opened the cage door. "Come on, boys," the blonde guy said.

The other man stepped out and Mick followed. The dumpy guy cuffed them and pushed them against the wall in turn and frisked them, then led them away.

"Where are we going?" Mick asked.

"Shut up," the dumpy cop said.

"Arraignment," the other prisoner said.

Mick walked along, thinking of the boys finding out he was in jail, and Constance. She wouldn't be shocked. Oh, God, he thought. He could lose his job. A teacher in jail. That won't fly. What would he do? Oh, God. And he thought about Angela, envisioned her smile, sweet and toothy, even her legs. This is just ridiculous, he told himself. How the hell could he be in jail? How the hell could those cops take that shoving match seriously? Maybe they were all pro-Bush. Maybe they arrested more people that day, although Mick hadn't heard of any arrests. In fact, he hadn't watched the news that night. He was a real journalist. He never watched TV news. Not local news. Worthless. "If it bleeds, it leads."

How the hell did this happen?

The cops took Mick and the other prisoner into a courtroom, with "Magistrate Martha Medwick" stenciled on the bubble-glass door. The cops pushed the two men into wooden chairs at the back of the courtroom. The room was not very full, just a few others, men and women. Mick tried to imagine what these other people had done. He soon tired of that and leaned his head against the wall behind him, thinking about everything and nothing. His life, his career, his future. Did he have a future? Was he going to be like the character Tim Robbins played in *The Shawshank Redemption*? Mick tried to think of the guy's name. He knew there was a mnemonic device that helped him remember. He ran it through his head. Duquesne. Dufresne. Andy Dufresne. Would he spend the rest of his best years behind bars for something he didn't do? He pushed the guy, maybe. No assault. Not real assault. He couldn't have hurt the guy. Not the way the soldiers were being hurt in Iraq, coming home without limbs. Shit.

Would he be thrown into some prison and unwittingly piss off some tough guy who would slice him to pieces? His knees shook. He could feel his heart rush and his breaths hurry through his chest. What a waste that would be. Even at his age, he had some potential. He still had dreams. And he had his sons, whom he wanted to see leave their marks in the world in something worthwhile. He wasn't crazy about Sean's girlfriend, but he thought Sean would eventually dump her and find a nice girl and give him grandchildren someday. Sam would give him grandchildren, too. Later, he hoped. If he came back. And maybe someday he'd meet someone and have another romance. Better than Constance. Maybe with — .

Finally, the magistrate entered the courtroom and climbed one step to her desk. She was ash blonde, older than himself, with a thin face. Her court clerk called out various names from a list she held, peering through black glasses. Then the magistrate read the charges for each person and set bail. The other prisoner's charge was attempted murder. Apparently, Mick concluded, he had beat up his dad pretty badly.

Then the clerk called his name. He stood up, with the help of the blonde cop, who grabbed his elbow. He heard the words, but his eyes started to blur and his head became light. Misdemeanor assault in the second degree. Did he understand the charge? Mick failed to answer. The blonde cop shook him and whispered. "Answer her. Do you understand the charge?"

"Yes, Ma'am," he said.

He heard an amount of bail and a question about paying. He said he had no money. He thought she said he would have a chance to make bail.

When everyone had been arraigned, the blonde cop and his dumpy friend rounded up all of the men in the room, maybe seven, Mick thought, and herded them back to the holding area.

They took the men to the cell Mick had tried to see into, but the men had to stand outside the door.

The dumpy guy frisked them all.

"I was frisked before I went in there," Mick said, regaining his composure. "You were with me upstairs. What do you think I picked up?"

"S.O.P., Pops," the blonde said. "Procedures are in place for a reason. How do we know Angel didn't pass you a knife before?"

"If Angel was frisked before he went in, how would he get a knife?"

"Pops, I'm gonna give you a word of advice: We don't need a lot of questions from you, and we don't need your critique of how we do our job or what our procedures are. The more you talk, the more difficult this will be for you. You got that, Pops?"

Mick saw the dumpy guy smile. "They're all smart guys, aren't they, Jerry?" he said. "Well, wait 'til he gets with the pimps and the rapists. He won't be that smart."

Mick smiled. "How do you know I'm not a pimp or a rapist?"

The dumpy guy finished frisking Mick and swung him around and let go of him, and Mick slammed into the small holding cell he had occupied with Angel. He felt the bars meet his face, unable to bring his arms around to cushion the impact.

The dumpy guy immediately pressed Mick into the cell.

"Pops," he said, "are you trying to escape? Where the hell do you think you'd go? You got so many steel doors between you and the street, you'd never get through them all even if you weren't cuffed."

"You did that on purpose," Mick said.

The dumpy guy swung him away from the cell and let him go into the wall, then pinned Mick into the wall.

"You tried that again? What did I just tell you? You'd never make it, Pops. You'd never make it if you were a young guy. Holy shit!"

Mick said nothing this time, and the dumpy guy pulled him off the wall and guided him toward the door.

The blonde guy reached out a hand to stop him. "You know what, Beans," the blonde guy said, "since he got away from you, you might have to frisk him again. You don't know what he might have jammed down his pants while he was out of your control."

"Ya think?" The dumpy guy pinned Mick against the wall and kicked his feet apart. Mick felt the forearm press into his back. He felt the hands all over him, briskly and lightly, then he felt a hand roughly jammed into his crotch and grabbing and twisting his testicles through his jeans.

"Oww!!" he screamed.

"No, Jer, nothing jammed down his pants, but, you know, it's always good to check."

He opened the door for all of them, then removed the men's cuffs, one by one. Mick stood in the door of the cell and looked into the enormity of the room, and he froze in his tracks as the collective body odor assaulted him. There must have been thirty guys in there. Some wore orange jump suits. Others wore street clothes like Mick did. The cell was the size of a high school classroom, with a cement bench running all around it, except for the breadth of the door. The blonde guy opened the door, and the dumpy guy pushed Mick in, then slammed the door shut. Mick stood at the door, not sure what he should do. He looked around. Some guys met his gaze, others did not. Some guys sat on the cement bench. A large man stood on it, bouncing up and down on the balls of his feet. Others milled around the room. One guy got up from the metal commode in the center of the cell, and flushed. Mick discovered there was no seat on the commode. The guy turned from flushing and scratched his nose. Mick cringed inwardly. Why didn't this guy wash his hands first? Then he realized there was no sink.

"Sit down, Dude," a voice said. "We ain't gonna bite'cha."

Mick surveyed the men, an eclectic bunch: white, black, brown, Asian. All sizes, some looking hard, others looking relaxed, still others anxious, as Mick imagined himself to look. One man in one corner talked quietly, but agitatedly, waving his arms, while another man looked at the floor and nodded at every gesticulation. A bronze body-builder type did sit-ups in another corner. One guy, short and slender, wore a short red dress so naturally, that at first, Mick thought he must be a woman. Except for the body builder type, who wore a dress shirt open from top to bottom, and the guy in drag, everyone wore denim, jeans or shorts. Mick suppressed the urge, fading as his sense of oppression grew, to ask which of them were pimps and which of them were rapists.

A man with the complexion of coffee with cream, probably in his late thirties, corn rows hugging his small, round head, oversized T-shirt hanging down to the knees of his jeans, motioned Mick to the bench. "Hey, your eye's bleedin', man. What the fuck?"

Mick sat down as near the man as he could and wiped blood from the cut. "They slammed me into the cell out there." He motioned with his head toward the smaller cell.

"They slammed you into the birdcage? Fuckers. Whad'ju do?"

"I asked why they frisked me so much." Mick looked at the blood on his hand and wiped it on the bottom of his shirt, then reached the shirt up to his eye and wiped away more blood. "That's all they do. Doesn't make sense. They frisk you when they — ."

"You think they ever get laid?" a pale-skinned guy wearing a tank-top undershirt and jeans said. "Those fuckin' losers? They like to touch us. Gets 'em hard. They're out there whackin' off right now. Whackin' each other off, right, Cuz?"

The first guy laughed. "Thass right. Palmin' each other's peckers."

Mick buried his head in his hands and gagged.

"You all right, man?" the black guy asked.

"No. I'm sick. Just sick." He gagged again and stood up to walk to the commode, but he lost his balance and veered to the left. His knees, always painful, now deserted him entirely. The guy in the dress reached up and steadied him.

"Sit down," he said in a surprisingly deep voice. "Take deep breaths. You'll be all right."

"Yeah, you'll get used to us," said a guy in shorts and sandals, "and pretty fuckin' soon, you'll smell as bad as the rest of us." He laughed.

"Especially if you're in here for a few days without a chance to shower," said the body-builder type, not even looking at Mick.

Mick smiled a little. He sat back down on the cement bench and the nausea passed. He folded his hands in his lap and stared at them. "I don't understand," he said. "They haven't let me make a phone call. Shouldn't I have been able to make a phone call? I never got a chance to close the windows. Oh, God."

"They came to your house?" the black guy asked.

"I had just got home from work and stopping at the mall for a couple of things. I hadn't even had time to start dinner."

"Work?" said a guy in a jump suit.

"Yeah, Alex," said the big guy jumping on the bench, "that's how you dress if you work."

"Work?" the Latino guy said again. "You work?"

"I teach."

The guy on the bench stopped bouncing and asked, "'Ju do something to one of them kids?"

"No. No." Mick buried his head in his hands. "This has nothing to do with the kids. Or anything about my job."

"Really?" asked the black guy.

"Honest to God. They just came and dragged me out of the house."

"You teach?" the guy in shorts said. "High school?"

"Yes. English."

"Where you teach, man?"

Mick answered all the questions: where he taught, where he grew up, where he lived. He heard the usual proportion of them, just as in the world at large, say English was their worst subject, blaming, "them fuckin' verbs and shit" or some "bitch English teacher" who made them memorize Shakespeare. One guy sitting on the floor screamed and pulled his hair. Mick stopped talking and watched.

"That's Ralphy. Needs his fix. He'll be okay."

"My God," Mick said, covering his ears as Ralphy continued to scream, "that's horrifying."

The guy with the corn rows shook his head. "Man, you don't belong in here."

XLII

Angela unlocked the passenger side door and Mick stepped into the car and onto the seat. He leaned his head back on the headrest. Angela walked around and got into her side of the car. Mick rolled down the car window, conscious of how he smelled, not wanting to offend the prettiest girl he knew.

She started the motor, and Mick said, without lifting his head or turning to face her, "Did you post the bail?"

"Yes."

"Where did — . Thank you," he said, "Where the hell did you get money to post bail?"

"I have a job, you know," she said, smiling at Mick.

"So, I've heard." Mick turned to look out his window as Angela waited to make a turn. "I wonder if I do."

"I called and told them you wouldn't be in," she said. "I just said it was personal business, but, um — ." Angela bit her lip.

"What?" Now he turned to face her.

"It was on TV."

"What?" Mick bolted forward. "My arrest was on TV?" He flung his hands into the air and onto his face. "What the fu — . Why was that news?"

"It was only on for a second. I saw it. The eleven o'clock news the night you were arrested."

"But, why? It was a little assault arrest. A bullshit charge."

"Well, what I didn't know until then was that all of the TV stations filmed you pushing that guy."

"Did they film him pushing me?"

"Not that I saw. It was on all three stations that night. I guess that's how the police knew who you were. Someone saw the news and called the police on you."

"That's not what the public defender said. She said one of the organizers identified me. They disavowed what I did. They said they did not want to be identified with someone who solved problems with violence."

"Oh, I'm so sorry."

They drove through the city and got onto the Parkway toward home.

"I wanted to call the boys," she said, "but I didn't know what phone book to look in. I checked the Internet, but they're not listed anywhere."

"I asked the PD to call. I doubt they're very proud."

"You missed a class, huh?" she asked.

"Yeah. Maybe I should just quit the program."

"Then you'll never get a job."

"I'll never get another job. Not in teaching anyway."

"Oh, right," she said. "The criminal background check."

They entered and left the tunnel in silence.

"When is your trial?"

"They haven't scheduled it. It won't be a trial, per se. They're going to knock it down to disorderly conduct, and I'll have to pay a fine."

They left the Parkway for Route 30.

"I shoved a guy who was giving me crap, a guy who shoved me. And I have a record." He turned back to watch the road and leaned his head back. He sighed.

Angela drove through a couple of intersections, then, stopped at a red light, she asked, "Do you think he'll sue you?"

Mick turned his head toward the window and dropped it into his right hand. "I never thought of that."

He turned his attention back to the road. "Well, I guess he can sue all he wants. I have no money. I guess he can take the house. I wonder how that works. I still have twenty-eight years of payments to make on it. Maybe it will just wait 'til I sell it and he'll get all the proceeds." He sighed again. "I'm guessing he doesn't want the Neon."

Angela could not suppress a giggle, and Mick discovered that he didn't mind. He guessed it was good to make her laugh no matter the circumstances. He had thought about her the whole time he was locked up. He wondered if she was going to the next football game with some guy, if she had gone to previous games with some guy. He knew better than to ask. He had enough problems.

Angela pulled into her driveway and they both got out.

"Thanks very much," Mick said. "I don't know how long I could have stayed in there. I'll pay you back for the bail."

"Look, why don't you come over tonight for dinner? I put one of those frozen bag dinners in the crock pot. Surely, you're not going to try to cook anything tonight." Mick opened his mouth, intent on declining, but she jumped in first. "And I don't want you to be alone."

Mick nodded his head.

"Sure. I have a bottle of wine. I'll bring it over. Let me get a shower and change clothes."

"Oh," Angela called over her shoulder. "I have your mail. I didn't want it stacking up in your mailbox. You want it now or — ?"

"Yeah, I'll take it now so I won't forget it later."

Angela opened her front door and reached inside and pulled out a plastic bag full of circulars and envelopes. Mick walked up to her and she handed it over.

Angela's cell phone rang, and she opened it up and burst into a broad smile.

"Hi," she said. "It's really nice of you to call."

Mick allowed an "Aw, geez" to escape his lips as she turned toward the inside of the house. He hurried away so he wouldn't hear the rest of it, though he was dying to know what she would say, who it would seem she was talking to.

Mick picked out the envelopes as he walked. He stopped as he saw a return address from the West Suburban Area School District. He stopped in his tracks and ripped it open, tearing a corner of the letter inside. He tore the letter out of the envelope and let the envelope drop to the ground. He unfolded the single white sheet with red letterhead.

"Dear Mr. Mackintosh:

"Due to your recent arrest on charges of assault, you are hereby suspended without pay, effective immediately, pending official action by the West Suburban Area School Board.

"Sincerely,

"Dr. Loretta St. Joseph

"Principal"

XLIII

The mailman turned away from Mick and walked toward Angela's, thumbing through his handful of envelopes, circulars and magazines, separating Angela's from the rest of the pile. Mick's gaze followed him for a while, as though he could discern whether the mail included anything for Angela from whatever guy was making her smile. Then he looked down at the certified letter. The return address told him all he needed to know. This was the official letter dismissing him from his teaching job.

He opened it to confirm. Yep. Signed by the board chairman. Well, at least he'd had a few weeks' salary until the board could meet.

He called Eddie Webb. Of course, he got the secretary.

"I'll give him the message, Mr. Mackintosh."

"Ma'am," Mick said. "I'm not calling to ask him for a job. I'm calling to ask him for direction. Any thought he might have for what I should do. He'll understand."

Mick heard silence, then for the first time he heard the secretary speak like a person instead of a programmed voice mail message. "I'll tell him that," she said.

Mick made some soup and sat on the couch to watch CNN. God, in heaven, he said to the TV, is this war ever going to end? But he knew it had really just begun, despite the president's declaration of "Mission Accomplished." Or was it the crew of the Lincoln, as the White House had said? No brainer. If they're talking, they're lying. Aaaah!

A while later, he heard Angela's car pull in, and he heard her voice. He got up to look out the door to see if she was calling to him, then he heard a male voice. That stopped him. He peeked through the blinds. He saw a young guy, very tall, very sleek, his movements athletic, his tie — blue striped, Mick thought — lying perfectly flat on his still perfectly pressed powder blue dress shirt. He put his arm around her and they walked into the house.

Mick sat back down on the couch. Like she was ever going to be interested in you, he told himself.

He watched the Cubs on WGN, not really caring who won, but just to have some noise in the house, to make an attempt to divert his mind from the loss of the job and the loss of the woman. What an idiot, he told himself.

And he thought of Ginny. Was he so stupid that he wanted a young woman who would never want anything to do with him, yet he pushed away a woman his age who had all but hung a "For Sale" sign around her neck? Ginny. Hell, she was very comfortable financially. She could take care of him until he got back onto his feet.

He picked up the phone book and looked up her number. He dialed the area code and the exchange, knowing that he could probably make no call that would be more happily received, that no woman — .

Then he hung up the phone. Ginny was the past. Like the steel mills, like the shopping mall that no longer stood. He needed to move forward. He just didn't know where forward was.

He stretched out on the couch and laid his head on the arm and watched the Cubs.

The phone woke him up. The game was still on. He checked the clock. He reached for the phone. It was Eddie.

Mick explained to Eddie about the letter.

"Any ideas where I go next?" Mick asked.

"Well, I can tell you that no public school around here would hire you. It's just disorderly conduct, but even so — . There's an outside chance — and I do mean an outside chance — that one of those districts in the hinterlands would hire you. One of the counties up in the middle of nowhere, maybe near the New York border. Not Erie. They get all the teachers they need out of Edinboro. Farther east, you know, where there are about 12 kids in the graduating class, no bookstore in the entire county, and the only entertainment is the annual tractor pull, unless you like to shoot deer. Do you like to shoot deer, Mick?"

"Not that much."

"Well, make sure you get cable up there. If, you know, there are any telephone poles up there to bring it to you."

"Can't do that. I have to finish the master's program."

"Well, then, you might want to practice these words: "`Four-ninety-five. Please pull around to the first window.'"

"Yeah, that'll look great on my vitae when I go looking for a college teaching job."

"Might not hurt that much, actually. You can explain that you were an anti-war demonstrator and that the pigs pulled you in. I think that would fly on a lot of campuses."

"You're secretly one of 'them,' aren't you, Eddie?"

"Whatever I am, it's a secret. Publicly, I am apolitical, the way my superintendent likes me. Something you might want to think about, my friend."

"Shit."

They said their goodbyes and Mick hung up. He ran his hand over his face and tried to focus on the game, which had gone to extra innings. He needed extra innings in his own life, he thought. Or a rainout, so he could go back and start again. A new life, like Angela had said.

The phone rang.

"Listen, Mick, I just happened to think after I hung up the phone: We send some of our kids to an alternative school. They're tough kids. We get them out of here to keep up our numbers for NCLB — ."

"Huh?"

"No Child Left Behind. We don't leave them behind. We move them out to make someone else deal with them. Nobody here wants anything to do with them. I've talked to the director over there from time to time, checking on our kids. She tells me they're always short teachers, even with the glut of teachers in this state. Hell, they don't even require that everyone have a teaching certificate, just one person in each department. You might give her a call."

"What's her name?"

"Rose Robinson."

"Do you have a phone number?"

"Not off the top of my head. Look for it on the Internet. Mon Valley Secondary Academy."

Mick wrote it down.

"Got it. Thanks."

Eddie did not respond.

"Eddie?"

The other end was dead. Mick hung up the phone.

Well, he thought, maybe this was his new life.

Acknowledgements

I am indebted to a number of people for the production of this, my first novel.

Professor Chuck Kinder, a member of my manuscript committee at the University of Pittsburgh, read the first version of this with care and understanding, then made many helpful suggestions for revisions. He gave me great words of encouragement, which have helped me to work through my doubts.

Early on in the writing process, Michael Byers, then a professor at Pitt, now at the University of Michigan, guided me toward the right direction for the novel. His inspiration was integral to my completion of the first draft.

My dear friends Bryan Denson and Kevin O'Connell, both very fine writers and astute readers, provided helpful remarks at various stages of the revision process.

I also appreciate the encouragement of my friends Adele Lynn and Cassandra Soars, as well as Patricia Hargest, early readers of the manuscript.

Also crucial to its publication is Lyle Applbaum, a friend and former co-worker who rescued me from the chore of formatting; and Kristin Stewart, who designed the cover.

Over the years, from the time I was first inspired by two wonderful elementary teachers, Ethel Frink and Rosemarie Bevil, to write, family, friends, colleagues and classmates too numerous to mention provided guidance, assistance, and support on my way to this point. Without them, this novel would have been impossible.

Finally, my late friend Emily Schultheiss, who left us before this work was completed, supported me in every way possible throughout our all-too-short friendship.

Made in the USA
Middletown, DE
03 October 2020